DESTINED TO THE WRAITH

The Shadow Realms

REGINE ABEL

CONTENTS

DESTINED TO THE WRAITH

Would he save her or be her damnation?

Hounded by a necromancer hellbent on appropriating her ancestral lands, Ronika must recover an ancient relic from a cursed mansion to keep her enemy at bay. To do so, she requires an escort. Convincing an enraged wraith to help seems like an impossible task. But she discovers that the being behind the billowing shadows is an honorable protector who moves her in an unexpected fashion.

After centuries of terrorizing the land while lost to madness, Asheron cannot believe this fragile human, with her weak green magic, has managed to bring back his sanity. Ronika's incredible strength, fearless determination, and the gentle way she touches him soothes the monster he has become and awakens a powerful longing and possessiveness in him. But she does not realize the deadliness of the deal she has struck to defend her land.

He will stop at nothing to protect the woman who has claimed his heart. But will Asheron's efforts bring about Ronika's salvation or doom them both?

DEDICATION

To those who strive to see beyond labels, appearances, and the often deceptive first impression. Some monsters cannot be redeemed. Others are merely deeply tortured and scarred souls hiding behind a hideous mask to shield themselves from further harm. The challenge is knowing which ones to cast out, and which ones to nurture back out of their darkness and into the light.

To mothers and fathers who will never give up trying to protect or save their child, no matter the cost, no matter how long it takes, and however arduous the journey.

CHAPTER 1
RONIKA

As my horse approached the wrought iron fences of the Hag's residence, the heavy gates barring the entrance to the domain parted on their own. No doubt, the imp-like 'statues' sitting atop the posts framing the gates had played a part in it. Their small bodies looked scrawny compared to their massive wings spread out as if they were preparing to take flight. Owlish eyes ate up most of their triangular faces framed by oversized, pointy bat ears. During the day, they seemed made out of oxidized wrought iron. But right now, under the soft moonlight, they appeared to be made of leather and stone.

I didn't doubt some form of life animated the imps, who acted as guardians to the estate. Whatever they were, magic oozed out of them—like with everything else in this place… in this town.

Although the imps remained immobile as I rode my horse past them, I could swear their intense gazes lingered on me. It didn't faze me. Beyond the fact that I sensed no malice nearby, so long as one didn't come to the Hag with evil intent, you'd be granted safe passage… if nothing else.

A luscious forest of the oddest trees lined both sides of the wide, two-hundred-meter path leading up to the house. Most magic users would kill to have access to some of this exotic vegetation. I'd never had the pleasure of working with a tenth of their leaves, sap, roots, or barks—to name a few—as the majority of these trees shouldn't be able to survive in our climate. Furthermore, the kind of magic required to successfully maintain such an eclectic combination of plants, many of which had completely opposite needs, defied comprehension.

But then, few things presented a challenge for the Hag.

The tree line finally gave way to a humble thatched-roof cottage, with walls made of a clever mix of wood, stone, and clay. Obviously, it was an illusion. I never understood why she presented that cliché witch hut front. The size of the domain implied a massive mansion hid behind the illusion. Whatever her reasons, I didn't care. So long as it didn't interfere with my life, she was welcome to do as she pleased.

I stopped Damar a few meters in front of the house before dismounting. Although the black thoroughbred wouldn't run or wander, I nonetheless tied his lead to the post outside the cottage. I caressed the bridge of his nose before heading for the door. Made of dark wood that looked deceptively worn-out, it creaked open with a drawn-out whine. Although invisible to the eyes, countless wards swept over me, making my skin tingle, as I entered the house.

The spacious room belied the small exterior. Surprisingly clean and orderly, distinctive sections divided the place. The far-left corner, a long counter laden with neatly organized vials ran the entire length of the wall. On each side, shelves contained various organic parts floating in colorful liquids on one end, and herbs, stones, and other magical paraphernalia on the other. On the opposite side, to the right, a voluminous grimoire sat on a pedestal, surrounded by bookshelves overflowing with ancient books and scrolls.

Straight before me, the Hag sat behind a large table that

clearly served as a desk. Once again, I repressed an amused smile at finding all the cliché items properly set up on it, from the crystal ball to the tarot deck, candles, small container with bones, another with runestones, and of course a grimoire or incantation book.

However, she wasn't working on it. Sitting in a low-back wooden chair, she was facing the right side of the room, while spinning the oddest 'yarn' into a glowing golden thread on a wheel. The Hag, legally named Cliona Nox—or so the records said—also known as the Weaver, was believed to be thousands of years old.

Of average height and slender, she had a timeless yet frightening beauty. Her silver-white hair plaited in one long messy braid fell to the floor. Surprisingly she didn't have the cliché black witch dress with rips and frayed edges around both the hem of the skirt and the wide sleeves, to go along with the rest of her theatrics. Instead, she wore a long, formfitting, beige dress embroidered with golden threads, and an elegant patch of fur around the collar and wrists. It had a medieval style to it, with trumpet sleeves. Although I could only see her profile from here, she didn't have the wizened features one might have expected. Barely visible wrinkles marked her forehead and the side of her eye.

Everything about her exuded danger and power, but not an actual menace. Where I didn't doubt she could turn me into ashes with a flick of a finger, I feared no harm so long as I didn't stir trouble.

"You came at last, Ronika Ortega," the Hag said without looking away from the thread she was spinning.

A shiver ran down my spine at the sound of the sultry, throaty voice, almost seductive. This was how I imagined a siren would sound.

Did it freak me out that she knew my name before I even mentioned it? Yeah, a little. You couldn't exactly make an appointment with her. You showed up and hoped she was available and willing to see you.

"At last? You expected me sooner?" I asked, stopping a meter away from her worktable while lowering the hood of my black cloak.

"Considering your plight, I didn't think you'd wait until the last minute to act," she said, still pulling the 'yarn' into a narrow thread.

"You heard?" I blurted out in shock, immediately kicking myself for stating the dumbest obvious fact.

The Hag lifted her foot from the pedal that activated the wheel and turned her purple eyes towards me, a less-than-impressed expression on her ageless features.

"*That's* the question you're going to ask?"

Ugh, by the Devil's horns, this woman sure knew how to make you feel lower than dirt without flinging a single insult. I needed to get my head together. Of the many things said about her, the one recurring theme was that she didn't suffer fools. If you tried her patience or struck her as being too dumb, she'd kick you out, and her gates would never open again for you.

"Right. Nothing that occurs in Willow Grove escapes your notice," I said sheepishly. "I didn't come to you sooner because I had hoped to resolve that issue on my own. I make it a point to avoid being indebted to anyone… especially in this town."

"A generally wise approach," she conceded in a slightly softer tone, though hardly friendly. "But less so if you wait until it is too late."

My heart dropped. "Is it too late?" I asked, worry seeping into my voice.

This time, the Hag fully turned to face me—or rather, her chair pivoted by itself and glided soundlessly over the polished floor to bring her next to the center of the table. Only then did I notice the red pentagram adorning the floor in the circular nook at the back of the cottage, behind her. I couldn't tell from here if it was drawn with blood, nor did I care.

The Hag shrugged. "It depends on which path you will follow once you have stated your request."

"I need an escort into Hemdell in two weeks," I said, lifting my chin with a hint of defiance.

A barely perceptible smile stretched her thin lips. Although she wore no apparent makeup, the vermillion of her lips would stir the envy of many a female.

"You need to be more specific, child," she said, her voice laced with a mix of a stern and taunting edge. "Hemdell's grounds? The crypt? The catacombs? Or the estate proper?"

"The estate," I replied in a non-committal fashion. In this town, it was never wise to reveal too much about your personal affairs.

"Let me guess," she replied, the taunting glimmer in her purple eyes cranking up a notch. "You want an escort to take you safely into Hemdell's observatory so that you may retrieve the Warding Microlith when the blood moon rises."

I felt the blood drain from my face that she should have guessed with such complete accuracy so cryptic a request. According to Willow Grove's legends, Hemdell contained innumerable magical artifacts of great power that countless treasure hunters and power seekers had lost their lives attempting to retrieve. How had she managed to guess this was the one I specifically sought?

"What I seek in Hemdell is my business," I said in a slightly clipped tone. "Can you find me an escort up to the task of getting me in and out unscathed or not?"

"The moment you came to me, you made it *my* business, little girl. You would do well to remember that," she said, her gaze hardening just like her voice. "As you stated so well, nothing occurs in Willow Grove that escapes my notice. Considering your current ordeal and the short time you have to resolve it, the only thing Hemdell has to offer you is the Microlith to ward Cornelius off your property."

My stomach dropped at having her once more figuring out my desperate plan so completely. Had it been so obvious? Could anyone else also suspect what I was up to? Could Cornelius attempt to beat me to it?

"There's really no keeping secrets from you, I see," I replied, trying to sound nonchalant about it. "But the question remains whether you can help me or not."

"I can do many things, Ronika Ortega," she replied with a dismissive wave of her hand.

Her claw-like nails shone under the light of the glowstones hovering overhead when she pointed at the chair I had not noticed by the entrance door. With a soft rubbing sound, the chair glided over the floor, stopping next to me in front of the table.

"Sit," the Hag ordered in a tone that booked no argument. "Do you have a type of escort in mind?"

Relief flooded through me as I settled in the chair. That she invited me to sit instead of kicking me out was a good sign. Maybe this would all work out in the end.

"I figured a gatekeeper demon would be strong enough to deal with anything that I might encounter there," I said feeling a little nervous.

As a low-level green witch, I didn't know much about spirits and demons. They loved to trick and deceive. Dealing with them held too many risks of you ending up on the losing end. I didn't crave power or wealth, just the basic human comforts. Therefore, I'd been content making a living selling potions, healing spells, and wards.

The Hag pursed her lips, her eyes all but stripping me bare as she gave me a slow, assessing look. I fought the urge to squirm.

"For your purpose, there are three viable options. You can go with a demon, a necromancer, or a wraith," she said pensively. "The question is what do you have to offer?"

I had dreaded that part. Fighting Cornelius had depleted all my savings. I didn't have anything left of value, but my house, and especially the land it was built on.

"I can pay you with potions and herbs," I said, my cheeks heating with embarrassment.

As a green witch, I had a natural talent to grow rare herbs highly sought-after for spells and potions. But after seeing the insane vegetation that thrived along the pathway to the Hag's house, she obviously had no use for whatever I could offer.

She scoffed, looking almost disgusted, if not offended. "I have no need for your herbs or potions. And the cost of *my* service depends on the choice you'll ultimately make. I am asking what you have to offer your escort."

I blinked, taken aback by that comment. "Well, isn't the whole point of summoning a demon the fact that you can control them for the duration of the summon, and that they have to obey your commands?"

No one in existence had ever made me feel so small and so ignorant with a single look as she did in that instant. She slowly shook her head, the slight twitch of her right hand making me think she was hitching to slap some common sense into me.

"For a Bruja, you're incredibly clueless and naïve. Controlling a demon requires a powerful witch—which you are not—and the performance of a complex ritual that you will never master in time. The slightest mistake could have dire consequences, not only for yourself, but also for the community. The last thing Willow Grove needs is for a demonic gate to lay open in Hemdell."

I flinched, feeling stupider with each word. A part of me had known this would be her answer, but I'd hoped she would have an alternative, some powerful incantation, a demonic stone, or some other arcane method only a being as ancient as she would have.

"Right. And I guess hiring a summoner isn't an option?" I asked in a subdued voice.

"With your limited means, any summoner you could afford would use that demon to claim the prize you seek for themselves," the Hag said with a dismissive shrug. "The trustworthy ones would likely refuse to take part in this venture or be well beyond your purse."

I clasped my hands in my lap, my chest constricting with growing despair. Why did I wait so long to come seek aid? Despite the witless way I'd been acting since arriving here, I wasn't brainless. I could have learned the ritual.

"Are you saying you can't help me?" I asked, my voice as tense as the muscles in my back.

The Hag leaned back in her chair with a slightly bored expression. "I'm saying that summoning a demon you can control is not an option for you at this point. That leaves you with trying to coerce or reward."

I shifted in my seat and flicked my blue hair over my shoulder. "Okay. How would either work? And doesn't that still require a summoning?"

"The summoning required in those instances are a lot simpler to perform than those that involve controlling a demon," she explained. "Both coercion and reward require the summoner to have something the demon fears, cannot resist, or desperately wants. However, as you do not dabble with spirits, I doubt you possess any relic they could be coerced or enticed with. The added difficulty is that each demon responds differently to whatever is placed before them. You would need the right trinket for the right demon. Your chances of acquiring such an essential element in time are slim to none."

I glared at her, feeling like she was making fun of me. "Then why bring it up since you know it's pointless, and I'm screwed either way?"

"Because you're not yet, but you could choose to be," she deadpanned with a taunting glimmer in her purple eyes.

I blinked again, this time with confusion. "Excuse me?"

"You do not have the magic level needed to summon and control a demon. You have no object of power to coerce or entice them. But you are an attractive female. You could seduce an escort. It is the fastest and easiest way for you."

My jaw dropped, and I gaped at her in disbelief, wondering once more if she was making fun of me. To my shock, she held my gaze unwaveringly with a serious expression on hers.

"Seduce as in… having sex with a demon?" I asked, my voice uncertain.

"Yes," she replied, matter-of-factly. "Is that a problem?"

I took a couple more seconds to let her words sink in before coming to a decision. I lifted my chin and squared my shoulders. "If it can get me what I need without me ending up maimed or dead, then yes, I'll fuck a demon."

An imperceptible smile stretched the corner of her thin lips, and something akin to approval—or was it triumph?—glimmered in her eyes. With a sudden bone-deep conviction, I realized she had always meant for us to get to this point.

"No, not a demon. For you, a wraith will be more suitable," she replied calmly.

I recoiled, my eyes all but popping out of my head in both shock and outrage. "A wraith? Are you insane?! They are mindless and constantly enraged. Merely touching them means death!"

Her smile broadened, and she slowly moved her thick and long braid in front of her shoulder, gently caressing it in the process. There was something sensual yet lethal in the way she moved, like a snake preparing to strike.

"That is true, unless you get them under your control."

I scrunched my face, completely baffled by that statement. "You just said I didn't have the skill to control them, and that it would take too long to find something to coerce them with!"

"I was speaking of demons. Wraiths are a completely different beast. There is no need for complex summoning rituals, and they have very simple needs," the Hag retorted with conviction. "They crave physical contact and peace in their tormented minds."

"Fine, I can see that. But wraiths are still rabid!" I argued. "I'll never live long enough to make the offer before he tears me to shreds!"

Actually, wraiths just sucked the life right out of you, leaving a desiccated corpse behind, and even a pile of ashes for the most powerful ones. A shudder coursed through me at the thought of facing such a being. A couple of them had been rampaging in the countryside for years now.

The speculative glint returned in the Hag's eyes as she observed me with an undefinable expression. "I will give you a soothing charm. It will help you in appeasing him long enough for you to make your offer."

I narrowed my eyes at her. As far as I knew, there was no such thing as a soothing charm for wraiths. They'd be selling like freshly baked lemon cakes. I would certainly want to offer such a product in my store.

"I've never heard of such a thing," I said, careful not to let my doubts seep into my voice to avoid offending her. "But don't you have something similar for a demon?"

She waved a dismissive hand and leveled me with an annoyed expression. "Forget demons. They are not the solution for you. And no, there is no such charm for them."

I pinched my lips, my own annoyance wanting to surface. Why in the world was she so set on a wraith? My gut told me she could have found a solution involving a demon if she wanted to. But what did she have to gain in forcing me to go with a wraith?

Did she truly have a hidden agenda or was she merely insisting on it because she knew it to be my only viable option?

"Assuming your charm works, and I manage to strike a deal with a wraith, can I even survive the encounter?" I asked, my tone slightly clipped.

Her annoyance faded, replaced by that obnoxious teasing smirk.

"Of course, so long as you make a good deal," she replied before gracefully rising to her feet. She headed towards a heavy, ornate chest on the floor, near the shelves overflowing with scrolls. "In exchange for your favors for one night, he must pledge to ensure your safety while he takes you to Hemdell's observatory, protect you while you attempt to recover what you came for, and then safely escort you back out of the estate grounds. Throughout the process, and after, he must pledge not to harm you."

As she spoke, the Hag rummaged through the chest. I couldn't see its contents from here, but her words held all my attention. I wished I had brought a pen and paper to write it all down. Still, her words gave me a sudden boost of confidence. They accounted for everything that concerned me. I especially liked the fact that it specifically spelled out that he couldn't harm me at any point, even after our deal was concluded.

But I still have to lie with a wraith.

I didn't want to imagine just how unpleasant that experience would be. Would he reek of death and decay? Would his skin be slimy or rotting in places? Would he be writhing with maggots? Would he…?

"Wait a minute, how do I even touch a wraith?" I asked, struck by a sudden thought. "Aren't they ethereal, like ghosts?"

The Hag straightened and observed an object she had picked up from the chest. A pleasant chiming sound emanated from it.

"A wraith has both a physical and ethereal form," she replied, her back still facing me.

She closed the chest before turning around. Her purple eyes almost seemed to glow, giving her ageless face an even more mythical aura. A shiver ran down my spine as she returned to her seat. My brain insisted that she had walked back, but my eyes swore she had merely glided over the floor.

My gaze zeroed in on the object in her hand, which she placed on the table in front of her. It was some kind of bronze charm bracelet. Every charm—nine in total—resembled a small sphere with slits on both sides, and each one bore a different runic symbol like I'd never seen before.

"While enraged or when going into battle, the wraith will remain in its ethereal form. You will know you are succeeding in appeasing him once the shadows shaping his body fade, giving way to his true form."

"Alright. But..." For some silly reason, my cheeks heated as I forced myself to speak the next question. "Does he even have a penis?"

The Hag chuckled. For the first time, a genuine smile lit up her face. It softened it in the most incredible fashion, giving me a glimpse of the stunning young woman she had once been.

Or does it?

For all I knew, this face, this body were complete illusions, just like this witch hut I was sitting in.

"Of course, he does. There would be no 'screwing' happening, otherwise."

She grinned further at my discomfort of having her use that word. I wasn't prudish in any way. But I made it a point to be respectful in front of elders. And Cliona Nox exceeded any definition of elder. So having her speaking the crude term I previously used made it all the more awkward.

"But do not worry, he cannot impregnate a human."

She hesitated, as if looking for her words. That immediately got all my senses on high alert.

"Coupling with a wraith might feel... strange. His touch will likely be uncomfortable—if not unpleasant—at first. Do not let that trouble you. It will pass. Just make sure you hold your end of the deal. The value of your offer is not just physical contact, but that it's voluntary and consensual. Do not give him grounds to think you failed to deliver. It will make your agreement null and void."

I swallowed hard and gave her a stiff nod. I had absolutely no intention of subjecting myself to this only to have him walk out on our deal because I didn't fake it well enough. Simultaneously, I kicked down the dreadful images of a decomposing zombie rutting over me which kept flashing through my mind.

However, the way the Hag had described it made me wonder if she had lain with a wraith before. It didn't sound like hearsay, but a firsthand experience.

She pushed the bracelet towards me, refocusing my wandering thoughts.

"And this will help you to get him to calm down. Wear it and shake it when he approaches."

I picked up the bracelet. It was light and exquisitely crafted. Each sphere contained a small ball that acted like the clapper of a bell. Within seconds of holding it, a frown creased my forehead.

"I sense no magic within it," I said, confused.

The oddest expression fleeted over her features and vanished too quickly for me to interpret it.

"When the time comes, it will serve its purpose. But remember that the burden remains on you," she warned. "No one can ever guarantee your success when dealing with the nether-world or the occult. Wraiths feed on sorrow, fear, and despair. You must remain calm and confident in your ability to soothe him. No amount of magic will save you if you cannot keep your composure. Remain *calm* and *confident*."

"Calm and confident," I echoed, understanding this would be the true test. I glanced at the charm bracelet before looking back at her. "And what is the cost of *your* assistance?"

I braced, my stomach flipflopping when a mocking smile—with what resembled a hint of malice—stretched her lips.

"My price is a strand of wraith hair," she said in a mysterious tone. "You must bring it to me within a month of having completed your journey into Hemdell."

"That's it?!" I exclaimed, having expected her to ask me for a finger or an eye.

The Hag snorted, and my uneasy feeling came back with a vengeance. She had that look that implied I had no idea what this truly entailed. I mean, the whole point was to have a wraith rutting over me for a while. Surely it wouldn't be too hard grabbing a strand or two while doing the deed? After all, if I touched him like a lover did, I'd be running my fingers through his hair, so…

But do wraiths even have hair?

That gave me pause.

"Yes, that's it," she replied in a factual tone.

I narrowed my eyes at her. "Wraiths do have hair in their physical forms, right?"

Her face hardened. "I never lie, Ronika Ortega. If I ask you for a wraith's hair, it's because they have it."

I flinched and lowered my eyes, feeling duly chastised. "Very well. I will get you a strand of a wraith's hair."

"Then we have a formal deal. In two days, at midnight, under the full moon, you will go to the sacrificial altar near the Duskwallow burial grounds," she continued, her voice back to a conversational tone. "Light candles at the four corners. You will then call out Asheron's name and shake the bells on the charm. Although it is not needed, you may cast a protection spell."

I definitely would. Too many foul things lurked in the forest surrounding Duskwallow.

"Thank you, I will," I replied in a subdued voice.

"And remember well that fear and despair fuel a wraith's rage and hunger. Calm and confidence appease them, and joy repulses them. Do not make the mistake of thinking the wraith your servant. He will be your temporary partner. Treat him accordingly. You will only have one chance. Do not fail."

With those final words, the Hag turned her back to me. Once more, her chair appeared to glide over the wooden floor before stopping next to her spinning wheel. She picked up her strange yarn and resumed spinning it, my presence apparently forgotten.

Feeling dismissed, I rose from my chair. It automatically slid back to its prior position by the door, confirming our audience had ended. Without a word, I turned on my heel and headed for the exit while pulling my hood over my head. The door opened on its own upon my approach. I stepped outside, hope and fear warring in equal measure within me as I inhaled deeply the fresh evening air.

As I detached Damar and hopped onto his back, a nagging voice at the back of my head said that I had doomed my soul by agreeing to sleep with the damned and by entering into a deal with the Weaver. If I failed to honor my end of our agreement, what she could do to me paled in comparison to even the worst death at the hand of a wraith.

And yet, as I rode back home under the moonlight, hope and a sense of purpose dominated my thoughts.

CHAPTER 2
RONIKA

The two days to the full moon flew by much too fast. I devoted most of them to reading up on wraiths and looking for whatever spells could be used to control or appease them. Unsurprisingly, everything confirmed the Hag's warning that only a calm and collected demeanor stood a chance of piercing through their rage and lust for destruction.

As soon as the sun began to lower on the horizon, I took a long bath, cast a spell of stoicism on myself, then donned a sheer bridal robe. The white fabric hid nothing of my curves or even the dark circles of my nipples. A button held the plunging collar closed between my breasts, hidden by the delicate, narrow row of floral lace that lined the edges of the garment. A second one did the same right below my navel. The long skirt pooled around my feet like a wedding train. And long, puffy sleeves fell to my wrists.

I didn't bother with any undergarments as they would defeat tonight's purpose.

I gave myself a critical look through the Psyche mirror. Pursing my lips at my wavy blue hair, with a hint of purple, I considered pulling it into a bun but decided to leave it cascading freely down my back.

Had I been meeting with a human, or at least a mortal, I would feel fairly confident about my current appearance. Like the Hag had stated, I was a reasonably attractive woman, with curves at the right places, and with just the right amount of meat on me for a man to get a good grip.

But I'm not meeting a human.

After nearly five years of celibacy, I never imagined I'd get back on the saddle with a demonic ghost. I just hoped the encounter wouldn't leave me mentally scarred for life.

With three hours to go before midnight, I slipped on my cloak and a pair of flat shoes, then carried my bag to my phaeton. I'd debated long and hard whether to use my small carriage or simply ride Damar to Duskwallow. In the end, I settled for the former as it would be more stable to transport the candles and vials I was bringing with me. Furthermore, as I didn't know what state I'd be in once the wraith was done with me, riding back home on the cushion of my phaeton would likely be more comfortable than a saddle.

To my relief, I didn't run into any of my nosy neighbors as I exited the residential area. I didn't doubt one or more of them spied on me on Cornelius's behalf. The man had been a thorn in my side since my father's passing three years ago. To this day, I believed foul play had sent him to an early grave. The physician had declared it a stroke, but Father had always been the healthiest of men. Had I been near him, I could have intervened. Sadly, he had conveniently been out of town. The following week, Cornelius was banging down my door with offers to purchase the property.

The forty-minute journey to Duskwallow gave me far too much time to think, and especially to question the wisdom of my current course of action. What did I really know about the Hag aside from rumors? Desperate people, or those with challenges deemed impossible to overcome would go knocking on her door. No one truly knew why she agreed to receive some callers while ignoring others. You knew she'd agree to grant you an audience if the front gates of her estate parted for you.

The fact that few people openly admitted to using her services—like I never would—made it even harder to get a good sense of the types of ordeals she would assist with. The only recurring fact was that she always honored her agreements. But like when dealing with a demon, you needed to make sure that what you had agreed to didn't exceed what you were willing to pay. A single play on words could cost you dearly. For such an ancient and powerful being, common compensation would never suffice. She already had in abundance most of what regular mortals could offer her. So that she had merely requested a wraith's hair had been a major relief.

But what will she do with it?

What kind of powerful magic could she perform with it? Truth be told, it didn't really matter to me. If she wanted to wreak havoc in Willow Grove, she would have done so centuries ago. According to legends, Cliona Nox had lived in this location for at least three centuries. As she had come here already a full-grown adult, who knew how many more centuries she had lived before then?

Still, I'd agreed to lie with a demonic ghost…

I didn't care so much about the sex part. While I'd never been the promiscuous type, I also didn't attach a great deal of importance to intimacy in a transactional context. Granted, I'd never used it that way before and never imagined that day would come. However, it was the nature of my partner that distressed me. Wraiths leeched the lifeforce of their victims, ate their souls, or flat out stole them.

If that Asheron craved contact and companionship as the Hag implied, why would he settle for a night of sex instead of stealing my soul and turning me into his servant for eternity?

Because stolen souls turn into wights, not wraiths…

And wights were mindless, wandering souls, filled with anger and despair. What would be the point of him turning me into one of those if it was companionship he wanted?

Misery loves company…

Blast it to hell… I needed to stop trying to talk myself out of this. Considering I'd entered into a deal with the Hag, there was no backing out now. I had committed to this course of action and would see it through. Anyway, I had exhausted every other option. Whatever the cost, I couldn't allow Cornelius to get his claws into our property.

Vigil—the Warden Tree in the backyard—had watched over my family for centuries. Beneath its roots, my father and our ancestors were buried, fueling him—and me—with their magic. Upon my death, I would also be buried there, to add my humble contribution to the magic that would be passed down to the children I hoped to have one day.

Considering what a formidable warlock and witch had conceived me, I never understood why my magic was so weak. But I couldn't let them fall into the hands of Cornelius. As a powerful and unscrupulous necromancer, he would undoubtedly raise my father and ancestors as his servants on top of harnessing the power of our Warden Tree in a way that I never could.

And all of it for evil.

The tall silhouette of Duskwallow's own Warden Tree appearing in the distance put an end to my somber thoughts. It was thousands of years old, with thick, knotted limbs spreading high into the sky. It measured at least twenty meters tall, and its trunk's circumference easily reached ten meters or more. Thick leaves with a mix of green and gold filled the branches like the luxurious mane of a wild beast.

But it was the giant face shaped by the knots in the tree that held my attention. Although it felt undeniably male, I couldn't say if it was human, demonic, or beastly. Some runes appeared around the face, their symbols and meaning as obscure to me as the ones on the charm around my wrist. Like the face, they had not been carved or woven by magic. They had appeared on their own over time. Thick, gnarly roots protruded from the ground, spreading far and wide, as if attempting to reach for something in the distance. Some were shaped like human silhouettes.

According to legends, the bodies of sacrificial virgins—both male and female—had been placed at its feet as an offering for the spirits believed to dwell beneath its roots. The souls of the sacrificed would have then given a new god-like life to the tree. As it faced both the sacrificial altar—located a little over a hundred meters from it, and the gated entrance of the burial grounds, the local population had named him The Watcher.

Despite how imposing and intimidating it looked, I stopped my carriage in the shadow of the tree. So long as you didn't threaten it, it wouldn't harm you. And in exchange for an offering, it might even grant a limited amount of protection and luck.

I didn't have much to offer, but placed the fresh corpses of three pigeons, fruits picked this morning, and dried medicinal herbs in the small cradle shaped by its roots at the base of the trunk.

"I have little to give, oh great Watcher. But please accept this humble offering. I seek nothing for myself but would be grateful for whatever protection you may grant my horse, Damar, during my short stay here, were you so inclined."

In seconds, the ground appeared to soften below my meager gift, and they slowly sank, soil and moss quickly covering them. My heart soared at this prompt display of acceptance. I could only hope it was a sign of more positive outcomes tonight.

But with time ticking, I needed to prepare for what awaited me. The first order of business was to cleanse that altar of negative magic and energy lingering from whatever rituals had been performed on it. The second was to physically wash it. The Hag had not needed to spell out she expected us to do the deed on top of that altar. I had no intention of getting pounded by a wraith while lying on the blood and grime of others.

That second task completed, and with barely thirty minutes left before midnight, I lit up the candles at each corner of the altar—as per the Weaver's instructions—then set up a series of wards on a wide radius around the altar. I held no illusions that they would stop a being as powerful as a wraith, but it might slow him down, giving me extra time to try and appease him before he chewed my face off.

In the ten minutes remaining, I knelt in front of the altar, my back to it while I faced the forest from whence the wraith would likely come. Despite the impressive effects of my stoicism spells that kept me from giving in to the panic that should be choking me right now, I reached deep for inner peace with meditation techniques.

Calm and confident… I mentally repeated those words like a mantra, the fingers of my right hand caressing the spheres of my charm bracelet for further reassurance. If the Hag hadn't believed I stood a chance of success, I doubted she would have sent me to a certain death. Therefore, it was up to me to make it happen. I had the tools. Now, I only needed to show my confidence.

The sudden rustling of the Watcher's leaves had my eyes snap open. A glance at my watch—which was hooked to the cinching hem at the waist of my robe—indicated two minutes to midnight. While I couldn't say for sure, my gut said it had just warned me of someone approaching.

I rose to my feet, discarded my sandals, and removed my cloak. After folding it, I placed it neatly by the altar with my sandals next to it and resumed my position facing the forest. With deep, controlled breaths, I kept my pulse slow while staring at the needles of the watch racing to the hours that would decide my fate.

As soon as they struck midnight, I raised my left hand and

shook it, the bells of the charms resonating with a beautiful crystalline sound. Although I still felt no magic emanating from the bracelet, the sound it created had a mythical quality to it. In itself, that bolstered my confidence. Its power was likely undetectable by a low-level green witch like me but would affect a powerful entity such as the wraith.

"Asheron! I humbly stand here with an offering. Will you heed my call? Asheron!" I called out, still shaking the charm at regular intervals.

The Watcher shook its leaves again. I glanced at him over my shoulder. My innards twisted at the sight of its runes beginning to glow. Had he sensed something so evil he already felt the need to activate its protection for Damar? Was this merely the manifestation of its watch beginning? Could it be that—?

A distant sound from the forest reclaimed my attention. Straining my eyes to discern any movement in the darkness of the thick forest, barely pierced by moonlight, I resumed calling on Asheron. The whole time, I silently prayed Asheron—and not some other fiendish creature—would answer my summon.

Moments later, a bone-chilling screech answered me. My stomach dropped. If not for the stoicism spell, I would have screamed with fright. Instead, a wave of peace washed over me, even as the red glow of the interloper's eyes appeared in the distance. They were approaching much too quickly, accompanied by further terrifying shrieks.

The temperature of the otherwise warm summer night suddenly dropped. A chill ran over my skin as a thin sheet of frost settled over the short, yellowish grass covering the clearing in which the altar sat. The sky darkened, as if from the gathering storm. The sudden surge of hopelessness, anger, and hatred attempting to engulf me confirmed my deadly wish was about to come true.

A wraith was approaching.

Had I not known the cause of that sudden sense of despair, I would have unwittingly fed the creature exactly what it needed to further unleash its bloodthirst. No wonder a single one of those beings could wreak so much havoc whenever they descended upon unsuspecting villages or hamlets.

Between my stoicism spell and sheer willpower, I shrugged off Asheron's debilitating aura and continued to call to him in a firm and confident voice.

"Asheron, peace! Cast away your anger. Heed my voice! I am not your enemy. Asheron, come peacefully to me."

A dark figure finally emerged from the tree line. Once more, I swallowed down the fear desperately trying to take root deep within. Even though it was still a hundred meters away, the wraith appeared a lot taller and broader than I expected. Billowing shadows gave him a more-or-less human upper body that faded into a flowy, skirt-like lower body, typical of those creatures. But it was his head and chest that fascinated me.

While his glowing red eyes constituted his only definable facial features, the long pair of shadow horns jutting from the top of his head took me aback. I couldn't recall ever finding a case of a horned wraith in the lore. And his chest appeared to have fractured right in the middle, the fissure akin to one left by an earthquake. Within, a pulsating red light seemed to mark its heartbeat, which also highlighted the bones of his ribcage.

That, more than anything, confirmed he was neither truly dead nor alive.

I could feel my fight or flight instincts increasingly battling my stoicism spell as the wraith continued his threatening approach. This was the moment of truth. I would either succeed in appeasing him or die trying. Forcing myself to remain focused on my target, I reminded myself that fleeing at this point was no longer an option. He would tear me to shreds before I even managed to cross half the distance to my carriage.

As I continued to shake the charm and entice him to come in peace, I noticed his speed had lessened, as well as the luminous pulse in his chest, and the red glow in his eyes. This *had* to mean my efforts were getting through to him. It gave me a much-needed surge of confidence that rang loud and true to my own ears.

In turn, it seemed to further slow his approach.

Words freely flowed from my lips, more soothing and seductive, as if a greater power had taken over me. Although I still didn't perceive any magic from the charm, I began to wonder if it was turning me into this assertive siren. Whatever the cause, I embraced it.

As did the wraith…

His advance faltered when he reached the first ward. For a split second, I wondered if I had somehow managed to cast something powerful enough to stop him. But his annoyed—maybe even offended—sneer as he glanced at the ground gave me a first glimpse of his mouth.

He closed the remaining distance between us almost at a leisurely stroll, although glided would be a more appropriate term. He stopped barely a couple of feet in front of me. His cold aura had my skin erupt in goosebumps and made my nipples pebble under my sheer robe. My breath fogged, and my bare feet felt unpleasantly frozen. He literally towered over me, the top of my head barely reaching his shoulder. Nevertheless, I bent my head back to lock eyes with him, refusing to acknowledge the five-inch claws at the tips of his fingers, or the dagger teeth that peeked through his still snarling mouth.

How in the world am I supposed to lie with that?!

At least, his presence didn't make me gag with the stench of rot and decay I had dreaded. Instead, a rather pleasant scent of smoked wood with a dab of fresh thyme wafted to me.

"Greetings, Asheron. My name is Ronika Ortega. Thank you for granting me the honor of an audience. I want to strike a deal with you." Once more, the poise in my voice genuinely impressed me.

By the way he tilted his shadowy head to the side, I could only presume it surprised him as well.

"Ronika Ortega, what makes you think I want to strike a deal with you?" he asked, his voice deep and otherworldly, filled with malice.

"Because I've already helped you reclaim the peace you haven't felt in a long time, and I am here to grant you a favor in exchange for one of your own," I said with an assurance that bordered on arrogance.

I was playing a dangerous game. Based on the Hag's statements, I assumed he had wandered in endless rage for months, years, maybe even decades. If I had misread her underlying meaning…

I nearly jumped out of my skin when Asheron lunged forward, stopping a breath's hair from me. Simultaneously, a wave of fear and despair crashed over me. By who knew what miracle, I remained rooted in place, despite my slight movement of surprise. I closed my eyes and willed happier thoughts to silence the dread he was attempting to stir within me. He emitted a hissy growl, his face so close to mine our lips almost touched.

Heart pounding, I held his gaze unwaveringly and even attempted a slight glare.

"Do not waste your energy trying to scare me, Asheron. The time for that is long past," I said defiantly.

"You think yourself able to stand against me?" he hissed in a soft voice laced with disbelief, his ethereal body inching even closer to mine.

My stomach churned from the distressing sensation of his aura wrapping around me. It felt like my flesh was shifting in and out of existence with each beat of my heart, and that my organs wanted to fall out with every other beat. But that, too, I clamped down on. If I allowed my mind to linger on this, despair would indeed engulf me. After all, if his mere proximity made me this nauseous, how would I survive embracing and kissing him?

The Hag warned of this and said it would pass.

I latched onto that thought to further help me through this.

"I'd be a fool to think I can best you. What I meant was that if I intended to give in to fear, I would have done that long before you exited the forest. It would be pointless now. As I stand no chance of defeating or outrunning you, all I can do is strive to convince you to accept my offer."

The red pulse glowing from his chest slowed further, reaching almost half the normal rate of a human heartbeat. The shadows forming his face seemed to deflate as if getting partially absorbed by his skull, making his features a bit more defined. The cold aura that had me freezing to the bone abated.

"What could you possibly have to offer that I may want?" he asked in a haughty tone, his voice dripping with contempt.

Bracing mentally, I detached the two buttons of my sheer robe and pushed the fabric down my shoulders, keeping it hooked at my elbows. Despite my arms being partially folded before my stomach, my breasts were fully exposed to his view, and the parted panels of my robe hid nothing of my sex. Asheron's red eyes widened.

"Physical contact. The warmth of a woman's touch, and the embrace of a willing lover," I said factually, annoyed by the sliver of tension seeping into my voice.

To my surprise, he recoiled and moved a step back away from me. This was *not* the reaction I had anticipated. Had the Hag been wrong about what he craved? Did my appearance repulse him? For a split second, I considered pulling my robe back on, to cover my nudity—not that the sheer fabric would achieve much of that.

"You are offering me your favors?" he asked, sounding like he thought I had lost my mind.

Which wasn't too far from reality.

"Is that so outrageous? When was the last time you were held, caressed, and kissed by a woman eager to please you? Years? Decades? Centuries? When was the last time a woman came to you, offering herself?"

"Are you so clueless as to ignore what happens to a foolish mortal when touched by a wraith?" he asked, the glow in his eyes strengthening while his pulse picked up.

I swallowed hard, refusing to contemplate the possibility that this reaction implied his anger was resurfacing.

"I know the touch of an enraged wraith will drain the life-force of a mortal, turn them into a desiccated corpse or even ashes in seconds. But you are no longer enraged," I added quickly when he seemed ready to call me out further. "You are having a rational conversation with me, with a clear and sound mind. It is well within your power not to harm me with your touch, if you so choose."

The oddest glimmer flickered in his eyes. To my relief, their glow and the pulsing in his chest diminished again.

"I can feel the nausea twisting your insides. You can barely stand my presence, and yet you offer to lie with me?" he challenged.

"I have never been in such proximity to a wraith," I replied, proud of the assurance in my voice. "It is true that your ethereal aura unsettles me. But it is already far more bearable now than it was when you first approached me. I believe once you fully shift into your physical form, it will fade away."

"And if it doesn't?" he insisted.

"It will not stop me from holding my end of our deal," I said.

He remained quiet for a moment, apparently weighing my words. Then the billowing shadows around him faded, along with the pulsating glow on his chest, as if a door had closed before it. The vanishing shadows gave way to what resembled grayish-beige bones on his forehead and shoulders. For a split second, my heart sank at the horrified thought I'd be lying with a skeleton. But wonder quickly replaced it as Asheron's true physical appearance was revealed to me.

Although there indeed were bones around the bridge of his nose and forehead, flowing into his pair of horns forming a V on top of his head, skin otherwise covered the rest of his body. Long, mostly straight black hair fell loosely to the middle of his chest. No eyebrows or eyelashes framed his entirely red eyes, sclera included. But with the glow having receded, I could now see their dilated pupils. If not for the unusually broad bridge of his nose made of bones, the rest of his nose could have passed for a human's, as did his sexy and perfectly drawn lips.

To my relief, on top of his surprisingly attractive face, Asheron's body was in no way the putrid walking corpse I had dreaded. He was fit and muscular. It struck me as odd that he didn't have nipples but possessed a navel. That confirmed he had been naturally born before turning into a wraith. Bone-like scales formed beautiful patterns the entire length of his shoulders, arms, and parts of his chest and sides. The same patterns lined his legs, and bony scales covered part of his feet. Sharp claws tipped both his toes and fingers. But thankfully, they were no longer the five-inches daggers he'd displayed in his wraith form.

At first, my mind froze at the sight of his smooth crotch covered in bone scales and devoid of the necessary organ to perform the deed. Then my jaw dropped when the scales parted, and his manhood extruded. I forced myself to avert my eyes as a massive club jutted out between his thighs. Even soft, his shaft appeared thick and long. Its shape seemed to match that of a human penis, with a slightly pointier head. But the chevron-shaped ridges covering the upper side appeared made of the same bone-scales on his forehead. How hard would they be? How much would they hurt inside?

Asheron raising a hand towards me, as if to fondle one of my bare breasts snapped me out of my shameless examination of his body. I promptly took a couple of steps back and closed the panels of my sheer robe in front of my chest, covering my nudity. The bells of my charm jingled, as if in further disapproval of Asheron's attempt to touch me. His sensuous lips twisted into a sneer, baring sharp teeth framed by a pair of fangs. They still looked intimidating, but not terrifying like the dagger teeth he had in his wraith form.

He advanced towards me, the red glow of anger returning in his eyes. I took a couple more steps back until the edge of the altar stopped my retreat.

"You cannot touch yet," I said firmly, hoping it came across with far more assurance to him than the weak way it sounded to me. "We must make a deal first."

"Or I could just take you," he countered, invading my space.

The mere heaving of my chest as I breathed had my nipples almost brushing against his torso.

My stomach knotted. "You could," I conceded. "As you already can with anyone else. But that would defeat the entire purpose. Don't you want a willing partner? To be embraced, kissed, caressed, and… fondled?" I added, casting a meaningful glance at his crotch.

He clenched his jaw. By the look on his face, he appeared to be debating whether he really cared about my consent or lack thereof.

"And what is the cost of your favors?" he asked at last.

I flinched inwardly at how it sounded when worded like that. But then, I was indeed trading my favors for something of value to me.

"I need a powerful protector to escort me safely to Hemdell's estate on the eighteenth of the month, under the blood moon."

Asheron snorted, and the oddest expression flitted over his features. "You want help retrieving the Microlith in the observatory."

I silenced a groan. Was there anyone who didn't know about the Warding Microlith?

An almost malicious smile stretched his lips. "Very well. In exchange for your favors, I will safely take you to Hemdell's observatory on the eighteenth. Deal?"

"Not so fast," I said sternly. He narrowed his eyes at me. "In exchange for *one night* of me granting you my favors, you will ensure my protection from the outer gates of Hemdell to the observatory, watch over me while I retrieve what I came for, and safely escort me back out of the estate and its grounds."

The way he smirked and the shameless glimmer in his eyes confirmed he had indeed worded the deal in a way that would allow him to demand my favors whenever and as often as he wished. While I knew to try to account for every loophole when dealing with demonic entities, I still felt grateful to the Hag for spelling it out to me.

"That is acceptable," he said. "Is that all?"

"No," I said, my heart soaring at the thought we were about to seal the deal. "Furthermore, you also pledge to do me no harm, tonight, in the time leading up to the eighteenth, or after our business is concluded."

My spine stiffened when his face closed.

"That is too broad a pledge," he said, his tone making it clear he wouldn't consent to this.

I blinked, baffled by what could make such a simple request so abhorrent to him. Was he so determined to do me harm?

"How is it too broad?"

"Should you decide to attack, enslave, or otherwise wrong me in any way once our deal is done—or at any time leading up to it—I will be unable to fight back. Such a pledge would leave me no choice but to flee. I *do not* flee before anyone," he said in a hard tone.

My jaw dropped. I had not thought of that. Why would I? To do such a thing would have never entered my mind to begin with. Had our roles been reversed, I would have given this ridiculous amount of power over me to my temporary partner.

"Fair point," I conceded. "Then I'm happy to amend it to where you will be free of your pledge should I *willfully* attempt to harm or wrong you."

Asheron snorted again, an amused smile settling on his face when I stressed the word *willfully*. I didn't know what foul creatures we might run into in Hemdell, but I wouldn't be accused of breaching our agreement over some monster mind-controlling me into attacking Asheron.

He pursed his lips, while studying my features. I could see his wheels spinning as he searched for any other loophole.

Or is he looking for a workaround to take advantage of me?

Not for the first time since the beginning of this entire ordeal, I felt way out of my depth. But there was no turning back now. I reviewed the terms of our agreement in my mind and couldn't think of any weaknesses that might endanger me. I could only take a leap of faith and hope for the best.

"Any other terms you haven't mentioned yet?" he asked at last.

I shook my head. "No, that's all of it."

"Then, with the Watcher as our witness, we have a binding deal, Ronika Ortega," Asheron said.

Something in his tone made me uneasy. It was the smug, satisfied edge, like the cat that got the cream. Somehow, I had missed something that would come back to bite me later.

"Now it is time for you to deliver on your end of our deal, little human," Asheron said in a taunting voice.

His hands reached for the top of my robe, still wrapped around my shoulders. I dropped my hands, which held the front panels closed over my chest. Asheron lowered the fabric, and I let it slide down my arms. It pooled around my feet with a soft rustling sound.

My stomach fluttered as a hungry look settled over Asheron's otherworldly face.

"Touch me, Ronika."

CHAPTER 3
RONIKA

My hands shook slightly as I raised them towards his muscular chest. I wanted to believe it was the lingering effects of the chilling aura that previously emanated from him. Granted, apprehension gnawed at me. There was something dangerous—not to say maliciously evil—behind his unexpectedly attractive façade… at least for a demon.

As soon as my palms made contact with his chest, an intensified version of that queasy feeling of my skin oscillating between dimensions coursed through me. My stomach roiled, and my gorge rose. I steeled my resolve, inhaling deeply to regain control while my hands continued to roam over his skin. I focused on its unusual texture to distract myself from the distressing sensation touching him awakened in me.

His skin was soft and pliable, in an almost leathery fashion. It gradually became somewhat grainier and a bit harder in the areas covered in bony scales. But even those were not unpleasant to the touch. If not for that dreadful aura, I'd be marveling at the way flesh and bone formed the most unusual tapestry on his muscular body.

Asheron's hissy breath claimed my attention. I lifted my eyes to peer at his face. His upper lip was raised in a snarl, once more exposing his sharp teeth and fangs. His red eyes glowed again, and an almost savage expression had settled on his face. It should have frightened me, but I instinctively recognized this as him trying not to let himself get overwhelmed by powerful emotions.

Eyes glued to his face, I ignored the unsettling crawling sensation skittering over my palms and arms as I gently caressed his broad chest, on an upward path towards his neck, then his cheeks, before sinking my fingers in the long strands of his hair. He closed his eyes, his head tilting back as he breathed in through his teeth. A violent shiver shook his body, and a sense of triumph surged within me. As he could read my emotions, I'd feared my discomfort at his touch would ruin his enjoyment of mine.

The texture of his hair between my fingers took my breath away. No word could properly describe the feel of it as it flowed over my skin. Each strand was incredibly thin, almost translucent. You'd think I was running my hands through a curtain of water, without the moisture, and that acquired a bouncy, almost spongy consistency once you tried to grab a fistful of it.

However, Asheron placing his hands on my hips and drawing me against his body put an abrupt end to my exploration. For a second, I thought I'd go into shock from the violence with which full contact with him affected me. My skin burned, and I almost expected it to turn to ashes and fall off my bones.

He swallowed my strangled gasp in a voracious kiss. I parted my lips to cry out in pain, but his tongue invaded my mouth. With it, his cold breath raced down my throat, through my lungs, then radiated outward throughout my body. The burning pain instantly faded. I moaned in relief and clung to him, my legs feeling wobbly. I felt him chuckle against my lips, the sound smug with that hint of malice I'd perceived earlier.

His tongue dove back into my mouth while his left arm held

me tightly against him. With the other, he caressed my body with a mix of roughness and possessiveness. One part of me believed Asheron was trying to make me tap out early on while he still had some control over himself, rather than later, when he'd be—hopefully—lost in the throes of passion. The other part speculated that he was trying to put me through the roughest phase now, so we'd get to the stage the Weaver had claimed would become more comfortable for me sooner.

Whatever his motives, I would see this through. I hadn't gotten this far only to be defeated by a bit of pain and discomfort. Thankfully, like with his scent, Asheron's taste also proved rather agreeable. Thyme and peaches came to mind, with a touch of cool mint. But the latter could merely be a misinterpretation due to the coldness of his breath.

As an additional pleasant surprise, the wraith turned out to be quite the skillful kisser. With his sharp teeth and fangs, I'd worried he would lacerate my tongue and lips. But the moment the pain of his aura faded, I caught myself pressing my body against his, my tongue happily joining the dance with his, and my hands resuming their exploration of his unusual skin.

Although a sliver of the discomfort from his contact lingered, it had dwindled to a weak enough level that a timid arousal sparked low in my belly. I willed it to grow into a raging brazier that would facilitate the completion of my end of the deal.

I didn't know if empathic power was the right term to define Asheron's ability to sense my emotions, but the way his touch became more feverish and bolder hinted he had felt the shift in me. He broke the kiss, and his hand fisting my hair yanked my head back. His lips kissed a path down my neck before he sucked on the palpitating artery there.

His fangs grazing my skin sent a thrill down my spine. With a single bite, he could end my life. I'd crossed paths with the occasional vampire and always wondered what it would feel like to have their fangs sink into me. Why did that thought stir up such an irrational appeal?

The strange mix of relief and disappointment fleeted through me when he didn't bite me and reclaimed my mouth in a possessive kiss instead. I caressed his back, the protruding bones of his exposed spine tickling my palms. On the journey down, my fingers encountered a bump which ended abruptly. My gut said it had been meant to extend into a tail. Did Asheron possess a retractable tail? Had it been severed in the past?

Despite my curiosity, I continued my exploration, reveling in the way he shivered beneath my touch. I didn't need to be an empath to sense how much he enjoyed that still mostly innocent contact. My hands settled on his behind. They were sinfully round and firm. The smattering of bony scales that fanned out from the base of his spine tapered off right where his behind began to round.

I gave his cheeks a good squeeze. In response, his shaft jerked against me. Too focused on controlling my negative reaction to his aura and on my journey of discovery of his body, I had locked out the thought of his cock. This sudden reminder piqued my curiosity. While my left hand continued to fondle his left bum cheek, the other slipped between us to cover his sex.

Asheron gasped against my lips. His body tensed, and he jerked his head up to stare at me. Teeth clenched, his upper lip curled up, he appeared to struggle to remain stoic... and failing miserably. I held his gaze, studying his features intently as I slowly began to rub my palm over his length. His hand fisting my hair on my nape tightened. It stung and hurt a little, but in a good way.

To my pleasant surprise, the bony ridges lining the top of his shaft didn't scrape my skin. In fact, the bumps felt wonderful to the touch. My mind immediately wondered what it would feel like inside me. But Asheron's breathing becoming shallower and louder drew my eyes back to his face.

He almost looked in pain as he pursued his losing battle for control. By the gods, seeing how my mere touch could make such a powerful being tremble and nearly come undone was both thrilling and emboldening. The all-consuming desire to see just how far I could push him took over me. As much as I hated to look away from his haunting face, I leaned forward and pressed my mouth to his neck.

"Yes… Touch me…" Asheron whispered, his voice trembling, almost pleading.

I complied, my left hand releasing his behind to resume caressing his back. My mouth brushed over the leathery texture of his neck. The tiny scales interspersed over it made my lips tingle. I blazed a trail down his chest, kissing, licking, and nipping his flesh. He tasted a little salty, with that same thyme undertone, but this time without the hint of peach. As a proud licker and kisser, it pleased me tremendously. Unfortunately, he didn't possess nipples. I had a thing for sucking on a man's taut little buds.

I rubbed my face over his chest before continuing my journey downward. When my lips closed around his navel, Asheron exhaled a shuddering breath before inhaling sharply. That sound resonated directly between my thighs. He knew where I was headed. Feeling the trembling of his body steadily increasing did insane things to me. But seeing him bend over me to support himself with one hand on the edge of the altar at my back turned me on beyond words.

By the gods, his cock was massive. That my fingers couldn't fully touch around it had made it obvious but seeing it up close as I crouched before him took it to another level. My inner walls contracted. The rational part of me believed fear prompted that reaction. But the twisted part of me knew better.

His cock was literally a work of art.

Where a human male would have a happy trail of pubic hair leading to his manhood, Asheron had a few small bone scales scattered in the area around its base. They gradually blended into the half-ring bone scales forming a straight line up to an inch from the head. At that point, wavy bones, almost chevron-shaped, circled the area normally covered by foreskin, before widening into the triangular head. It, too, had a series of tiny ridges. Arched scales delineated the left and right sides of the half-ring scales of the shaft, dividing the ridged top from the smooth underside.

Unable to resist, I leaned forward and gave it one long lick. Asheron's body jerked, and he emitted a feral cry. I gave him another lick, analyzing the taste and incredible silkiness of the underside. Here, the smoky flavor was more dominant with a hint of peach. And yet, the scent of thyme dominated despite it being absent on my tongue.

I stroked Asheron a few more times with my hand before taking him into my mouth… or at least what part of him I could. The sound he made had my nipples instantly harden while mois-ture pooled between my thighs. His hand fisted my hair painfully, and a grating sound behind me revealed the claws of his other hand were likely scraping the stone surface of the altar.

Ignoring the stinging pain in my nape, I started bobbing in front of him, opening my mouth as wide as possible. To my chagrin, I could barely take more than a quarter of his impossible length, not to mention his insane girth. Judging by the growly moans tumbling out of Asheron in a continuous flow, he didn't seem to care. What I couldn't fit between my lips, I stroked with my hand in counterpoint to the movement of my mouth. My other hand caressed the bone scales of his legs before reaching for his testicles. Although comparable in shape and size to those of a man, the skin of both sacks wasn't wrinkled, but as soft and smooth as the underside of his shaft.

By the urgency of his moans and the way his body trembled, the imminence of Asheron's climax loomed near. Normally, although it didn't feature in my top favorite things to do, I didn't mind swallowing. However, I had no idea what to expect with a wraith's seed. The Hag had confirmed it wouldn't impregnate me and no harm would come to me from coupling with a wraith. That still left me with many unanswered questions. Naturally, none of the lore I'd been able to get my hands on regarding those creatures mentioned what would happen if you decided to swallow a bucket of fresh wraith sperm. After all, what sane person would deliberately seek to perform fellatio on a demonic ghost?

I never claimed to be sane.

As if he'd read or sensed the conflicting thoughts racing through my mind, Asheron suddenly shouted out angrily and pulled away from me. Startled, I looked up just in time to see him bend down, pick me up, and slam me on the edge of the altar. I barely managed to hang on to his shoulders before he crushed my lips in a brutal kiss. Even as I opened my mouth in response to his imperious tongue demanding entry, Asheron slipped his arms behind my knees, spreading me wide open.

In the brief instant it took me to realize his intentions, true fear that even my stoicism spell couldn't quell blasted through me. He was too big. And despite my blossoming arousal, I was nowhere near ready to receive him. I should have rubbed my clitoris to at least get me properly wet while I'd been sucking him off. But I'd been too focused trying to pleasure him, both to fulfill my end of the deal and—it shamed me to admit it—to sate my pride that my ministrations could make a terrifying wraith come undone.

My ego had killed me.

As if in slow motion, I felt Asheron's pelvis move back before charging forward in one powerful thrust. His mouth swallowed my terrified scream. But the pain of his cock tearing me asunder never came. Instead, the burning sensation of his phasing aura spread throughout my pelvic area, followed half a beat later by the impression of being full to bursting.

Neither my body nor my mind could comprehend what was happening, but both concurred it wasn't right. And yet, I rejoiced that it hadn't killed me outright. I wanted to clench my teeth through the pain and bury my face in his neck while waiting for this storm to pass, but Asheron insisted on kissing me. Irritated by my involuntary attempts to turn my face away, the wraith let go of my legs to grab my neck and squeeze it. My lips parted in a startled gasp to have my airway thus constricted. His tongue seized the moment to once more invade my mouth. With it came the blast of cool air from his breath.

Seconds later, the burning sensation of his aura faded. After a brief instant, my frazzled brain finally remembered his kiss also previously appeased the distressing feel of physical contact with him. Had I not been so panicked, it would have dawned on me sooner. I stopped fighting. My hands, that had been pushing back on his chest with a will of their own, glided back over his broad shoulders to hang on to him. He tilted his head to the side to deepen the kiss in a commanding fashion. I gladly submitted to his dominance.

With the pain of his brutal—and especially unnatural—possession of me receding, I was finally able to get a better sense of what he was doing to me, and why he hadn't split me in half even though he continued to pump in and out of me at a frantic pace.

And then I got it.

Asheron's lower body was shifting to its ethereal form while penetrating me, then turning back to its physical form once inside. That explained the sudden burst of feeling impossibly full. But he would shift right back before the stretching actually damaged me. The gods only knew how long he kept it up. However, the amount of time he remained tangible inside me gradually lengthened, and with it, the feel of him grew stronger.

The sound of my moan took me by surprise. I couldn't tell when the discomfort had given way to pleasure. All I knew was the bony ridges that had so fascinated me on his cock were now doing quite a number on my inner walls. The ones on the head were particularly wicked, grazing the sensitive bundle of nerves deep within me with each thrust, both on the way in and out. It sent electric sparks throughout my pelvic area.

I whimpered when Asheron broke the kiss. His eyes had darkened. Beneath the hungry, borderline feral expression on his face, I didn't miss his smugness. Considering how he had me quickly cresting, it was justified. With my body having adjusted to his girth, my lover picked up the pace, taking me faster and harder. He bent me backward, his hand behind my nape supporting me as his mouth greedily dove for one of my breasts. He alternated between sucking the nipple gently, forcefully, then nipping at it with his sharp teeth, before soothing it with a lick of his tongue.

I held on to his shoulders, my hips gyrating with a mind of their own, chasing the bliss quickly building within as his thrusts grew even more urgent. My climax crashed into me with sudden and brutal force. I cried out, my back arching while my nails dug into the leathery skin of his shoulders. In the distance, I heard Asheron growl angrily. Whatever the reason, I didn't care. In that instant, I was flying high, my body singing from the unnatural pleasure of his cock wrecking me.

As I began to come down, I vaguely felt the polished stone of the altar slide under my back. I realized that, with only the briefest pause, Asheron had moved me to the center of the altar and joined me on top before resuming rocking in and out of me.

"Touch me," he hissed as I refocused on him.

A sliver of shame washed over me as I realized how I'd shirked my duty to give in to the pleasure he was lavishing on me. This night wasn't about me, but him. That I got any gratification from it just happened to be a bonus. I complied, my hands roaming feverishly over him, exploring every inch of his body. It was no chore. Asheron was a fantastic lover. Too great in fact.

Despite my recent climax, his lips over my neck and chest, and his cock pounding into me already had me nearing the edge again. At least, his growly moans reassured me that he, too, was finding pleasure in my arms.

But even as I prepared to give in yet again to ecstasy, a sudden pulling sensation steadily grew within me. It tugged at my soul. My skin tingled, and my head spun the way it did moments before losing consciousness. The jarring clash of these new sensations with the waves of pleasure crashing over me left me reeling and disoriented. It took me far too long to understand the cause.

My nails dug into Asheron's back while my spine seized with horror.

"You're draining me!" I whispered.

Without slowing down the punishing pace with which he was taking me, Asheron stopped kissing my neck, and lifted his head to peer at me. A single look at his face confirmed my worst fears. His eyes glowed with great intensity. Even the luminous pulse I had witnessed earlier radiated through the skin of his chest.

A malicious smile stretched his lips. "I am."

"You... you pledged—"

"Not to harm you," he said, interrupting me. "I never promised not to feed from you. Fear not, my little human. You will not be harmed this night."

His mouth crushing my lips kept me from answering. Pleasure and fear raged through me in equal measure, casting me down a vortex of conflicted emotions and sensations. An all-consuming fire coursed through my veins. Electric sparks fired off on each of my nerve endings. Through the waves of bliss sweeping through me, I could feel my soul getting sucked right out of my body.

Had I made a mistake? Was he killing me despite giving me his word? Did he...?

A sharp pain in the crook of my neck snapped me out of my

frightened meanderings. Asheron had sunk his fangs into me. The tingling sensation intensified. He would suck me dry, leaving my desiccated husk on the altar.

The Hag had lied to me.

And yet, I found myself taking solace that overwhelming pleasure rather than pain would be the last thing I felt before I died.

Just when I thought I would pass out, Asheron suddenly pulled his fangs out of my neck. He slammed himself deep inside of me and threw his head back. A powerful roar tore out of his throat at the same time his cold seed shot out inside me. The shocking sensation turned into liquid bliss spreading outward, seeping into every inch of my being. A blinding light exploded before my eyes as an ultimate orgasm swept me away. I embraced it.

Asheron shuddered over me, and I felt myself falling out of my body.

"You are mine," the wraith whispered as a veil of darkness descended before my eyes.

CHAPTER 4
ASHERON

A primal roar tore out of me as I surrendered to ecstasy. Every inch of my body vibrated with intense pleasure, down to my bone scales. Was I not already undead, the nearly unbearable bliss of my essence shooting into my female would have slain me.

To be touched again… To feel the softness of a woman's body, the passion of her embrace, and the searing tightness of her sheath gripping me from all sides as I lost myself in her…

By the gods, it had been so long… too long.

I felt her consciousness fade as I continued to rock in and out of her a few more times until the last of my seed was spent. As much as it frustrated me, I had expected it. In fact, I had provoked it. As I loomed over Ronika's inert body, my cock still buried deep inside her, I fought the burning urge to drain her. Even though I had fed from both her lifeforce and life's blood, I remained famished.

As a wraith, I was plagued by a deep and insatiable hunger that felt like a gaping hole not only deep inside my body but also within my very soul. Nothing could fully sate it. The pain, terror, and despair of my victims dampened it, and devouring a soul temporarily appeased it.

I could feast on her and get my fill.

From the moment Ronika beckoned me, the feral beast in me kept repeating that thought. Yes, we had made a deal. But so what if I broke it? I was already damned. Once dead, she couldn't exact revenge. That she was here alone while possessing such weak magic further indicated she had no one of consequence—if at all—to seek retribution on her behalf.

Yes, I could feast on her.

Propping myself up on one hand, I caressed her face and then her breast. A shiver coursed through me. She was so warm, so soft. My cock jerked inside her as memories of how she touched me, moaned in my ear, and writhed beneath me flashed through my mind. But as much as it turned me on, it also rekindled my anger.

I felt cheated out of the night of passion she'd promised. I still wanted her hands and mouth on me. The night was still young. She should have granted me her favors until dawn.

You knew it would never happen.

I did. In truth, I never thought she would last as long as she did. Most humans would have gone insane from such prolonged contact with a wraith's phasing aura. If not madness, her fight or flight instincts would have driven her to flee. The predator in me wouldn't have been able to resist and would have devoured her.

However weak her powers, Ronika had been wise to cast some kind of soothing spell over herself. I couldn't say for sure what the spell had been, but I felt it trigger every time fear surged within her. As much as the rational part of me had been grateful for it, my wraith had resented it. And as I began to feed, her fear had steadily grown. The wraith had relished it, salivating as my resolve weakened, and the predator came to the fore. Had I not deliberately overwhelmed her, I would have given in to my instinctive urge to kill her.

For all that, Ronika held her end of the bargain while it lasted. In fact, she went above and beyond what I ever could have hoped for. I still couldn't believe she took me in her mouth. I wanted more… so much more. Technically, I had the right to continue enjoying her for a few more hours. But necrophilia held no appeal to me. Even though she was still alive, rutting over an unconscious partner would feel just like it. Anyway, the whole appeal of the deal was her consensual participation.

With much reluctance, I pulled out of her and stepped down from the altar. She looked excessively delicious lying helplessly on the stone surface, her nudity caressed by moonlight, and her disheveled hair sprawled around her attractive face. They were an unusual color. I couldn't recall ever meeting a human with blue hair and hints of purple.

My gaze roamed over her smooth, flawless skin. It slightly glowed under both the effect of the moonlight and especially of my essence coursing through her. I could feel it claiming her, forming a bond between us. A malicious grin stretched my lips as a wave of possessiveness swelled within.

Such a naïve woman…

She had no idea how many loopholes she had left in our agreement. And I had no qualms exploiting every last one of them. But how in the world did she know my name or to come to me here on this night?

As if in response to that question, Ronika shifted slightly. The little bells of her bracelet jingled, drawing my attention. My eyes narrowed as I leaned in to get a closer look. A flood of ancient memories flashed before my mind's eye as I recognized the trinket.

"The Weaver…" I whispered in shock.

Only she could have possessed that bracelet and given it to Ronika. What was she up to? Why would she seek me out after all those years… or rather so many centuries? Why had she sent this clueless mortal to me?

Memories of how Ronika had shaken the charm as she called my name and spoke soothing words replayed through my mind. The foolish woman had clearly believed the charm to have some kind of power over me. But why? The weakness of her magic couldn't justify her not being aware that the bracelet held no power of its own. What in the world had the Weaver told her? Granted, the sound was pleasant and could help in appeasing me. But in the end, the only thing that truly mattered were Ronika's emotions. Had she given in to fear, panic, or despair, no amount of magic would have saved her from my rage.

An explanation lurked at the edge of my mind. Unfortunately, I'd been feral for so long, I struggled with rational thinking. The hunger still gnawing at me only made it harder. I needed to feed some more, and urgently before the madness overtook me once more. If it did, I would likely never manage to rein myself in again in time for our venture into Hemdell.

That, too, brought a malicious smile to my lips. Her request had opened the door to many possibilities. I reached a hand and gently caressed the soft skin of her stomach. Although I couldn't have her one more time tonight, I certainly intended to do so again soon. She had been clever enough to limit my free access to her favors to one night. But I felt her response to me. While her pleasure was irrelevant to me when I first entered into this agreement, feeling it grow within her and then seeing her falling apart for me changed everything.

Yes, I will have her again. I will claim her and bind her to me.

For now, I needed to hunt. One glance at my woman's unconscious form made me hesitate. It would be at least an hour or two, maybe more, before her body and soul recovered from the shock. If left alone, she would be vulnerable to whatever might lurk in the shadows. I hunted in this forest for a reason. While her face remained relaxed, Ronika shivered, and goosebumps erupted all over her skin.

I reached for the cloak neatly folded at the foot of the altar and laid it over her. That instinctive action took me aback. I hadn't felt the need to protect in centuries. The last time I had done so had cursed me to eternal damnation.

Casting away those dark thoughts, I circled around the altar, pouring my own magic into the weak wards Ronika had placed around the clearing in protective rings. Sensing them upon my approach had been somewhat offensive. Had she seriously thought they could have stopped me? Had she not displayed such self-control and confidence, those wards would have merely fueled my rage.

In a flash of clarity, it dawned on me that, like with her soothing spell, Ronika had merely sought to stack what little magic she could perform to increase her chances of getting through to me before I ravaged her.

And it worked.

Just as I was finishing enhancing her wards, the Watcher started shaking his leaves in a familiar warning.

Prey was approaching.

My predatory instincts and an anticipatory bloodlust surged forward. At the same time, I'd berated myself that the Warden Tree should have warned me of nearby danger. I was an Ancient Wraith. I should have sensed it long before the Watcher even could. However, the tree appeared to have taken a liking to my woman. Its runes had glowed red, and its face had grown ominous when my wraith had threatened to take over and harm Ronika.

Despite its displeasure, the Watcher couldn't have done anything to me had I chosen to devour her. After all, she came to the sacrificial altar of her own free will. Whatever I chose to do with her automatically became my discretion. But it made me curious as to what had earned her his affection.

Such musings would have to wait until later. I shifted back to my ethereal form. It was easier to maintain than my physical form, but also made it harder not to give in to the rage and madness that constantly simmered inside me. I didn't go towards the forest, but away from it. I wanted my prey to expose itself in the clearing. Too many other fiendish creatures could be roaming around in the hopes of sneaking in on two opponents already engaged in battle and score an easy kill.

As I inched closer to the Watcher, its runes—which had turned blue once I had clamped down on any thought of harming Ronika—turned red again. That baffled me. Surely he didn't think I had ill intentions towards him?

Then I noticed a carriage led by a single horse. The Warden Tree's large trunk had hidden it from view. I instinctively knew it belonged to my woman. Had she made an offering in exchange for protection for her mount?

"Peace, Watcher," I whispered in a slightly taunting tone. "I will not feed on the horse. Much more satisfying prey approaches."

My words appeared to mollify him, making me smile further. It felt odd. I couldn't recall the last time I smiled, let alone felt amused. I wanted to hang on to this peacefulness of the mind. And it would require me to keep my woman, my anchor bound to me.

"Hello?" called out a faint female voice in the distance.

I stiffened upon hearing the frightened tone. By the sound, it belonged to a young woman, in her late teens or early twenties. She was likely frail and lost, fighting back tears of terror as she wandered aimlessly in the darkness.

An irresistible appetizer for monsters such as I.

Or the perfect bait.

I phased further into the void, making my ethereal form nearly invisible to the naked eye, and crouched down to the ground. If anyone could perceive me at all, they would confuse me for being part of the thin fog crawling over these cursed grounds.

I lay in wait while the voice grew clearer and louder. Time stretched as my hunger and impatience intensified. I would feast this night once my suspicions were confirmed.

After what felt like an eternity, the delicate silhouette of a woman finally appeared at the edge of the forest. She advanced with an unusual gait, as if walking barefoot on the sharp rocks and uneven terrain of the forest, or after an injury. She stopped by a tree, her features hidden by darkness as she remained out of the path of the moonlight.

"Hello?" she called once more, her voice clear, but more hesitant, like when you are wondering if the person standing in front of you truly didn't hear you the first time around.

It took every ounce of my willpower for me not to give chase. If I attacked now, she would turn around and run deep in the forest. While I loved a good chase, I wouldn't be lured into a trap. An hour ago, before meeting Ronika, I would have lunged at the woman in a mindless frenzy. Even now, my wraith rattled and raged for me to attack.

But I silenced him. It had been too long since I'd played little games with my prey. I would savor all that my current 'sanity' allowed me to enjoy again.

Moments later, she stepped forward into the light, and as expected, she remained a dark silhouette. Two red orbs appeared in the face of the woman, where the eyes would be. They were indeed eyes, but certainly not human. Now that she had locked on a target, the 'woman' revealed her true appearance—a Shadow Flayer—by shedding its camouflage. Like with the West African Gaboon vipers, the dark scales covering the Shadow Flayer's skin absorbed any light that hit them while reflecting none. It made it impossible to see the true horror of its appearance, even in broad daylight, until it so chose.

A second pair of slanted red eyes opened in the monster's forehead, its entire face below splitting into a gigantic mouth filled with impossibly big and sharp teeth that put even those of my wraith to shame. What had passed off as straight long hair in the shadows turned out to be shorter tentacles that stood on end above its head. The tips gradually lit up in a slow pulse that was hypnotic to many beings.

The arms, legs, and luscious curves of the woman's body unraveled as the Shadow Flayer unfolded the dozen tentacles that lined its body, and which it had cleverly wrapped in a way to give the illusion of a human silhouette. Its petite woman's height increased by a couple of feet as it unfurled the two tails it had been walking on, giving itself that drunken gait. Propped on top of both tails, like a snake standing up, the creature revealed a second nightmarish mouth, which opened vertically where the woman's belly had previously been located.

Both mouths opened incredibly wide, and the Shadow Flayer released a dual, blood-curdling screech. Ronika didn't stir, but her horse—still hidden by the tree—neighed nervously. The Watcher shook its leaves in a soothing fashion. This further confirmed it had taken the mount under his protection. Nothing would survive long enough to get to the horse.

The Shadow Flayer charged, slithering at an impossible speed towards the altar. Malicious glee, a rabid hunger, and fevered anticipation animated the beast at the prospect of an easy meal when Ronika remained still. I surged forward in my invisible vaporous form. I didn't rush, but leisurely floated towards my prey, on a wide radius so it wouldn't sense my presence too soon.

I wanted to play…

My night with Ronika had been cut too short. I would find a different type of satisfaction elsewhere. And the Shadow Flayer would entertain me for daring to threaten what was mine. In its greed to feed, the stupid creature didn't sense the first ring of wards and ran straight into it. It looked as if it had slammed into a wall and got zapped by lightning.

The repelling magic flung the Shadow Flayer back. Its tentacles writhed and flailed as the creature screeched in shock and pain. After regaining its balance, it carefully slithered forward, its tentacles wiggling in every direction as it tasted the magic. The creature emitted another shout, this time fueled by frustrated anger. Even as it circled around the ring in the search of a weak spot he could sneak through, the Shadow Flayer kept casting famished glances at Ronika. And while the fool longed after its unattainable prize, I closed in.

Swooping in behind it, I materialized my wraith's right arm with five-inch-long, razor-sharp claws at the tip of each finger. In a flyby, I swiped them at the beast, and reveled in the orgasmic sensation of my claws slicing through scales, flesh, and muscles. The shrill scream that tore out of both the creature's mouths resonated like the most divine chorus to my ears as one of its left tentacles fell off. It writhed and flopped on the ground in reaction to involuntary spasms.

The Shadow Flayer turned around in shock, its four eyes flicking this way and that in search of the source of this unexpected pain. As it surveyed the clearing, failing to find me as I had once more faded to my invisible state, the creature covered the gaping wound left by the severed limb with one of the thicker tentacles from its right side. Thick gobs of dark blood fell like blotches of tar on the ground. Although unpleasant, its sulfurous stench nonetheless fanned the flames of my bloodlust.

As the creature slithered around, its limbs spread out, it opened its stomach mouth. The high-pitched sound that came out wouldn't be audible to most creatures, and certainly not humans. I didn't know how it worked, only that whenever the Flayers did that, it received some kind of response through the tips of its outspread tentacles. I only knew that the creature used that method to detect the location of prey. But it couldn't detect me in my invisible, vaporous form.

I flew up and swooped back in, this time coming from above, chopping off the antenna tentacles on top of its head. It doubled over, screaming in pain. Simultaneously, it swiped its limbs in every direction, hoping to make a lucky strike with the sharp claws at the tips.

Killing a wraith was nearly impossible. While my physical form could be damaged, you couldn't harm us in our ethereal form. Or rather, you could only achieve the latter by striking true, using a holy weapon wielded by someone with a pure heart. Holy knights had grown quite scarce over the centuries.

I toyed a while longer with the Shadow Flayer, severing three more of its tentacles, before chopping off one of its tails. Its agonized scream was suddenly echoed by the voice of another Flayer. An evil grin settled on my face as I materialized in my wraith form in front of the maimed creature. It was time to put an end to its misery so that I could go play with its kin.

A powerful aura of sheer terror exploded out of the beast when its four eyes settled on me. My blissful moan at the waves of dread and despair pouring out in droves from my quarry sounded like a growly, demonic chuckle. I absorbed it all, gorging on its helpless emotions as it attempted to flee, half-crawling and half-slithering on its remaining tail. Already weakened by pain and blood loss, panic made its movements even more erratic, further impairing its ability to escape—not that it could have.

I slowly advanced, invoking my powers to spread my chilling aura towards the monster. Frost covered the ground in a straight path towards the Flayer, who vainly attempted to outrun it. A thin white sheath of frost coated the creature's severed limbs which littered the clearing. They shriveled as I glided past them, sucking out their energy with a mere brush of the billowing shadows of my wraith form.

The theatrics weren't just for my amusement, but also heightened my target's terror. I gorged on every ounce of it. Too weak to go any further, the Shadow Flayer collapsed and rolled onto its back to look at me with an air of pure despair. As I towered over the creature, I smiled at the heart-wrenching wail of defeat that it bellowed with both its mouths.

Yes. Call your friends to me.

I heard their answer from a very short distance. Eyes locked with my victim, I brushed the shadow skirt of my wraith against the Flayer's tail. Like a chain of tumbling dominoes, its body collapsed on itself from the tail up as I drained every last drop of its lifeforce.

"No one threatens my woman," I hissed as I watched the light fade from its eyes.

It wasn't as satisfying a meal as draining a human or a demon. Devouring a soul provided true nourishment. A single soulless being such as this one merely appeased the more vicious pangs of my hunger. But stacking a few of them made for a decent meal.

I could have fully drained the Flayer, which would have turned the creature into ashes that the wind would scatter. But this was the first of many trophies I intended to leave for Ronika. She would know I had already gone above and beyond the duties of our agreement. Considering the extra… compensation I would collect from her, it was only fair.

I sensed the first of two more Flayers approaching the clearing well before it exited the forest. A malicious chuckle tickled my throat as I turned back to my vaporous form and stalked my new prey.

Yes, I will feast well tonight…

CHAPTER 5
RONIKA

Damar's aggravated neighing pulled me out of my restless dream. My eyelids felt heavy as I regained consciousness. But it was the coldness of the hard surface beneath me that snapped me awake. The open sky overhead—streaked with yellow, orange, and pink—screamed of early sunrise.

I gasped and shot up into a sitting position. The sharp pain that radiated from my back and behind tore a hiss out of me. No injury had caused it, but spending the night on the cold stone slab of an altar would do this to you. Judging by how low the sun still hung on the horizon, it was just a little after five.

As memories of the previous night flashed through my mind, I jerked my head around to see if Asheron was still nearby. To my shock, instead of the wraith, I found the desiccated remains of what seemed to have once been Shadow Flayers. They'd been dismembered, their limbs scattered around the clearing surrounding the altar. Judging by the number of larger pieces which could have been torsos, at least three or four Flayers ventured into the clearing.

And I slept through it all?!

The state of the corpses testified a wraith slew them. My

heart swelled with gratitude that Asheron protected me during my vulnerable state, at the same time confusion settled within me. He pledged not to harm me, but I didn't request he shield me from any lurking abominations last night. His protection was only compulsory on the eighteenth. Had he let the Shadow Flayers eat me, Asheron would legitimately have been freed of our contract without ever having to fulfill his end of the deal.

I never should have required it. In my mind, I would have limped back home straight after we'd done the deed. Once again, I realized how out of my depth I was with his whole ordeal that I hadn't accounted for the fact that I would be too out of commission to even ride back on the padded seat of my phaeton.

My gaze dropped to the dark fabric that had slipped down from my chest and into a puddle on my lap when I sat up. My cloak… I clearly recalled folding it neatly by the altar before the wraith's arrival. That could only mean *he* covered me with it before leaving, once again going beyond his contractual duties. He even picked up my sheer bridal robe from the ground where I'd left it and placed it on top of the altar, at my feet.

I took stock of myself, still stunned to be alive and unharmed. I found no bruises, lacerations, or other signs of injury on my body. Even running two fingers over the curve of my neck and shoulder where Asheron bit me only met with smooth, undamaged skin. Last night, in the final moments before my ultimate orgasm, I'd been certain Asheron was devouring my soul. Yes, he fed from me but kept his word to do me no harm. Remembering the way he used his ethereal form to ease penetration added to my confusion.

Many demonic creatures craved human suffering. He could have hurt me without causing harm. In truth, I expected him to deliberately derive much satisfaction from making it as painful for me as possible without damaging me. Instead, he multiplied the ways to keep me safe.

Another aggravated neigh from Damar put an end to my

wandering thoughts. The poor sweetie was likely starving. I winced at the soreness in my back as I turned my legs to the side so that I would sit at the edge of the altar before sliding off. My muscles complained, feeling both numb from the cold and stiff from lying on such an uncomfortable bed.

I stuffed my feet into my shoes, slipped on my robe, and then my cloak. A grateful moan vibrated through my chest from the warmth it provided against the morning chill, especially against my back.

Ignoring the underlying stench of sulfur the early morning breeze wafted to me—no doubt from the dead Shadow Flayers—I made my way towards the Warden Tree with a stiff gait. To my shock, my wards remained strong. Correction, they'd grown stronger than when I'd set them. They should have faded by now.

Asheron... He reinforced them.

Another wave of gratitude swept through me at that realization. He had been so cold, almost evil when interacting with me last night. Who would have thought he could be so kind and considerate? But then, was it kindness or did a different motivation drive him?

However, the soreness between my thighs quickly distracted me from those thoughts. I had expected to feel a significant amount of pain and maybe even suffer some tearing. Taking Asheron's massive girth after quite a few years of celibacy should have left me raw and achy. Instead, a delicious soreness lingered. With each step, my inner walls appeared to rub against each other, like a flint trying to rekindle the fire that had previously burned so bright.

By the time I reached the tree, not only had the stiffness from my uncomfortable night faded away, but I felt light, with a spring in my step. Considering Asheron drank my blood and drained part of my lifeforce, I should be weak and dizzy, not feel this... strong. Whatever the cause, I welcomed it.

I stopped by the Warden Tree, and gently rubbed my hand on its bark. "Thank you, Watcher, for looking after Damar."

A deep rumbling sound emanated from him, and he shook his leaves in a brief but playful fashion in acknowledgement of my words. Warmth filled my chest as a smile settled on my lips. I let my hand drop and closed the short distance to my carriage, partially hidden by the tree.

"Sorry," I said sheepishly to my horse when he glared at me.

Having not expected to be gone this long, I didn't have food for him, aside from a couple of apples. He accepted them and grumpily made the long journey home, where I gave him plenty of fresh hay.

The following days proved uneventful. I kept a close eye on myself, looking for any sign of negative side effects from having lain with a wraith. When none appeared, I finally started relaxing a little.

To my dismay, I found myself in an almost permanent state of arousal. It disturbed me that I should constantly fantasize about Asheron. Sure, scratching that itch after a long period of abstinence had awakened that dormant side of me. But there were plenty of decent, mortal men who could feature in my raunchy dreams instead. After all, sex with a wraith had oscillated between both extremes of mind-blowing bliss and intense discomfort, not to say pain. And yet, my mind was idealizing what had occurred, making me crave another round.

Over the last couple of nights, some of those dreams had been so vivid, I'd awakened with a start, convinced Asheron had just been in my room, even though it now stood empty. A quick self-assessment confirmed my body had not been touched, at least not physically. And a tour of my house reassured me that none of my wards had been disturbed.

By the gods, if I kept this up, I'd drive myself into paranoid insanity.

In truth, I was already well on the way there. As the eighteenth drew near, the fear that Asheron wouldn't show up kept growing. He didn't have a steady address—at least that I knew of—where I could send a raven or a note reminding him of our appointment.

On the eve of that fateful day, I'd almost talked myself into riding back to Duskwallow and calling on Asheron to make sure he hadn't forgotten about me. To be fair, I didn't actually think he would forget. But what if he'd lost himself to madness again? I doubted he had the ability to just snap himself out of it.

The Hag didn't tell me to follow up with him.

That felt like a weak argument, but she'd been so clear about everything else, surely she would have mentioned the need to check up on him if she believed it to be a potential issue?

My stomach dropped at the sudden realization that I still needed to compensate the Weaver. At a visceral level, my gut had told me something was missing in the list of requirements of our agreement. How could I have forgotten such an essential element?

Even without making it part of our deal, I had the perfect opportunity to just snag a hair. My wretched hands had been buried deep in Asheron's unusual mane while he unleashed his passion on me. But I'd been so lost in a whirlwind of pleasure and pain that night that I'd completely forgotten to snag a hair from him. Even then, a few strands had likely fallen during our tumble that I could have simply picked off the altar or the ground.

After wasting a few more minutes berating myself, I settled on a course of action. First, assuming he met me in his physical form tomorrow, I'd try to discreetly pluck one from him. As he craved touch, I could pretend to feel generous and give him a couple of free caresses or a hug as a sign of gratitude. However, if he only showed up in his wraith form, I'd have no choice but to flat out ask him, even if that meant granting him my favors a second time.

My cheeks burned with embarrassment at that last thought. If I were being honest, a part of me hoped I'd fail to steal a strand. Then I'd have an excuse to offer myself to him and sate the desire that had been plaguing me for days. I couldn't decide if that obsession stemmed from a need to find out how much better it could be to couple with him because I *wanted* to, or if it was because I'd set him up on some sort of pedestal for watching over me in my moment of vulnerability.

Since my father's passing, I felt so lonely and abandoned. In Willow Grove, no one ever did anything if they didn't stand to benefit in some way. But a wraith had protected me when he had nothing to gain from it.

Heaving a sigh, I locked the front door of my shop, and flipped the sign hanging on the window to CLOSED. I'd kept it open much longer than usual to keep me distracted from my distressing thoughts. Night fell an hour ago, and no one would show up now unless someone got hurt with something Dr. Fallwell couldn't or wouldn't handle.

My father had built this shop as an extension to our cottage. It proved quite convenient and far more cost-effective than paying separate rent elsewhere. I entered the house through the communicating door and went upstairs to pour myself a hot bath.

The flicker of a few aromatic candles projected dancing shadows on the wall as I slipped into the water. I rested the back of my head against the edge of the free-standing tub and closed my eyes. To my dismay, I could swear the burning candles smelled of thyme and smoked wood. It wasn't the case at all, but my mind latched on to that and refused to let go.

I'd meant to relax and meditate but ended up fantasizing about my wraith. Before long, one hand slipped between my legs while the other settled on my breast. My fingers scissored my little nub a few times, then parted my folds to sink inside me. My inner walls constricted in protest. After the impossible fullness of

Asheron's cock, stretching me to the limit, what use were my tiny fingers?

I pinched and rolled my nipple, regretting I hadn't prepared a colder bath instead to recreate the illusion of Asheron's cool skin against mine. Pulling my fingers out, I started rubbing my clitoris and pressed my lips, rubbing them a bit too forcefully against each other to rekindle the sensation of his brutal kisses.

By the gods, what was wrong with me? Had he somehow cast a seduction spell on me?

I accelerated the movement of my fingers between my legs as pleasure gradually built. It significantly paled in comparison to the earth-shattering sensations Asheron had awakened in me, but at this point, I'd settle for anything that could appease this relentless hunger. The sound of water sloshing around me soon mingled with my loud breathing as I chased after my impending climax. It was close, so close, yet eluding me. Each time I believed I would fall apart, it slipped away, just out of reach.

A startled cry shot out of me when the door chime suddenly resonated in the house. In my shock, I abruptly straightened, and water splashed onto the floor. I grabbed the sides of the tub with both hands, breathing heavily while trying to get my erratic heartbeat to slow down.

I jumped as the chime went off again. Muttering a series of less-than-ladylike curses, I stepped out of the water and wrapped myself in a thick bathrobe. I put on my slippers and flinched at the icky feeling of my damp feet on the padded lining inside. Hurrying down the stairs, I wondered who in the world this could be and why so persistent when the chime rang for a third time.

I mentally reviewed my clients who could have urgent need of me. A couple of them came to mind. They always wanted the more complex treatments but refused to follow instructions. Then they'd come crying for help when their hair fell off, or their magic-assisted erection wouldn't go down for a few days, preventing them from urinating. I'd already treated Kaspar twice for a ruptured bladder over it.

Annoyed by the disturbance and being cheated of the climax that had eluded me, I tried to ignore the angry throbbing of my clit. I reached for the doorknob, ready to berate the eternally horny old man. Once I'd finished healing him, I'd warn him that the next time he got himself in a bind for continuously exceeding dosage, I'd refuse to treat him, like Dr. Fallwell, until sepsis kicked in. Maybe then he'd learn his lesson.

I yanked the door open, but the sharp words on my tongue died at the sight of my visitor.

"Cornelius!" I whispered, shocked.

"Ronika, my dear... What a nice welcome!" he said in his suave and polished voice with a hint of a foreign accent.

The lurid expression that settled on his handsome face as he undressed me with his eyes made his meaning crystal clear. My skin crawled with disgust, and I instinctively closed the panels of my robe more tightly around my body.

Tall and lithe, with pale skin, black hair, and deep blue eyes, Cornelius Cromwell perfectly matched the profile of the rich, ancient vampire. As was his wont, he was fully dressed in black, from the fancy high-collared tailcoat to the fitted pantaloons and embroidered gloves. The only hint of color came from the white cravat, and the dark purple of his waistcoat. His propensity to only prowl around town after nightfall reinforced that impression.

But Cornelius was no undead. He merely enjoyed playing with them.

Leaning on the polished skull of the ungodly small creature that served as the pommel of his walking stick, Cornelius absent-mindedly fingered the pocket watch dangling on his hip. Many a woman would have deemed this a seductively virile pose. It just stirred another wave of disgust within me.

Despite his youthful appearance, Cornelius had to be at least two or three hundred years old. The necromancer had mastered the art of cheating and manipulating death.

"You interrupted my bath," I said in an icy tone. "What do you want?"

"Your bath?" he echoed with false commiseration. "My apologies. I could make it up to you by washing your back."

No sooner did he speak those words than he jerked his head to the right, as if he'd heard or seen something. My gaze followed his, finding nothing but the plants in my flowerbed gently swaying under the pleasant evening breeze.

"I'd rather have a Chimera give me a full body massage than let you touch even an inch of my skin," I hissed, when Cornelius returned his attention to me, having apparently also concluded there was nothing there. "Now what do you want?"

"Tsk, tsk, tsk," Cornelius said with that obnoxiously patronizing air he loved to take whenever someone resisted him. "Such pointless aggression. A pretty woman like you should learn to show her more agreeable side. You would have more suitors knocking on your door."

"The last thing I need is a suitor. And I'd especially appreciate seeing less of a specific man come calling," I snapped, giving him a meaningful glance.

His face lost some of its smugness to take on the hard edge truer to his cold and cruel nature.

"You might want to rethink your position quickly, Ronika," he said in a harsh tone. "You have four days left before I get to seize this house. I would rather not toss you out on the street, but I'll have no qualms doing so if you insist. You fought hard and well, but it's time to admit that you lost. Despite your less-than-charming disposition, you are an attractive enough female. I can take good care of you and even allow you to continue residing here. Make this easy on all of us. Be smart. Sign over the title to me, and you'll be fairly compensated. If you wait to be evicted, you'll lose everything."

Each of his words struck me like a dagger to the heart. If Asheron didn't come through for me tomorrow, I would indeed lose everything. The thrice damned vermin had depleted all my savings by multiplying the legal procedures to seize my home. From miraculously discovered unpaid taxes to obscure cadastral infractions, and random conformity non-compliance, I spent every penny I owned fighting back. I even had to let go of my lawyer as I could no longer cover his fees.

The Warding Microlith wouldn't help me pay the new taxes and legal fees Cornelius had managed to conjure up and get added to the city's financial records, but it would make it impossible for anyone but me to enter the house, unless I expressly granted them access. No amount of magic could lift the ward. Anyone with ill intentions towards me or the house would find themselves turned around or paralyzed.

The necromancer would have no choice but to set his sights elsewhere.

Sure, life would be a bit difficult for me in the days and months after that. I wouldn't be able to leave the house without risking getting arrested. But I was self-sufficient here. Between the garden in the backyard for fresh produce and herbs, my henhouse, and my goat, I could comfortably get by until I figured out the next step.

I raised my chin defiantly. "Like you said, I fought hard and well and have no intention of stopping now. I will never sign the title over to you, and you will never get your slimy paws on my home. If I have to whore myself out to a pack of trolls to keep you from achieving your goal, I'll gladly do it. Now get the hell off my property. You are not and never will be welcome here."

My spine stiffened as the skin of his face shifted. It had been brief, as if a creature behind a mask had moved. An imperceptible smile filled with malice stretched his sensuous lips.

"I will have your home, Ronika Ortega. And I will have *you*. When I'm done playing with you, I will grant you your wish and hand you over to a pack of trolls. My friends and I will enjoy watching you get wrecked by their wart-covered cocks. Sweet dreams, my pretty."

Without another word, he turned on his heel and walked away in an elegant and leisurely stroll. That he'd spoken those words in that sweet, polite, and polished voice he usually reserved for esteemed business partners made it frightening. That he meant and would go through with everything he'd said made it even more terrifying.

Feeling shaken to my very core, I closed the door a bit more forcefully than intended, locked it, then pressed my back against it. Fear and despair crawled over my skin and carved a path into my heart.

"Please, Asheron, don't let me down," I whispered.

CHAPTER 6
ASHERON

As I flew through the sky on my way to Ronika's dwelling, I surveyed the city and its inhabitants. The first time I'd made the journey revealed just how long I'd been out of touch with reality. Eleven days later, I still struggled to comprehend some of the things I saw.

Finding out I'd given in to madness over three hundred and twenty-five years ago still rankled. The castles and mansions of my former patrons had been razed to the ground, turned into something unrecognizable, or remained stranded in time like Hemdell.

The quaint little hamlet of Willow Grove easily quadrupled in size. They split previously large lots into smaller ones to accommodate a greater number of residences. Sectors once overrun by squalor and crime had evolved into upscale neighborhoods where the wealthy strutted with an air of entitlement. Other areas reeked of magic, with peddlers of the occult openly running their business with their storefronts lining the winding streets of Charmers District.

Charmers... a pretty euphemism for conjurers, witches, alchemists, and necromancers.

In my days, those who practiced the dark arts dwelled in the shadows for fear of persecution. More disturbingly—but also intriguingly—undead, fae, and various otherworldly beings hid in plain sight among humans. Vampires, doppelgangers, and fae easily blended with the masses. But demons and other interlopers with far more conspicuous appearances used glamour spells and illusions to fool the mortals.

This held an undeniable appeal for one such as I.

However, the technological advances confused me. I was familiar with clocks and gears. But this era took them to another level. Various contraptions devoid of magic combined clockwork mechanisms and steam to operate on their own. Some of them even flew. In the streets, I'd spotted the occasional carriage moving without horses. Thankfully, they still seemed quite rare. Considering only the wealthy owned them, they were likely unaffordable to commoners.

As I approached Ronika's residence, I began my descent. The chaos of emotions from the locals immediately prodded my wraith. While the negative ones stirred his need to hunt and leave a carnage in his wake, the positive ones repulsed him and made him want to leave.

To me, they were appeasing.

It had been so long since I'd been able to roam the street of any town without leaving a trail of death and devastation. I wanted more of this. I wanted to belong again.

An eager thrill coursed through me when Ronika's home finally came into view. Judging by the darkness through most of the windows, she would be going to bed soon. I loved watching her sleep. Would she whisper my name again, like she did a few times over the past few days?

The arrival of a dark carriage right in front of her house crushed those pleasant meanderings. I could see right through the glamour spell on the two undead horses pulling it, which gave them a lustrous black coat. Mortals would be fooled. Ronika might not even notice it either. But what did the necromancer want at this hour with my woman?

Cornelius stepped out of his carriage. A wave of hatred welled within me as I watched him saunter up the path leading to the front of the house. He walked with the confidence of a proprietor, like the master of this domain. The foul male had not aged a day. He'd already been a couple of centuries old when I was damned. But unlike his horses, no glamour or illusion granted him this youthful and handsome appearance. He had delved deeply into the darkest arts and struck the type of deals no amount of penance and purification could ever absolve.

The necromancer had been powerful back then, but his magic now was truly a force to be reckoned with.

But so is mine.

I didn't need complex spells, incantations, and raising an army of undead to fight my battles. With a touch, I could turn even my most powerful enemies into ashes. With a single breath, I could freeze the land and turn the mortals in contact with it into blocks of ice. With a wave of my hand, I could gather the storm and unleash a shower of lightning on my foes. And with a single thought, I could fill the hearts and minds of the throngs with dread, despair, and madness.

Cornelius had better tread carefully where my female was concerned. I was no longer the compassionate soul I had once been.

Remaining in my invisible vaporous form, I hovered over the flowerbed lining the front of Ronika's house. I couldn't get too close for fear he might detect my presence. While all mortals and most otherworldly creatures would fail to sense me in this form, a powerful necromancer such as he potentially could. But his mastery over the dead only went so far with me. After all, I was neither dead nor alive—just an anomaly that hovered between the two states of existence.

I watched him ring the chime repeatedly before Ronika

opened the door. A possessive anger surged through me at finding her dressed in nothing more than a bathrobe, water still dripping from her hair and down the visible parts of her legs. The tension I felt instantly drained when she visibly recoiled at the sight of her visitor. Until then, I hadn't even realized a part of me had dreaded she'd been expecting him... in more ways than one.

The self-righteous fury I felt at the prospect of another man touching her made no sense. We weren't a couple. She made no pledge of loyalty or exclusivity to me. She also never claimed to be single. Such an attractive female could easily be in a committed relationship. I barely managed to quell the murderous rage that exploded inside me at that thought.

But I had detected no scent of another male on her, no man shared her house, and none had visited the private section of her residence over the past few days.

A pox on sense or logic. She's mine.

She became mine the moment she willingly gave herself to me and took my seed on that sacrificial altar before the Watcher and the Moon Goddess.

"You interrupted my bath," Ronika said. "What do you want?"

The coldness and contempt in her voice as she addressed him pleased me tremendously.

"Your bath?" Cornelius replied with fake surprise. "My apologies. I could make it up to you by washing your back."

You dare?!

I almost surged forward to tear him to shreds that he would dare make such disrespectful advances to my woman. My wraith shouted for me to indulge in our bloodlust, to teach him the error of his ways. But seeing both Cornelius and Ronika suddenly look in my direction had me instinctively fading deeper into the shadows. I knew better than to give myself away by failing to control my emotions.

Ronika's snarky reply and the contemptuous way she sent him away appeased me. I loved her spine, the fierceness of her convictions, and the sharpness of her tongue.

That mouth and that tongue that had given me so much pleasure…

But the distress the necromancer caused her angered me. Her despair felt like a living entity had entered her home. Had she been anyone else, my wraith would have been unable to resist its beckoning call and gone in for the kill. Thankfully, as much as he hated how Ronika's presence brought order into the chaos of our mind, he wanted her more. Like me, he'd claimed her as ours.

I watched Cornelius get back inside the cabin of his carriage. His driver—another glamoured undead—closed the door behind him, then climbed onto the driver's seat before riding off. Considering his propensity for ostentation, I would have expected the necromancer to travel in one of those mechanical carriages. But they wouldn't respond to death magic… Or at least, he had likely not yet figured out a way to do it.

No matter, I'd make him regret coming after my female.

Malicious glee filled me at the thought of the secret plan I'd put in place for Ronika. Yes, that would properly punish him. It was a good thing I'd had the past ten days to look into the necromancer. At first, it had merely been out of curiosity. Now, it was personal.

I lingered outside a while longer until the lights in her bedroom went out. Despite knowing it would take her some time to fall asleep, I gave in to my urgent need to see her and glided to her front door. The wards barring entry possessed a respectable level of power but held no sway over me. I effortlessly passed through the door and floated up the stairs to the four bedrooms of the house.

Contrary to popular belief, wraiths weren't ghosts or incorporeal entities. In our purest ethereal form, we were comparable to vapor. We couldn't pass through solid objects, just like vapor couldn't escape a properly closed container. However, we could seep through any space that wasn't hermetically sealed. No door, no window, no matter how well designed—was ever fully sealed. But magic could make up for it. My clever female had accounted for that weakness, just not for the fact it wouldn't work on me.

My anticipation and hunger grew exponentially as I flowed through the upper floor hallway down to her room at the end. The lingering scent of herbs and burnt wax wafted to me as I passed in front of the bathroom. I squeezed through the narrow space under the door and entered Ronika's bedroom.

My rabid hunger warred with a wave of possessiveness as I peered at my woman curled up in her large bed. Judging by the restless energy filling the room, sleep still eluded her. I had barely advanced by a couple of feet before Ronika's eyes snapped open, and she jerked her head towards me. Thanks to the darkness and my vaporous form, she couldn't see me. That she could sense my presence so clearly testified to the strength of the bond that had already formed between us.

It should concern me, but it pleased me a great deal instead.

Her understandable fear didn't trigger my predatory instincts. The underlying fierceness that emanated from her certainly helped.

Ronika abruptly straightened on her bed and waved a hand towards her nightstand. A sliver of magic crossed the short distance to the lamp sitting on top, lighting it. She blinked at the sudden brightness filling the room. Her eyes flicked this way and that, searching for what had alerted her, although her gaze kept returning to where I stood, invisible.

She blindly reached for the silver dagger that sat next to the lamp on the elegantly carved wooden nightstand. I saw it every time I visited her. She fisted it, ready to stab at the intruder, and slipped out of bed with a determined look on her pretty face.

That turned me on.

It wouldn't be too effective against one such as I, but it would be perfect against undead creatures. Considering her current predicament and how she had bruised Cornelius's overwhelming ego, a sneaky retaliatory attack made sense. Not wanting to unnecessarily prolong her fear, I partially shifted out of my vaporous form, materializing before her from the waist up. The billowing shadows of my wraith form swirled where my legs would have been.

A slew of conflicting emotions flitted over her features. The oddest mix of shock, joy, fear, and confusion warred within her.

"Asheron," she whispered in a disbelieving tone.

"Ronika," I replied as a greeting with a slight taunt in my voice.

She blinked, visibly trying to make sense out of something that didn't. Her gaze flicked to the closed door behind me before returning to me. A frown creased her forehead while she lowered the silver dagger, pressing it against her chest like a shield.

"What are you doing here? And how did you get past my wards?" she asked, a touch of wariness audible in her voice.

I couldn't say if the relief she felt flattered me more than her distrust irked me.

"I hunger," I replied in a factual tone, unsure why I felt the need to further needle her. "I must feed."

This time, true fear crossed her features before she quickly clamped down on it.

"You pledged not to harm me," she said, taking an involuntary step back.

I waved a dismissive hand, making no effort to hide my annoyance. "I've already told you that our deal did not exclude feeding from you. You need me strong tomorrow."

That last comment sent a wave of relief surging through her. However, it didn't lessen her confusion.

"Right. But why from me? There are countless criminals and other fiendish creatures you could grab and make this town a bit more secure in the process," she said, while absent-mindedly putting the dagger back down on her nightstand.

I smiled. "Because feeding from them will fuel my rage and reignite the madness. If I allow rage to overtake me, I may be unable to honor our deal. But do not worry, little witch, it will not harm you. After all, I have fed from you every night since our first encounter."

Her right hand flew to the side of her neck where I had bitten her in Duskwallow. It stirred a deep and gnawing hunger, the hollowness almost tearing a rabid growl from me.

Instead, a rumbling purr vibrated through my chest. "No, I didn't drink from you."

Her shoulders slouched with relief. "But how? How did you get in? My wards have not been disturbed!" she exclaimed.

"They wouldn't be," I said smugly. "But do not panic. They are decent wards. They simply will not work against me because you granted me access to you when we struck our deal."

I didn't add that her taking my seed had created a bond between us.

Ronika's face paled. The way she wrapped her arms around her chest as if to cover herself over her warm cotton nightgown hit me in the most unpleasant fashion. Where the horror and outrage I awakened in others usually pleased me, I hated how they felt emanating from her.

"I granted you access to me? You've been taking advantage of me during my sleep?!"

I recoiled, offended she would assume such a thing from me.

"I did not," I hissed. "Yes, I fed from you, as I already stated I could back in Duskwallow. But I haven't touched you. Should I ever once again enjoy your favors, you will need to grant them."

By the look on her face, I could tell she wanted to believe me. However, her lingering doubts couldn't be denied. It took me a second to realize the reason behind it.

A taunting smile settled on my lips. "You are wondering if I speak the truth because of the intense state of arousal you've been in every night."

The crimson shade that crept up on her cheeks confirmed I had guessed accurately. A smug chuckle rolled out of my throat.

"Do not fault me for your own desires. I am a wraith. I have no aphrodisiac pheromones or seduction magic," I said, slowly gliding towards her. "I haven't touched you since that first night… but I wanted to."

I stopped barely inches from her, and fully shifted into my physical form. Her breath caught in her throat. Her eyes flicked to my nether region. Although I hadn't extruded yet, she swallowed hard then jerked her head back up to look at me with conflicted emotions.

I had not come here with any intentions other than to feed and be on my way. But now that I had her awake and aware, I craved much more than sating my eternal hunger.

"Since our first night together, I haven't stopped thinking about you. I ache for your hands on me again, your warm skin against mine, your mouth swallowing me, and to lose myself inside you," I whispered in a pressing tone while further narrowing the distance between us, invading her space. "Touch me, Ronika."

For a split second, she looked like she would comply, then fisted her hands. She licked her lips nervously before a glimmer of defiance sparked in her brown eyes.

"I already paid for your protection," she said in a calm but firm voice.

Anger flared within me, and I bared my fangs at her.

"I didn't ask for payment," I hissed. "Touch me because you *want* to. And I know you do. I have smelled your arousal every night. You have no idea how many times I fought the urge to wake you and claim you. Touch me. I need your hands on me."

To my shock, instead of further challenging me as I expected, Ronika let her gaze roam over my body with a possessiveness that had blood rushing to my groin. My breath caught in my throat as she slowly lifted her hands towards me. When the searing heat of her palms settled on my chest, my knees nearly buckled. A bolt of lust exploded in the pit of my stomach. I closed my eyes and tilted my head back, my teeth clenched while an almost pained moan vibrated through my chest.

She rubbed her hands in the most exquisite fashion over my chest before trailing a caress down to my stomach. Seconds later, the softness of her mouth settled at the base of my neck. I wrapped an arm around her waist, drawing her tightly against my body. My free hand slipped through the soft strands of her blue hair, in an unconscious effort to keep her from stopping what she was doing. I stretched my neck giving her better access while she kissed and nipped the curve of my shoulder in a path up my neck and to the side of my jaw.

With a hungry groan, I fisted her hair at the nape and bent her head back before claiming her mouth in a savage kiss. By the gods, how I had longed for this. She tasted light and fresh, like an early morning breeze. Better still, I had stabilized enough, and she had sufficiently bonded to me that she no longer felt nauseated by my phase shifting. Only pleasure and a burning desire radiated from her as her hands feverishly explored every inch of my back. Her blunt nails raking the sides of my exoskeleton sent a fiery jolt straight to my cock. I extruded, unable to withstand the painful pressure of its confinement.

The sound of tearing fabric vaguely registered in my mind. But it wasn't until the exquisite feel of Ronika's naked skin pressed against me that I realized I had ripped her nightgown off her. The guilt that started rearing its head vanished the moment my hand slipped over the round mound of her behind to find she wasn't wearing any undergarments.

Something snapped inside me.

I lifted her up, slammed her back against the wall, and rammed myself home. In a split second of lucidity, I partially shifted my cock to my ethereal form as I penetrated her before materializing again. We both cried out in that brief second from the crushing pressure of her inner walls closing all around me. I repeated the shift a few times until she adjusted to me.

Despite the burn of my brutal possession, Ronika wasn't fighting back but welcoming it. She was clinging to me, her nails digging into my skin, while our tongues warred with equal fervor. Unlike our first night, it only took a little over half a dozen thrusts before her body relaxed around my cock.

By the gods, she felt so insanely good!

I had meant for our second time to be done properly, with lengthy foreplay and a gentle touch. But I wanted her too much. Every time I felt the softness of her hands on me, any rational thought fled my mind. The primal need it invariably triggered overtook everything. Liquid fire swirled in my loins, spreading throughout my body with each thrust. Her tight sheath stroked my length, squeezing its sensitive ridges, which further fanned the flames of the inferno raging inside me.

And her hands on me… Seven hells, by that alone she owned me. It went beyond my ardent longing for physical contact after centuries of loneliness and rage. Even though our first time had been a contractual agreement, the fervor she'd touched me with had gone beyond duty. Ronika had derived genuine pleasure from our coupling. She had craved the feel of my body against hers, despite the great discomfort of my aura.

And now, even as I pounded into her, my woman hung on to me as if she feared I might vanish, as if she couldn't get close enough to me. After centuries of being nothing more than a half-dead abomination, I felt wanted… worthy… alive.

The way she shivered and moaned every time the head of my cock struck the sensitive bundle of nerves inside her acted as the most potent aphrodisiac. I could feel the bony ridges of my glans rub against it both on the way in and out. Even in my lust-addled craze, I instinctively targeted it, wanting to feel her fall apart around me.

As she began to crest, I once more reined in my wraith shouting for us to feed. There had been no greater bliss than when I'd had both my cock and my fangs buried deep inside her on that altar. And I would… soon.

The tremor coursing through her legs announced her imminent climax. I crushed her lips in a voracious kiss and ground my pelvis against hers between thrusts. The bone scales scattered at the base of my shaft worked their magic, giving her clitoris the extra stimulation she needed to topple over the edge.

Ronika cried out, her body seizing around me. I shouted as her inner walls clamped down on my cock, squeezing it with delightful brutality. My abdominal muscles constricted painfully in an effort to keep myself from spilling my seed. I wasn't ready to yield to ecstasy just yet. Nowhere near…

With a savage roar, I sank my fangs into the tender flesh at the base of her neck. The decadent taste of her blood exploded on my tongue. A voluptuous moan tumbled out of me as I gorged on this nectar worthy of the gods themselves. Her lifeforce flowed through me, saturating every cell of my body, filling the gaping void of my insatiable hunger. I wanted to drink her dry, devour her flesh, absorb everything that she was and ever would be so that she'd forever be a part of me.

My balls felt heavy, and my loins burned with the urge to fill her with my seed and further bind her to me. But that would wait. I was nowhere near sated. Ronika would scream for me over and over again before sunrise, as she should have on our first night.

As she started to come down from her high, I first pulled my cock out of her, then my fangs with a feral growl, and licked the wound shut. Ronika gasped with shock and fright as I turned away from the wall I had her pinned against and threw her. She landed on the soft mattress of her bed. I lunged at her. The startled cry that rose from her throat shifted into a rapturous moan when I buried my face between her legs.

Her dainty fingers wrapped around my horns as my tongue darted in and out of her. Blast it! She tasted divine. The intoxicating scent of her musk had my already engorge cock grow even more painfully hard. Her hips gyrated in response to my mouth feasting on her. I pulled my tongue out, replacing it with my fingers and sucked instead on her little nub. The strangled sound of her moans washed over me like a heated caress, seeping into me, and rushing down to my shaft.

I ached and throbbed with the need to take her again, but I couldn't stop devouring her. As pleasure steadily built within her, my woman involuntarily tugged at my horns. Her grip tightened as she clung to them with the desperate strength of one on the verge of drowning. She shouted my name as ecstasy swept her away in a tidal wave.

I lifted my head to admire her beautiful face dissolved in an expression of pure bliss. My fingers frantically rubbed her clitoris to keep her flying high a little longer while I kissed and caressed every inch of her body. She was so soft, so warm, so fragile...

My mouth watered as it reached the hard little bud of her nipple. I greedily licked and sucked on it before shifting my attention to her other breast. My hands and mouth were all over her, worshiping the precious gift she had granted me. Her sighs of delight, her shivers in response to my touch, and the way she whispered my name spurred me on. But Ronika closing her legs around me and lifting her pelvis against mine, while begging me for more undid me.

I gladly complied and pushed myself inside her welcoming warmth, this time with far more restraint, despite the volcano threatening to erupt in my loins. I lost myself inside my woman, our bodies rocking in this immemorial dance. Pleasure almost too much to bear ebbed and flowed as I wrested one climax after another from her. But still, I refused to surrender to my own orgasm.

I was claiming her, branding her, ensuring she would never want another but me. All the while, I drained more of her life-force. Too little to harm her, but enough to feed and to make her an indelible part of me. Her pleasure made her taste even more delicious. Time stretched and lost all meaning. Nothing else mattered other than Ronika and I becoming one, the enthralling sound of her voice whispering my name, her labored breathing in my ear, the searing feel of her skin covered in a thin sheath of sweat, and her body writhing beneath mine in the throes of the unbridled passion consuming us.

When bliss finally swept me away, I slammed myself deep inside my woman with a powerful roar. The exoskeleton of my spine felt like it was getting torn right off my back from the violence of my orgasm. One tremor after another shook me to my very core as liquid ecstasy shot out of me. I peered at Ronika's face while pumping in and out of her with erratic movements until the last of my seed was spent.

By the gods, she was beautiful!

Back arched, her blue hair splayed over the pale bed sheets, and her lips swollen by my kisses parted in a silent O, she looked like a goddess. The soft light of the lamp gave an almost magical glow to her flushed and glistening skin.

"You are mine, Ronika," I growled in a hushed tone, my body still shaken by the spasms of bliss.

She didn't respond with words but merely slipped shaky fingers through my slightly damp hair and drew my face to hers. She claimed my lips with a tenderness that wrecked me. The spark of a timid emotion I hadn't felt in centuries ignited deep within me. She broke the kiss, and our gazes remained locked for who knew how long while a silent communication passed between us. I couldn't have translated it into words, but it didn't matter.

I rolled onto my back, holding her tightly in my embrace, with my cock still buried deep inside her. Ronika snuggled against me, her head resting on my chest while my thundering heart slowly calmed down. I could feel my essence coursing through her, strengthening our bond while replenishing the energy I had siphoned from her.

A sliver of guilt tried to take root. One more night with Ronika, and I could initiate the ritual that would bind her to me for eternity. I wanted to, desperately. The thought of returning to the mindless rage, despair, and senseless killing knotted my insides. I loved the peace her mere presence gave me, the feel of her in my arms, and that wonderful way she looked at me, spoke to me.

I swore to do her no harm.

But I wouldn't be.

She might resent me for not giving her the choice.

So what? She would still be mine. In time, she would see all the ways it also benefited her.

But a willing partner would be better.

And that was the crux. My kind—both before and after my damnation—never worried about how others felt. If we wanted something, we just took it. I'd always been an anomaly. Even now. Yet, I couldn't feel any real shame at the prospect of binding her to me for eternity, with or without her consent. Ronika being mine felt too right.

I will decide once the matter of Hemdell is settled.

Three more times that night, I made her mine.

As the first rays of the rising sun colored the horizon, I pulled myself out of her embrace with much reluctance. I had a few things to take care of before our venture into Hemdell later tonight. I drew the cover over my sleeping woman, brushed my lips against hers one last time, then shifted into my vaporous form to go on the prowl.

CHAPTER 7
RONIKA

The joyous chirping of birds outside drew me out of a lovely dream. I couldn't recall any of it and didn't care. My entire body thrummed with energy and an incredible sense of well-being. A contented sigh tumbled out of me as I lazily turned to the side, the softness of the blanket caressing my naked skin in the process. I stretched my hand in search of Asheron only to find his side of the bed cold and empty.

I cracked my eyes open, disappointment flooding through me that he had left like a thief in the night. However, judging by the light noises seeping in from the outside, morning was fairly advanced already. I stretched noisily, tossed the blanket off me, and sat at the edge of the bed with a slightly frustrated sigh. For all that, the wondrous soreness lingering between my thighs brought a wistful smile to my face.

Asheron had wrecked me and exceeded even the wildest of my fantasies.

My cheeks should be burning with embarrassment for the shameless way I had given myself over and over again to the wraith. Instead, I only regretted he hadn't awakened me so that we could have one more round before he left this morning. His stamina was ridiculous. In fact, I believed he only relented out of pity for me, not that I would have stopped him had he continued, even if it killed me.

After his initial roughness—not that I minded it in the least—Asheron had been incredibly gentle and tender in his passion. I nearly felt worshiped. That his aura didn't bother me anymore either was a major bonus. I felt a negligible discomfort when he first used it to ease penetration. Then it completely faded away. It made me wonder how much better our next time would be.

Will there be a next time?

My stomach dropped. Assuming everything went as planned in Hemdell, there would be no more reason for us to see each other after tonight.

But he claimed me as his.

He had, both in Duskwallow and here, last night. Technically, nothing prevented us from pursuing whatever this was. But where would it lead? If he agreed to more encounters between us —which I strongly suspected he would—what would be his expectations? What about mine? What did I want out of this beyond sexual gratification?

Being rather picky when it came to men, I'd been celibate for years by choice. That I'd choose a wraith as a lover defied logic. Considering how much I loved my independence, was the appeal the fact that we could never have a relationship in the traditional sense? Would one even be possible? Would I want to?

Would HE want to?

"Stop borrowing trouble," I grumbled, chastising myself.

I had more serious matters to deal with instead of speculating about whether I got to draw Asheron to my bed on a regular basis.

To my pleasant surprise, I didn't feel exhausted after our endless night of sex or after he both drank my blood and drained my lifeforce. In fact, I'd never felt so full of energy. I quickly bathed and dressed.

"Blast it to hell!" I exclaimed as I started combing my hair.

The strand of wraith hair! I'd forgotten to grab one from Asheron during our countless romps. Tossing the comb onto the counter of my vanity, I jumped to my feet and rushed to my bed. Surely he'd lost a strand or two during our frolics.

To my dismay, I did find a few strands of lost hair, their tell-tale blue shade making all of them unequivocally mine.

How did he not shed a single one?

Even on the floor, by the wall against which he had so soundly ravaged me, I only found yet another strand of my own hair.

Frustrated, I finished getting ready and went down to my store. I only kept it open for a couple of hours to handle pick-ups from regular customers. With Cornelius so completely draining my finances, I needed every penny that came in. Sadly, the number of patrons who still visited me noticeably dwindled of late. The wretched necromancer made certain to spread the word that he would soon own my residence, including my shop. As Cornelius always got what he wanted, many of my customers apologetically sought comparable services elsewhere for fear they would be left hanging high and dry overnight once I lost my home. I was just grateful for those who remained loyal until the end.

An end that will never come if all goes as planned.

Time flew by way too fast. Before long, I closed the shop and went into my den. It was too humble to call it a temple, but it met my needs. I cast a series of protection spells on myself, equipped a couple of artifacts, and filled a pouch with a few vials of healing tonics and antidotes.

Unlike that night in Duskwallow, I didn't take my carriage. Riding on horseback would not only be faster in case I needed to make a swift escape, but it would also be a lot easier to hide Damar while we ventured inside the belly of that cursed place.

Luciana Delacroix had been a beautiful foreigner, married

against her will to the sixty-one-year-old Lord Frewin Hemdell. Having fallen madly in love with his much younger bride—only eighteen at the time—Lord Hemdell gave Luciana everything she wanted. When she expressed interest in alchemy, he brought the most renowned masters to Willow Grove as her private tutors. In light of her fascination with the stars, Hemdell built the most impressive observatory in their mansion as a gift for her twenty-first birthday.

According to history, things took a darker turn once Luciana became pregnant with their first child. By then, the lavish balls and elegant soirees the couple frequently held at their estate stopped, supposedly because the pregnancy was difficult. Being bedridden, the young woman lost herself in extremely rare books that her husband imported from remote places.

During those months, rumors started spreading about unusual occurrences at the estate. First, many servants nearly lost their lives in a series of strange accidents, leaving a couple of them permanently maimed. Then some sort of wild beast attacked their animals in both their barn and stables. The claw and teeth marks on the rare remains found didn't match any known creature in the area. A maid stumbling on the mangled corpse of the groundskeeper one morning marked the beginning of the end.

Multiple servants left, speaking of curses and dark arts. Those who remained either desperately needed their generous wages or were already too old to seek new employment, having served the Hemdell family their entire career.

On the night their son was born, a feral creature went on a rampage in a nearby hamlet. The creature was never caught. Witnesses spoke of some sort of demonic beast, but the tale was too formidable to be believed. That morning, Lord Hemdell announced that his son had been stillborn. As the pregnancy had been difficult, no one questioned it. When she had another miscarriage a few months later, people speculated that Lord

Hemdell's old seed was to blame. His quickly deteriorating physical appearance gave it credence.

On the day that should have been their son's first anniversary, Lord Hemdell died. Luciana dismissed everyone. In the following weeks, mysterious visitors were seen coming and going at the estate. Among them, dauntless treasure hunters known to only offer their services in the search of extremely rare or forbidden artifacts came knocking. Soon, blood-curdling sounds could be heard at night while ungodly lights emanated from the mansion. The once luxuriant gardens surrounding it withered, the proud ancestral trees turning into twisted, gnarly things, their branches like the skeletal fingers of some abomination.

Reports of more fiendish creatures lurking in the shadows and descending upon unsuspecting travelers abounded. When they started attacking farms and villages, the people rose against the young beauty they had once admired and pitied. As demands for her to leave remained unheeded, a mob gathered outside the gates. That day, more than two hundred people died, their ravaged corpses and severed limbs scattered on a two-mile radius outside the estate. Rumor claimed that this massacre opened a portal to the underworld that day.

Ever since, demons, ghouls, and various otherworldly beings became permanent residents of Willow Grove. In a vain effort to cleanse their lands and countryside from these abominations, the villagers called upon holy knights, exorcists, and Inquisitors. None of those who entered Hemdell returned.

Drawn by what they perceived as an opportunity, many who dabbled in the occult and dark arts flocked to Willow Grove. Witches, seers, necromancers, and alchemists provided alternative solutions where holy knights had failed. The sale of protective wards, cures and antidotes against the virulent toxins of demonic creatures grew into an extremely lucrative business. Demon hunting and the banishing of undead beasts also made welcome those people who were once considered sacrilegious.

People like Cornelius…

With time, as the demonic invasion went from critical danger to just business as usual, the local population shifted its attention to the other benefits of magic, from glamour spells to performance enhancing tonics, everyone wanted a quick fix to whatever woe or perceived shortcoming they possessed.

As magic gradually became an integral part of Willow Grove, more supernatural beings and magic users congregated here in search of safety or anonymity for some, and for a fresh hunting ground for others. I'd seen vampires and fae in the city but heard of Lycans in the forest and Wolfmoon mountains to the north.

In the years that followed, visitors continued to go to Hemdell, although Luciana herself was never seen. According to rumors, the Weaver also settled in Willow Grove around that time. On the night of the blood moon, a little over three hundred years ago, purple flames engulfed the estate. No one knew what caused the fire. Terrifying screams resonated through the night from the mansion. Witnesses claimed it was like a chorus of the souls of the damned screeching in agony from the deepest pit of hell.

The flames faded with the first rays of the rising sun. To everyone's shock, the house stood unscathed. No one ever visited the mansion again.

Popular belief claims that Luciana died that night or that she performed a summoning that went awry and ended up dragged to one of the seven hells. After a few months, the first pillagers ventured inside in search of the artifacts she had collected, and which had to be worth a fortune. Most of them didn't make it out alive. Those who did usually returned empty-handed, having chosen to flee with their lives rather than press forward to their deaths.

As far as I knew, only three of the hundreds of artifacts Luciana had collected had successfully been retrieved.

In the distance, the massive dome of Hemdell's observatory peaked above the dark limbs of the trees lining the long path to the mansion. I'd lie by denying that a hefty dose of apprehension weighed on me at the thought of entering that cursed place. As many artifacts—such as the Microlith—tended to bind to whoever released them from their previous confinement, I had to retrieve it myself.

Allowing Asheron to retrieve it on my behalf while I remained safely tucked away at home would have been much too easy. Anyway, he probably couldn't have completed the task. As was often the case with these types of magical items, unsealing or releasing them involved some sort of mortal sacrifice—blood in this instance. Although Asheron could bleed in his physical form, he technically wasn't mortal anymore… at least not in the traditional sense. Therefore, an offering from him would likely be rejected.

I was just glad he would be the one escorting me inside. In theory, we only had a non-committed sexual relationship. In practice, I felt a genuine bond was forming between us. In a way I couldn't fully explain, I trusted him. His visit last night cemented that conviction. There were so many ways he could have screwed me—well, figuratively speaking—but he had not.

My head jerked up at the sudden darkening of the sky, ominous clouds gathering at an unnatural speed. The temperature dropped, making my breath smoke in what had otherwise been a comfortably warm summer night.

Two weeks ago, this would have filled my heart with terror. Tonight, it fluttered instead with wistful anticipation while a delighted smile stretched my lips. As if called by my thoughts of him, Asheron was approaching.

Movement at the edge of my vision drew my attention. I turned my head to see the air blur before a shadowy figure materialized a few meters to my right. Asheron's red eyes glowed as he flew alongside me in his wraith form. Totally unfazed by such a terrifying presence, Damar didn't slow down, continuing to gallop at a steady pace towards our destination.

I beamed at Asheron. The palpitating red glow between the exposed bones of his chest grew in intensity as he returned my smile. The endless rows of dagger teeth thus bared should have turned my blood to ice and sent a chill down my spine. Instead, it further appeased me. This was *my* wraith, *my* monster. And those terrifying teeth would wreck any fiendish creature that dared stand in our path.

I no longer feared his wraith form. Last night, when Asheron partially shifted before asking me to touch him, his lingering wraith's lower body had brushed against my legs. It made my skin tingle. The sensation had been strange but not unpleasant. Above all, it hadn't drained the very life out of me or turned my skin to ashes. A part of me knew the final step to break whatever barriers still existed between Asheron, his darker side, and me was to fully embrace him in his wraith form.

I was ready and willing.

As my gaze shifted back to his ethereal form gliding through the air, a potent wave of possessiveness swelled within me. Yes, he was mine. Whatever the future held, I would claim all of him.

I wondered if he had summoned his frost and gathered the storm clouds to let me know of his presence, as a warning for the creatures we would encounter to scatter, or a mix of both. It didn't matter. That display of power further comforted me that he'd keep me safe inside that wretched place.

A few minutes later, we reached the tall gates of the estate. They'd been all but torn off their hinges years ago. I couldn't tell if it had been by creatures attempting to escape or looters trying to get in. After multiple failed attempts at replacing the gates by more solid ones, the villagers had called upon a coven of powerful witches for a more permanent solution.

There was no such thing when dealing with this level of magic.

The witches had set up a magical barrier that prevented monsters from getting out, and made it extremely hard, if not impossible for people without spellcasting abilities to enter. The goal had been to keep our reckless youth and clueless travelers from venturing into these accursed grounds and meeting an untimely demise.

Asheron landed at the same time I dismounted from Damar. He shifted into his physical form while I loosely wrapped my horse's lead around a branch of the bushes lining the exterior of the fence. Their lush and healthy leaves contrasted sharply with the barren and gnarly branches of the trees just on the other side, their limbs stretched towards the sky like in a desperate plea for mercy.

I caressed Damar's face and fed him a few apples. He was well-trained and understood that my loosely looping the lead the way I had meant he was to remain here but could leave if threatened by any danger. He would return for me as soon as things were safe again. But I prayed that it wouldn't be needed.

For added safety, I cast a camouflage spell over Damar, which would make him invisible to the naked eye and mask his scent. To my utter shock and complete delight, my magic burst forth with unusual strength. Something this finicky usually took me a while to cast and stabilize. I especially struggled with the opacity of the illusion that made my subject invisible. This one went off with the ease of a low-level light spell, like the one I used to turn my night lamp on and off.

I gave Asheron a speculative sideways glance. The smugness of the discreet smile on his lips appeared to confirm he'd guessed what thought had just crossed my mind. An undeniable shift occurred over the past couple of weeks. Without a doubt, he enhanced my magic.

I approached him and let him draw me into his embrace. The

possessiveness and protectiveness of the gesture warmed my chest. No lust lurked in his red eyes, only focus and a smidge of wariness.

"So long as we stick to the main path, we should be relatively safe up to the house," Asheron explained in a serious tone. "The barrier erected by the witches prevents most of the lesser creatures from leaving the garden. But they may try to scare you or lure you off the road into the trees. *Do not* stray from the path, no matter what you see or hear."

"I won't. I will stick to the path," I said, my stomach knotting with blossoming apprehension now that the reality of the moment was sinking in.

Having likely perceived it, Asheron frowned.

"You also must control your fear. Aside from the fact it will attract more abominations to our location, I would rather not have to fight the urge to attack you," he warned.

"I will," I promised. "But I know you won't attack me."

"Of course, I won't. But that's not the point," he retorted sternly. "Always stay behind me. Once we're inside, if I am fighting, keep a wall to your back so that nothing can sneak up on you."

"Okay. I was planning on using some repelling spells and protection incantations during that time. Would that be acceptable?" I asked in a sheepish voice. "It won't disturb you?"

He snorted, his face softening in the sweetest way. "Your spells cannot negatively affect me."

I stiffened at that. "My magic is not *that* weak."

His face took on a mysterious expression laced with amusement. "It has nothing to do with that. Your magic can no more affect me than the wards in your house did. I am a part of you."

"A part of me?" I echoed, taken aback.

A shrill scream beyond the gates prevented him from answering. We both glanced in the direction the noise emanated from. Silence returned immediately thereafter. Asheron peered at the sky. Although his dark clouds still covered most of it, they didn't hide the moon.

"The eclipse begins," he said, a slight tension in his voice. "We must go. The moon will turn red in about an hour. We want to reach the observatory and secure it before it does. Then you'll only have ninety minutes to recover what you came for before the moon turns black again. Let us not dally."

I nodded stiffly and absentmindedly fingered the mojo bag in the pocket of my dress, which contained a moonstone, quartz crystals, moonwort, and a silver bead. It would help harness the power of the blood moon to further protect me.

Asheron turned into his vaporous form. Despite sensing his presence nearby, it disturbed me to have him go invisible as we approached the magical barrier that blocked the otherwise broken gates. It allowed him to go through anything not perfectly sealed and reduced his vulnerability to wards. I cast a safe passage spell on myself before walking past the mangled remains of the former gates. My skin tingled as I crossed the barrier. As intended by the witches who erected it, the barrier clearly wanted me to turn back but held no power to compel me to do so.

To my relief, Asheron materialized into his wraith form a couple of steps ahead of me as soon as he cleared the gates. The air instantly shifted as if we'd entered another world. Technically, we had. It felt muggy and humid, filled with a sickly-sweet scent, like overripe fruits.

The deafening silence gave the impression all sounds had been sucked right out of the world. Even my footsteps on the packed dirt of the path came out muffled and barely audible. That suited me just fine. The less attention we brought onto ourselves, the better.

Dead trees with ebony bark lined both sides of the wide path, big enough to allow two large carriages to ride side by side. At their feet, reddish moss covered the dark soil and their thick, twisted roots. It could easily be mistaken for blood.

Maybe it was.

I snapped my head to the right as I detected movement at the edge of my vision. Failing to see anything notable in the stillness of the night, I looked back ahead. Asheron advanced with his head straight, seemingly oblivious. Had I just imagined it? Was he deliberately ignoring it?

To my relief, he adopted a brisk but comfortable pace. The last thing I needed was to be winded by the time we reached the three-story mansion. As they'd built the observatory on the top floor, a long and perilous climb awaited us ahead.

Movement, this time to the left, startled me. My heart leapt at the sight of a series of tree branches bending like dark skeletal hands towards the path. I barely managed to squelch the instinctive urge to run to the right, away from the threat. Asheron looked at me over his shoulder, his red eyes glowing. In his wraith form, his facial features were too blurred to allow me to clearly read his emotions. But that didn't prevent me from perceiving the stern warning emanating from him.

He'd cautioned me about the scare tactics the damned entities lurking in the gardens would use. I needed to bury the natural inclination to assess and detect potential threats and act like Asheron. He was keeping his head straight, looking ahead, and ignoring whatever horrors lurked in the shadows.

They are barred from the path. Ignore them.

That resolution appeared to set the lurkers in a frenzy. At the edge of my vision, on both sides, the trees bent their trunks at impossible angles, almost folding in half as if in an attempt to swipe at me. Considering their incredible heights, they should have been able to reach me, despite us walking in the middle of the path. Just when I thought they would strike me, they suddenly seemed to be a lot farther away than my eyes led me to believe.

Large branches severed themselves from the trees, then jumped onto the ground. They stood on two or three offshoots of their limbs in an almost humanoid position. Seeing them dart towards us at lightning speed nearly had me screaming in terror. But I kept my head straight and began to whisper a calming chant, repeating the incantation in a loop.

If not for Asheron continuing to stoically glide forward, I might have given in to panic as two of the 'walking' tree branches closed the distance between us. Vicious thorns dripping with what could only be a deadly poison or lethal toxin extruded all over their surface seconds before they leapt at me.

This is an illusion. This is an illusion.

Just as they would have crashed into me, lacerating me with their thorns and sharp limbs, the creatures vanished in a puff of smoke without ever making contact.

Deep down, I had known them to be an illusion, as I kept repeating to myself. But that confirmation erased any power those creatures might have had over me. Although I continued to whisper my calming chant—you could never be too prudent—I no longer felt any fear. Even when the trees appeared to physically move closer to the path, I didn't blink. The only strong reaction they got out of me was when multiple trees launched various branches at me like harpoons. I gasped in shock as they brutally stabbed into the ground barely inches from me with a thundering sound.

Those, too, were illusions.

I couldn't tell if some creature with eldritch powers was playing with my mind or if those trees were really the ones trying to lure me. So long as they couldn't get to me, I didn't care. However, had Asheron not warned me, I would have undoubtedly tried to run away from the limbs rushing me, which would have instinctively been towards the woods.

Sadly, at the same time the rows of twisted trees thinned, and the path opened into the wide courtyard of the manor, the repelling magic of the witches increasingly faded. Whatever crawled in the shadows ahead would not be hindered in its effort to reach us.

They wasted no time manifesting their presence.

Although I couldn't see them yet, the clicking of small feet scurrying about, and muffled croaking sounds that faded into a kind of rattling went off in various areas around the manor.

As claustrophobic as walking along the path framed by the creepy forest-like garden had been, entering the imposing circular courtyard left me feeling exposed and vulnerable. Water, black as sin, shot out of the fountain and into the wide basin which occupied the center of the courtyard.

Behind it, the elegant lines of the tall gothic building rose in a foreboding fashion. Despite the vines crawling over the intricately carved pillars framing the large doorways, along the tall arched windows, and wide balconies, the structure itself seemed to have been frozen in time. There was no visible tear, damage, or rot one would expect to find in an abandoned and haunted house. While the previously light-beige stone building had now turned black—likely from the magic fire that had preceded Luciana's disappearance—it didn't look charred or burnt and had kept some of the lighter color in some wall panels visible beneath the vines. Bright, powerful yellow lights illuminated every window, as if a brazier was raging inside.

As we grew closer to the house, I didn't miss how Asheron gave the fountain a wide berth. A hint of sulfur emanated from the dark pool. Although I perceived no heat from it, thin plumes of smoke crawled over the oily surface of the water.

What I first assumed to be the glow of green, magical flames of the sconces and torches scattered around the mansion soon proved to be the source of the scurrying and croaking. I couldn't fully make out the creatures they belonged to. However, the rapid movement of the 'lights' between the bushes and the dark shadows of the manor's terrace reminded me of the waddling of a duck.

Still looking ahead, Asheron slightly turned his face sideways to address me over his shoulder.

"There are bile spawns ahead. Prepare to run," he whispered. "Once we reach the house, press your back against the wall—the *wall*, not the *door*—and cast the Shield of Azriel on yourself. If anything comes at you, use a repulsion spell."

"Understood," I replied, forcing myself to silence the fear rearing its head.

As soon as we finished circling around the fountain, and with less than twenty meters from the short flight of stairs up the large porch, the first bile spawn emerged from the bushes lining the left side of the house. I had never seen or heard of such monsters before.

The nightmarish creature vaguely reminded me of a small ostrich, the size of a five-year-old child, with much thicker legs and vicious talons. Its body stood mostly upright, with thick scales and spikes on its back, but a translucent, bulging underbelly filled with the glowing green substance I'd previously mistaken for magic lights. Scythe-limbs similar to a praying mantis' front legs replaced the wings. A long tail trailed behind it, tipped by a humongous dart shaped like a dagger. But it was the head attached to its long neck that had my blood curdling. Round and pitch black like the rest of its body, the face had an eerily human quality to it, with large, green eyes without pupils. It didn't possess a visible nose or ears, but a round mouth— almost like a pig snout, but fully hollow.

The creature emitted that croaking shout again, quickly echoed by many others on both sides of the house.

"Now!" Asheron ordered before darting forward.

I didn't question him and just ran.

Like an army of ants rushing out of a disturbed anthill, the dreadful creatures emerged from the shadows in numbers far too great to count. My stomach dropped, and my pulse raced with fear. As powerful as Asheron was, how could he handle such throngs?

As if in direct response to that unspoken question, Asheron summoned his frost. A thin sheet of black ice quickly spread over the stone pavement on each side of us, leaving a safe path straight to the stairs. The bile spawns in the front of the pack—running at mind-boggling speed—lost their footing, falling face first onto the ground. The other monsters following behind tripped over them in a chaos of tangled limbs.

Straight ahead, a dozen creatures pushed and shoved at each other in greedy impatience as they ran down the stairs towards us. Asheron dashed forward with a blood-chilling scream. The billowing shadows of his wraith form seemed to expand as he flew straight into the incoming swarm. Their vicious shouts died as abruptly as they began. Asheron flew up the stairs, leaving a trail of ashes in his wake where the spawn had previously stood.

I covered my nose as I raced up the steps both to avoid inhaling the clouds of ashes rising up and to block the foul stench they had left behind. As soon as I reached the porch, I slammed my back against the wall, between the door and the first window to the left. Ignoring the terrifying screeches of the bile spawns quickly approaching, I cast the Shield of Azriel spell over me. A barely visible dome formed around me. Once more, the ease with which I performed the spell left me reeling.

But now wasn't the time to reflect on such things.

Asheron's dark silhouette flew at impossible speed this way and that, first over the porch to wipe out any imminent threat to me, then down into the courtyard. I hated not being able to help him—not that he looked like he needed me. But my staying put meant he didn't have to worry about my whereabouts or current situation. It allowed him to control the field and the battle as he saw fit without me getting in the way or messing up his plans.

Just as I was resuming my calming incantation, the clouds

overhead grew even thicker and darker, blocking out the moonlight. The brightness of the lights inside the house didn't radiate outside, as if magically stopped by an invisible wall.

A thick and opaque blanket of darkness descended over the porch and courtyard. I might as well have been blindfolded as I couldn't even see my own body. The only things that remained visible were the glowing bellies of the bile spawns. In this complete obscurity, their numbers seemed to have multiplied exponentially.

While countless creatures congregated towards Asheron, far too many glowing bellies were veering towards me. Seeing them floating in the darkness at high speed, swaying in that typical way an ostrich's body moved as it ran, made it all the more distressing. Although this lasted mere seconds, it felt like an eternity had gone by.

A thunderous sound ripped through the sky, then a blinding light stabbed my eyes as a myriad of lightning bolts shot down to the ground. Right before I shut my eyelids, I witnessed countless spawns explode, their bellies bursting, and the green bile they contained spraying outward. In their midst, Asheron floated upright, his arms spread out, and his terrifying mouth wide open in a feral expression.

I blinked, blinded for a few additional seconds after the intense brightness that had assaulted my eyes. The clouds scattering overhead helped clear my vision. To my horror, the bile acted like bubbling acid, burning through the skin of the mangled remains of the spawns that had exploded under the lightning blast. The others still moving around appeared unscathed by it.

However, the ones closest to Asheron spit their greenish bile at him through their round mouths. The spatter flew right through his vaporous form, some of it falling to the ground and some landing on the bile spawns amassed on the other side of the wraith. Unfazed, Asheron swept through them, eviscerating them with his claws, and draining every ounce of their lifeforce with the dark shadows of his skirt.

It was terrifyingly mesmerizing.

My head jerked to the right at the pitter-patter of quickly approaching footsteps. To my shock, the incoming bile spawn's belly didn't glow, which had allowed him to fully hide in the shadows. Its bigger size marked it as older than the ones we'd encountered so far. Once it realized I had noticed its presence, the creature gave up its 'camouflage' and its belly lit up, from the center outward.

As I whispered a repelling spell, it spat a stream of bile at me. It struck my protective shield—making it shimmer—at the same time my spell sent the spawn flying backward. It screeched in pain and anger. My shield flickering again, and a dull thud had me jerking my head left. My stomach dropped at the sight of three more older spawns. The one closest to me, his belly glowing green, had spat some bile at me while sneaking up from behind. His two companions in the back were just now illuminating their bellies, ready to get into the action.

Even as I cast the repelling spell on the closest one, I knew there wouldn't be enough time for me to cast it on the other two before they got to me. And that didn't account for the first one behind me who was undoubtedly recovering from the impact. Although my magic had grown stronger since meeting Asheron, I doubted it had made my Shield of Azriel strong enough to sustain a prolonged attack by many of these creatures.

My spell hit the closest spawn. Luck being on my side, the monster knocked back one of the other two shadowing him. The third one sprayed its acid at me, covering my shield with a heavy coat.

"Asheron!" I called out before my shield violently shuddered.

A glimpse behind me turned my blood to ice. The first spawn had run up to me and stabbed my protective shield with a huge needle-like protrusion that shot out of its round mouth. In a flash of understanding, I realized the creatures likely used it either to inject prey with their acid, or to drink their victims' liquified insides when done. The dart of its tail also stabbed at my shield.

Not even a second had gone by since calling Asheron—the longest of my life—when the creatures attacking me from both sides collapsed with agonizing screeches. Stunned, I stared at the spawns writhing on the stones covering the porch. Their legs and arms had been broken in half, the shattered bones piercing through flesh and scales. Their necks suddenly snapped. A violent shudder coursed through their broken bodies, and they went still.

A wave of cold engulfed me while a looming shadow blocked part of the moonlight. I looked up to find Asheron towering over me. His eyes and palpitating open chest glowed with the same savage intensity as the first time we met in Duskwallow. He emitted a steady, menacing growl, his rows of dagger teeth bared at me.

The madness is overtaking him.

In an instant, I realized his wraith was fighting the urge to kill me. The logical fear that should have gripped me never came. I smiled, letting my body relax, and projecting as much calm and assurance as I could muster.

"It's me, Asheron. *Your* Ronika," I said in a soothing voice. "You are my protector. You've kept me safe so far. I trust you with my life."

Although the glow in his eyes and from his open chest intensified, the palpitation slowed down. He moved closer to me. My Shield of Azriel collapsed as soon as his aura touched it. The freezing cold of his presence went up another notch, chilling me to the bone.

He raised a hand towards my face, his dagger claws coming within an inch of my cheek. Still, I didn't panic. A single touch would do irreparable damage to my face. Nevertheless, I remained stoic. In a way I couldn't explain, I knew he wouldn't harm me.

"My Ronika," he whispered, his voice sounding doubled.

"Yes, Asheron. Your Ronika," I said, my eyes flicking between his.

The five-inch claws at the tip of his fingers receded as did the shadows around his monstrous wraith hand, revealing the gray-ish-beige skin of his physical form. He placed his palm against my cheek. I leaned into the coolness of his touch and trustingly closed my eyes. His thumb slid down to my lips, gently brushing over them.

I slowly opened my eyes and found his face but an inch from mine. I didn't move, even when he menacingly bared his teeth at me.

"You are mine," he hissed.

Asheron didn't give me a chance to respond. He dropped his hand, turning it back to its frightening wraith form as he straightened. His shadow skirt spread in an arc around me, siphoning the lingering energy of the dead older bile spawns at our feet. He glided over to the door, freeing my line of sight. My jaw dropped at the tableau it revealed.

The entire courtyard was covered in ice. While the area closer to the fountain where Asheron had battled only showed piles of ashes beneath the ice, the outer edges held a completely different spectacle. Dozens of bile spawns, both old and young, were impaled in ice spikes that had shot out of the ground.

In my need to appease him, I'd completely blocked out the fact that we had been under a brutal onslaught. I wanted to believe that a subconscious part of me had realized the battle had already ended.

As the door parted open before Asheron, the ice spikes in the courtyard faded, leaving the corpses slumping onto the ground.

CHAPTER 8
RONIKA

I followed my companion into the manor, a million thoughts racing through my mind. The main one was how in the world he had shattered the bones of older bile spawns. Wraiths possessed the powers of frost, lightning, dread, draining one's lifeforce, and the ability to take, steal, or feed from souls. But their dominion over frost and lightning should never be as great as what Asheron had displayed. Judging by his physical form, he had not been human before his damnation. What was he?

After a couple of steps inside the manor, all those wandering thoughts flew out of my mind. This place reeked of malice. It had nothing to do with scent. Under different circumstances, I would deem the lemongrass aroma that lingered in the air rather pleasant. But evil permeated this place. It felt like a slimy, living entity crawling over my skin.

The great hall extended into a seating area in front of what I believed to be a library or spacious study at the back. Two large open doors gave us a glimpse into that room. On each side of the hall, intricately carved wooden stairs led to the second floor.

Like the exterior façade of the manor, the interior looked pristine. There was not a single piece of furniture out of place or the slightest speck of dust to be found. You'd think an army of maids regularly maintained the house. Based on images I'd seen and descriptions I'd read about Hemdell, Luciana had once again given a darker edge to the house after her husband's passing.

The once paler colors of the walls had been replaced by obsidian, deep purples, and burgundy shades. The bright lights we'd seen from outside stemmed from the imposing black chandeliers dangling from the fifteen-foot-high ceiling. The elegant furniture matched the gothic style of the house.

Once more, I cast my safe passage spell on myself. While the Shield of Azriel held undeniable advantages, it worked best if you stood still in one area. If on the move, the former spell offered greater protection.

By the glance Asheron cast my way, he seemed to approve of my choice.

Without hesitation, he started gliding towards the right staircase. I followed, curious as to what had prompted this choice. As soon as I set foot on the first step, my stomach roiled. I didn't feel any magic—negative or otherwise—radiating from it, but the cushiony feel of what should be solid hardwood made me uneasy. You'd think I had stepped on a living entity.

That creepy impression was reinforced moments later when the dark tapestry covering the wall bulged as if a limb pushed against it from within. It reminded me of a fetus shifting inside its mother's womb, and the outline of a tiny foot appeared on her belly from the internal pressure. The bulge inside the wall followed an upward path. The immediate thought that crossed my mind was that whatever lurked inside the wall wanted to beat us up the stairs.

Then, I finally noticed the first sign of desecration in the house. A few family portraits hung on the wall alongside the staircase. While I couldn't swear to it, their outfits with the colors and crests led me to believe they were all members of Lord Hemdell's family. Their faces were covered by a white mask with wide, narrow red eyes, two slits for the nostrils, and a long mouth that almost split the face in half. Black demonic teeth peeked between the lipless mouths. The masks had a reptilian quality to them, as if a snake had attempted to take on a human face. But the most disturbing part was that the masks didn't look painted on. It felt like I could reach a hand and take them right off.

But the gods knew I had no desire whatsoever of finding out what lay behind them.

Asheron, too, was keeping an eye on them. As he approached the first one, a growl rose from his throat, sending a shiver down my spine. He waved his palm in front of the wall, and a thick coat of ice covered it. I nearly jumped out of my skin when a loud groan resonated all around us. It didn't come from the wall, but the house itself. The spongy steps of the stairs undulated beneath my feet. It was subtle, but noticeable enough to make me queasy.

Behind the thick layer of ice, the masked Hemdell ancestors banged on their frozen prisons, their terrifying mouths open impossibly wide in a silent scream of rage. Heart pounding, I uttered my calming chant under my breath and forced myself to look straight ahead.

With a threatening hiss, Asheron suddenly surged forward. I raced up the stairs after him, refusing to be left behind. A high-pitched screech emanated from whatever creature had prompted Asheron to lunge. By the time I reached the landing, more dying screeches echoed the first one, a trail of ashes the only proof something living had once lurked here.

He used his frost to seal the couple of closed doors we passed to reach the second set of stairs on our way to the third floor. While I perceived nothing from that first sealed room, unmistakable scurrying sounds reached me through the second door. I could only pray whatever dwelled within wouldn't be able to break through the ice and attack us from behind.

Thankfully, no paintings lined those stairs as giant windows occupied the entire wall, giving us an eerie view of the sprawling dark gardens outside. It was only once we started climbing the second staircase that I finally saw what fresh abomination Asheron was culling here.

It resembled a human twisted into the parody of a spider. With arms serving as legs—which all ended with clawed hands instead of feet—it walked on all fours. Like an owl, its head could turn two hundred and seventy degrees. That its face matched the creepy masks on the painting knotted my insides. Its translucent white skin exposed the bluish-black veins running beneath it.

The creature leapt at Asheron from the landing with a blood-curdling cry. He caught the monster mid-air and effortlessly tore it in half. Black blood sprayed only to be instantly absorbed by the wall and stairs. The remains of the creature withered under the wraith's touch before crumbling into a shower of ashes.

Through the windows, I glimpsed the completion of the eclipse, and the moon turned red. A wave of energy surged through me, my mojo bag granting me the extra power it was harnessing from the blood moon.

Two more crawlers met a swift demise at the hands of Asheron before we reached the third floor. It couldn't have been soon enough. Nothing came at me from behind, but I distinctly heard shuffling sounds emanating from the second floor. It had been getting closer, although still too far to be a real threat. A part of me believed it belonged to something heavy. I didn't doubt for a minute that Asheron had heard it as well. Whatever it was, we'd deal with it on our way out.

The spacious landing had a large balcony looking down onto the lower floor. It split into two corridors on the left and right. In the distance, more of the crawlers poked out their heads to observe us. One of them climbed up the wall to hang from the ceiling. They clearly itched to come after us, but the brutal end of their kin seemed to deter them from attacking for fear of meeting a similar fate. When Asheron made as if to go after them, the crawlers scattered, vanishing through some hidden nooks or passages.

To my relief, he didn't give chase.

Anyway, our destination lay straight ahead of us. The rounded walls lining the back of the balcony enclosed the observatory. An artistic carving of the stars and constellations adorned the massive set of wooden doors. The gold leaf work on the carvings made them stand out even more against the dark wood.

I held my breath as Asheron pushed the doors open, dreading something foul might leap out and attack us. Tension bled out of me when only a stunning circular room greeted us. As soon as I stepped inside, Asheron closed the door behind us and locked it.

My gaze roamed over our surroundings with awe. Tall, floor-to-ceiling arched windows made up half the walls of the observatory. The dome overhead took up most of the ceiling. Alcoves harboring stunning, life-size statues of each zodiac sign stood between each window. Sconces with magical flames hung above the alcoves, lighting up the space. A giant telescope sat on a circular dais in the center of the room. Neatly organized nautical and celestial maps covered the tables on the left and right sides of the door. A large tapestry on the wall combined strange drawings of constellations, zodiac symbols, and the same type of odd runes etched on the charm the Weaver had given me.

On the left side of the telescope, an astrolabe sat atop a wooden pedestal. On the opposite side, an armillary sphere stood on a similar pedestal. I had no use for the astrolabe, but the telescope and armillary sphere would lead me to my prize… assuming I followed the steps correctly.

"Hurry," Asheron said in a tense voice. "The blood moon has already started. Time is ticking."

He didn't have to say it twice.

Heart pounding, I hurried to the telescope. I didn't know

much about astronomy but enough about astrology to hopefully be able to get through this. As was common during a total eclipse, the stars appeared so dimmed in the sky they were barely visible to the naked eye. But the telescope allowed me to see them more clearly. Once I peered through the eyepiece, it took me far too long to recognize the Gemini constellation as being the one closest to the blood moon.

I headed to the armillary sphere and started adjusting the rings. As the latitude and longitude were already set, I left them alone and rotated the ring to set the month and day to today's date at the equinox. In turn, that allowed me to find the time of both the sunset and sunrise.

Feeling both excited and a little apprehensive, I headed to the sculpture of the twin sisters. They faced each other, one hand resting on a two-ring disc. Only once within range did I realize the discs represented a total eclipse. Based on my research, I had known revealing the relic would have required entering the sunrise and sunset times in some sort of dial. But it said nothing about which, how, or why. A glance around the room at the other statues confirmed they also possessed overlapping discs. However, their placement varied, and only two other statues had both discs perfectly centered with each other.

As a mistake could have dire consequences, I pondered on which time to assign to which disk. Taking a deep breath, I decided to set the sunset time on the first disk and sunrise on the second one. As the eclipse occurred when the moon passed in front of the sun, the top disc had to be the moon. And the moon became visible at nightfall.

I jumped at the clicking sound that came from the statue, followed by the grinding of gears similar to that of a clockwork mechanism. Then the twins came to life, their wooden limbs covered in gold leaf rotating one of the two discs in opposite directions. A smaller ring in the middle of the 'moon' opened into a hole the size of a medallion. A tiny bowl—no bigger than a tablespoon—slowly poked out of the opening.

It's working! By the gods, it's working!

As soon as it stopped moving, the twins jerked their heads sideways to stare at me with a menacing expression. Their lips gradually parted, revealing needle teeth. Their nails lengthened into terrifying claws, and their features distorted, becoming monstrous. It was all the creepier that they remained wooden statues, but their teeth and claws seemed made of metal.

Forcing myself to remain calm, I retrieved the small dagger from my belt and sliced the tip of my index finger. Holding my finger over the small receptacle, I pressed its sides so blood would trickle down while I recited the incantation in a loop. The twins were growing increasingly frightening and detaching from the wall and their pedestal. Asheron's dark silhouette entered my line of sight at the corner of my eye, as he no doubt readied to protect me should I fail.

I blocked them all from my mind and focused on completing my task. As I spoke, the dials rotated, their hue shifting. As the 'moon' began to turn red, I realized the ritual would only be done once the dials emulated the blood moon. But it was taking so long... too damn long.

Like with everything else when dealing with the occult, fear was your greatest enemy. If I panicked and lost my concentration, it would make this take even longer. Then the twins would lunge at me.

To my eyes, the moon disc had now fully turned red, yet it seemed to want more. Doubt finally started taking root. Had I forgotten a step? Had I made a mistake during one of the previous steps?

Just when I thought the worst would happen, a loud clicking sound resonated. The Gemini froze. Then, as if the clock was being turned back, the twins slowly reverted to their almost angelic appearance and returned to their original position inside their alcove. The receptacle slid back inside the opening, which closed with a discreet sound. My face split in an ecstatic grin when the moon disc glowed then slid down inside the lower part of the sculpture, revealing a secret compartment.

I did it! I did it!

The nightmare would soon be over and…

My face fell when the recessed shelf turned out to be empty. I blinked in shock and confusion. I shoved my hand inside in disbelief and met nothing but air.

"That's not possible," I whispered, my chest constricting.

Struck by a sudden thought, I cast a revealing spell… to no avail. Crestfallen, I stared at the empty space, feeling too numb to think or otherwise react. I'd made so many sacrifices, put my life at risk in more ways than one, and beaten the mechanism for this? For nothing?!

"Ronika," Asheron said in a soft voice. "It is gone. Someone else took it already."

I jerked my head towards him to argue that they couldn't have. *I* needed it! It *had* to be in another one of the statues. But not a single word crossed my lips. He had partially shifted back to his physical form as his wraith's undefined features made it difficult for him to convey emotions. Something in the way he looked at me turned my blood to ice.

"You knew," I exclaimed, my voice barely more than a whisper. "You knew it was already gone."

The guilty expression that flitted over his face confirmed my accusation. I took an involuntary step back as I recoiled in horror. My heart shattered into a thousand pieces, and my vision blurred with tears of pain and anger.

"You betrayed me! I trusted you. I TRUSTED YOU!" I exclaimed, my voice filled with anguish.

"I did *not* betray you," he ground between his teeth, taking a step towards me.

I backed away. "You knew, and you led me on!" I shouted.

"No, Ronika. I did not *know*," Asheron replied forcefully. "I strongly *suspected* it might be, but I had no way of knowing for sure. Remember that I've been lost to madness for the past three centuries. This is the first time since my awakening that this repository has been accessible. I had no way of verifying if the Microlith was still there."

His words made sense, and yet, I still felt like he had betrayed me.

"But you suspected! You could have warned me! You could have—"

"*You* should have known," he snapped in a stern voice. "The minute you mentioned coming to Hemdell on the night of the blood moon, I guessed you were coming after the Microlith. I said as much. That I could so easily figure out which artifact you wanted and when it could be acquired, should have tipped you off that others might have already come after it."

Yes, a part of me had known. In truth, the minute the Hag had also guessed, the thought it might be gone had first entered my mind, reinforced by Asheron doing the same. I had been in denial because the Microlith had been my last hope.

And now…

My shoulders slouched while tears freely rolled down my cheeks. I wanted to scream and break things, but I felt too defeated.

"The Warding Microlith was never the solution," Asheron continued, his voice softening. "Granted, it would have kept Cornelius off your property for a while, but it would have made you a prisoner. The minute you left your house, you would be arrested and coerced into lifting the ward."

"But it would have given me time to find another, more permanent solution! I could have survived with the produce from my gardens. Now, I've lost everything. What Cornelius will do to my father, Vigil, and my ancestors…"

I fell to my knees, heavy sobs rocking my body. That my

weak magic was linked to my home didn't actually matter much to me. I never thirsted for power. My apothecary skills would suffice to keep me living comfortably if I so chose. But my Warden Tree, Vigil, was a younger version of the Watcher. It was sentient and powerful, a protector, and the embodiment of goodness. My father and his ancestors were buried beneath its roots, their essence flowing through him and through the land. Cornelius would harness Vigil's power, twist it, and raise my ancestors as undead servants.

Such desecration could never be undone.

"Stand up and get a grip of yourself," Asheron growled. He closed the distance between us, grabbed me by the upper arms, and effortlessly pulled me up onto my feet. "Your despair will draw the demons here."

"What does it matter?" I asked, wavering on my feet. "He won. There is no time for an alternative plan. I don't want to live in a world where I allowed my father to be turned into a zombie." I locked eyes with him, my heart shredded into a million pieces at the thought of all that could have been. "You have fulfilled your duty. I release you from your pledge."

Asheron bared his teeth, his fangs descending while the dark shadows of his wraith partially resurfaced. His hands gripping my upper arms tightened painfully. But I didn't care. The greater pain in my heart, in my soul, superseded everything else.

"Stupid girl!" he hissed. "How can you be so strong when facing ancient demons and so weak when confronted with temporary defeat? You're inside Hemdell! The Microlith was trash. There are countless more relics in here."

"Most of which are useless to me," I snapped back angrily. "Those I could use won't be accessible for weeks if not years, and the others I don't have powerful enough magic to unlock them or have no idea of the ritual required. Don't you think I would have gone for something better if I could have?"

The oddest expression flitted over his features. "I reject your release. Not once did I say I would help you get the Microlith. I pledged to take you inside Hemdell and protect you until you recovered what you came for. And I will fulfill that pledge."

I blinked in confusion before angrily wiping the tears off my face with the back of my hand. "What I came for is gone! Did you miss the empty shelf inside the statue?" I added, pointing at it.

Asheron shook his head and smiled smugly. "No, Ronika. You didn't come here for the Microlith, but for a way to defeat Cornelius. The Microlith never would have accomplished that. What you need is right over here."

He released my upper arms and fully shifted back into his vaporous form. Still sniffling, I wiped more tears off my face and instinctively followed him as he glided towards an ornate section of wall next to the table on the left side of the room. Seconds later, he vanished through the wall.

My eyes widened as I studied the wall for any sign of an opening that might have allowed Asheron to go through it. Wraiths could go through apparently solid objects only if they weren't completely sealed.

To my dismay, finding myself suddenly alone in this place had me feeling queasy. Barely a minute ago, I told him to abandon me here to be eaten by the human crawlers still scurrying outside the room. Now, I could swear the twelve zodiac statues were staring at me, ready to jump out of their alcoves and rush me.

My fertile imagination was already picturing the other statues turning into the horrible monsters the twins had morphed into while I was casting the spell. A clicking sound made me yelp, then a door—hidden in the pattern of the wall—slid open, revealing a narrow corridor. Asheron filled it almost entirely. He gestured for me to follow and floated down the short passage into the adjoining room.

Heart pounding with an impossible hope, I hastened after

him. My jaw dropped as I stepped into an elegant, but windowless study. If not for the giant pentagram in the center of the floor, where an area rug would have otherwise been, this could have belonged to a notary or an accountant. The same oppressive shades of black and dark brown dominated the room and furniture. A huge candelabra—similar to the one on the ground floor —hung overhead, flooding the room with a warm golden light.

Before I could fully take in my surroundings, Asheron pointed at the dark wood bookshelf which spread over the entire back wall behind the massive desk. At a glance, the inscriptions on the spines of the books indicated the bookshelf had been divided into specific sections: grimoires and magic compendiums, astronomy and astrology, alchemy, and necromancy. The considerable size of the latter section took me aback.

However, the ornate chest on the central shelf retained my attention. With a will of their own, my feet marched me over there. Undeniable magic oozed out of it. I cast a nervous glance at Asheron over my shoulder. He nodded encouragingly. I carefully reached for the latch, expecting it to resist my attempt at opening it. But it instantly gave, and I lifted the intricately carved lid of what could have passed for a fancy cigar box.

"By the gods!" I whispered, shock and awe audible in my voice in equal measure when I peered at its contents. Stunned, I glanced back at Asheron. "The Endless Purse?!"

His shadowy face split into his monstrous wraith grin.

My heart soared as I looked back at the small coin bag lying inside the box. This legendary pouch bestowed endless wealth to the owner in time of need. With it, I could pay off the crushing legal and administrative debts Cornelius had forced upon me in his efforts to seize my property. It would also allow me to face any future ploys he came up with to ruin me.

But how is it here?

As far as I knew, the Endless Purse never featured among the artifacts and relics Luciana acquired over the years. She had no use for money. Hunters worldwide would have descended like a flock of vultures upon Hemdell to appropriate this incommensurable treasure. How no one had been aware of its presence, or that it should have been so easily accessible, defied logic.

Grateful for this unimaginable blessing, I greedily reached for the purse.

"No!" Asheron exclaimed, startling me. "It is bound to its previous owner. You must release it first, then bind it to yourself."

My blood drained from my face, and I yanked my hand back. Obviously, it wouldn't be that simple. I knew better. Releasing the artifact wasn't a problem. No strong magic or defense mechanism leashed the purse. A simple incantation would do the deed. But binding it to me could take a long time. Some artifacts could take days or even weeks to accept a new master.

The intense wave of despair that crashed over me had tears welling up in my eyes again while an overwhelming urge to just curl up on the floor and cry settled heavily on me. I almost gave in to it when a sudden surge of outrage welled within me.

What in the seven hells is this?

When had I become such a weak and whimpering creature, falling apart at the first sign of adversity? I'd faced a feral ancient wraith wearing nothing but a sheer bridal robe without faltering, but the thought of releasing and binding a relic had me on the verge of beating my chest in despair?

The house is doing this...

In an instant of clarity, that answer came to me. The moment we'd entered the manor, I felt the stifling sliminess of the evil that permeated the very air within. I'd been so focused on staying alive on our way to the observatory, that I blocked out the pervasive way it seeped its way into me through every pore, every cell, all the way down to my bones.

I glared at the walls and ceiling, allowing anger to squelch the hopelessness that sought to cripple my will.

"Nice try. It will take far more than that to defeat me, you abomination," I hissed.

The rumbling purr of approval from Asheron behind me further spurred me on as I began the release spell over the purse. It felt like snapping tiny magical threads. Their great number meant its previous master had owned it for many years. But their flimsiness indicated either a great distance separated them, or its owner's magic was even weaker than mine. I suspected the latter to be correct. Those with advanced skills in the occult rarely bothered with such basic materialistic artifacts. They coveted things that further increased their power. Wealth-generating artifacts only appealed to the mundane and low-level spellcasters.

To my pleasant surprise, I burned through the threads in record time. Despite their flimsiness and the surge of power I'd benefited from since meeting Asheron, this was too fast. I pricked my index finger again and drew a rune with my blood on the pouch. The intensity of the magic channeling through me as I bound the artifact to me left me reeling. For the first time in my life, I had to rein in my power.

In moments, I'd completed my task.

"How?" I whispered to myself, equally awed and confused as I picked up the Endless Purse.

The pleasant tingling in my palm confirmed the bond was successful.

"Because you're in Hemdell," Asheron said softly behind me. "This entire house is a magic conduit. It augments everything. Plus you have your mojo bag that harnesses the heightened power of the blood moon, and the essence of a wraith coursing through you. Outside of Hemdell, it would have taken you days to bind this pouch to you."

Something in the way he said that last sentence struck me as odd. I wanted to dwell on it, but the lovely tingling in my palm reminded me that I now held the key to my complete freedom. A key that Asheron freely led me to when he owed me nothing.

My throat tightened as a tsunami of gratitude and affection rippled through me. "You saved me," I whispered in a choked voice.

"As you saved me," he whispered back, the words all the stranger that they should be spoken by a terrifying horned wraith.

I realized I'd run towards him when my arms closed around his shadowy form. In that brief instant, I felt his shock then horror before he roughly pulled out of my embrace.

"No! You fool!" he shouted as he glided away from me. "Do you have a death wish?!"

I gaped at him in confusion before understanding slammed into me. Arms spread wide, I jerked my head down to examine myself. No pain, no wound, or visible burnt skin indicated touching his wraith form had damaged me in any way.

But I had known that.

At a visceral level, I had indeed known no harm would come to me from him. With a boldness I couldn't explain, I slowly advanced towards him. Seeing him shift out of his wraith form and take a wary step back messed with my head.

"Not anymore, I don't," I replied in a factual tone. "I embraced your wraith, and you didn't harm me, as you pledged. I trust you, Asheron. All of you."

"You don't know what you're saying," he replied, his voice tense.

His back meeting a bookshelf ended his retreat while I continued to advance. I placed my hands on his hips and pressed my chest against his. Head tilted back, I locked eyes with him. The way he held my shoulders, he clearly itched to push me away.

"Let me touch your wraith," I said in a soothing voice.

He firmly shook his head. "Have you not seen what my touch has done to the creatures we fought on our way up?"

"I'm not one of those creatures. I'm your Ronika. Your

shadow has touched me before without harming me," I added quickly when he opened his mouth to argue. "On the porch, when you were fighting the madness, your wraith's skirt touched my legs and feet. You didn't harm me then, and neither did you just now. Let me touch your wraith, Asheron."

He swallowed hard, and his eyes flicked between mine, searching. The mix of worry and longing on his face tugged at my heart. I realized then that he wanted this as much as I did—to be fully embraced. Even though I spoke of Asheron *and* his wraith, I understood well that they weren't two separate entities sharing a corporeal form. They were merely the two facets of the same coin.

He lifted his hand from my right shoulder. His fingers lengthened, and the vicious claws of his wraith extruded from his fingertips while shadows wrapped around his hand. I could feel tension oozing out of him. I smiled as he hesitantly brought his index finger to the patch of exposed skin of my shoulder, at the edge of my round collar. He barely brushed it before pulling away. I chuckled and further pressed myself against him.

"Go on," I encouraged him. "It didn't hurt."

He swallowed hard again, then repeated the gesture, this time, his touch lingering while he studied my reaction. The powerful emotion that twisted his features when I simply smiled in response utterly wrecked me. He covered my shoulder with his full palm then caressed a path up my neck to my face. I leaned into his shadowy touch. It wasn't cold like before, but lukewarm and slightly pulsating.

Mesmerized, I stared at Asheron while he fully took on his wraith form. He possessively wrapped his arms around my body, engulfing me in a sea of rolling shadows. I no longer felt his legs against mine, only the caress of his vaporous skirt. A cloudy cushion padded his chest and arms embracing me. Then it felt like an invisible thread had shot out of the glowing pulse in his chest to drape around my heart. Its beat slowed down, until it matched his own heart rate.

Eyes locked, the world vanished. In that instant, we had become one. Asheron was both around me and in me, our hearts beating as one. The pulsating effect of his shadows swathing my body gave me the impression of gently being rocked by rolling water. I never saw him lowering his head. When the thin line of his wraith lips pressed against mine, I melted against him.

Never in a million years would I have expected myself to even contemplate sharing an open-mouth kiss with Asheron's wraith. And yet, my lips parted with a will of their own in response to his tongue teasing the seam of my mouth. The slight pricking of his dagger teeth against my lips didn't unsettle me in the least. With slow and careful movements, our tongues mingled. Like kissing Asheron in his physical form, his wraith tasted fresh, like thyme and peaches laced with mint.

It was possessive, tender, and protective, all words I never thought to associate with this terrifying being. Asheron broke the kiss, lifted me up, and buried his face in my neck. Eyes closed, I pressed my cheek against the shadows covering his head where hair would have been. His smoked wood and fresh thyme scent made me feel warm, safe… home.

"My Ronika," the wraith whispered, saying my name almost like a prayer.

I couldn't say what my response—if any—would have been. A loud, angry groan tore a startled gasp out of me, putting an end to the tender moment. Silently berating myself for once again allowing us to forget what hostile environment we were in, I jerked my head up to look around for the source of the threat.

Asheron chuckled as he put me back down on my feet. "Calm, my Ronika. The house does not approve of happy emotions. It is deeply offended by our actions."

I snorted, excessively pleased to have caused this thrice damned place any measure of distress.

"Good. It deserves it," I said without remorse. "But we should get out now. We've more than overstayed our welcome."

"Indeed," Asheron said before turning towards the secret passage back to the observatory.

"Wait!" I exclaimed, grabbing his wrist.

It still blew me away to be able to touch his wraith form fully unscathed when contact with his physical form had been nearly unbearable the first time.

He eyed me questioningly.

"You picked me up just now, and your wraith can fly. As I would rather not traipse through that horrible house again, is there any way we could fly out of here with you carrying me?" I asked sheepishly.

Under different circumstances, his stunned expression—made even more eerie by his undefined features—would have been hilarious. But I really didn't want to face what else lurked here.

His terrifying mouth suddenly stretched into a wide smile, exposing his even more terrifying teeth. A mouth I had kissed only moments prior...

And that I would kiss again.

"Brilliant idea! We should be able to open one of the windows in the observatory," Asheron said with a thrill in his voice.

I squealed with delight, the petty side of me feeling a bit cheated that my happiness didn't draw another disgruntled groan from the house. I secured the artifact in my shoulder bag and followed him back through the passage. Excitement bubbled within me at the prospect of flying. It had always been a dream of mine. The recent technological devices had granted the exclusive few members of the elite the possibility to do so. But even had I been drowning in money, I wouldn't have risked my life flying in those steam and clockwork devices. The technology was still too much in its infancy.

My wistful smile faded a few steps inside the massive observatory. Although I couldn't see anything different from how we had left the room, something had undeniably changed. Pure malice filled the air. Something evil had entered the room.

Asheron gestured for me to stay put.

As per his prior instructions, I backed up to the wall to prevent anything from sneaking up behind me. Keeping my voice low, I once more summoned my Shield of Azriel as it would be the best defense while remaining stationary. To my dismay, Asheron didn't prowl towards the main doors into the observatory, but towards the back, where the windows were located.

"Show yourself," Asheron commanded in a voice so menacing a cold shiver ran down my spine.

A strange tingle pricked at my nape seconds before the air across the room blurred, in front of the windows, slightly to the right of the telescope. My stomach roiled at the sight of the frightening monster.

For a reason I could not explain, I instinctively knew the creature to be a sentient female. She seemed to be made out of countless ropy tentacles, each one the thickness of a teenager's forearm. The best description I could come up with was that the tentacles had been bunched up as if to create a ponytail, and the top had been pinched into forming a dreadfully pointy face. The nose looked almost like a hummingbird's beak framed by two beady white eyes. A large, round mouth took up the entire bottom half of her round face, sharp teeth lining the entire circumference like a nightmarish version of a sea lamprey.

The tentacles draped around her entire body, falling to the ground like an oversized cloak. They curled back behind her, making it impossible to assess just how long they actually were. Excessively long arms with crooked fingers tipped with vicious claws were the only other visible parts of her. Oddly, a series of silver bracelets adorned her wrists. Considering her dreadful appearance, such coquettish accessories defied logic.

"Hello, Asheron. It has been a long time since our last meeting," she croaked in a highly unsettling voice like nails on glass.

I utterly failed to hide the shock I felt upon discovering she knew him.

"Chaerim," Asheron replied, his voice less-than-friendly, "what makes you think now is a good time to come pay your regards?"

"When else would be a good time?" Her innocent tone couldn't have been less sincere. "After your damnation, three hundred and twenty-five years ago, you vanished, never to be seen again. And then you visit twice in as many days. Am I to understand you are coming back home?"

Twice in as many days?! And what does she mean by he's coming back home? Was Hemdell his home?

It then dawned on me that I truly knew nothing about Asheron, aside from the fact that he had been turned into a wraith over three centuries ago.

"And who is that pretty little companion of yours?" Chaerim asked, leaning slightly to the side to peer at me behind him.

"No, I have no intentions of settling here. My business in Hemdell is at an end. We are leaving with no plan of ever returning," Asheron replied in a clipped tone. "Now leave this room. I would rather not hurt you."

"Aww, Lord Voror, what an unkind thing to say. After such a long absence, surely you would show a bit more generosity to your former dear friend. You could share the pretty," she added, a greedy hedge seeping into her voice while her beady eyes flicked towards me.

Lord Voror?

My stomach roiled, and the tingling in my nape cranked up another notch, turning into an unpleasant pressure. I rolled my shoulders to release the tension her unsettling presence was awakening in me.

"Touch her, and I will make you regret it in unspeakable ways. She's mine and under my protection. You have survived here for many centuries, Chaerim. Do not make me end you. Now get out!" Asheron hissed while taking a menacing step towards the demonic female.

"Why would you want me to exit this room?" she asked, tilting her head to the side with genuine curiosity. "If your plan is to leave Hemdell as you claim, you and the pretty human should be the ones walking out this door."

"For the last time, my business is none of your concern. I will not repeat myself again."

She pinched her monstrous face in what I could only interpret as a pouty expression. "Very well," she said at last, running her spindly fingers over one of the tentacles cascading down from the top of her head like one would run their fingers through their hair. "But you know, Asheron, you could reclaim Hemdell for yourself, now that your madness is under control. After what Luciana did to you, you deserve to own all of this," she said waving at the room. "The ease with which you come and go within these walls is proof that all its inhabitants would bow to your commands."

Luciana? She did this to him?

Even as those questions fired off in my mind, the discomfort at the back of my head turned into a painful pressure. Just as I was going to cast a healing spell on myself, my shield flickered. It was subtle but distinct enough for me to know something was tampering with it.

And then I realized I had moved at least a couple of meters towards the door.

"By the gods! You're controlling me!" I exclaimed, my head jerking towards the witch. "Get out of my head!"

"You dare?!" Asheron shouted at Chaerim.

Dropping all pretense of friendly demeanor, the demon went on the attack. To my horror, infinitely long tentacles that had been camouflaged by an invisibility spell or power suddenly appeared. They lined the walls, the ceiling, and even the floor. Three of them darted my way, their tips covered in sharp spikes battering my shield.

The triple simultaneous blow shattered my shield. However more powerful Asheron had made me of late, my magic stood no chance against such an ancient demon. The pain in my head multiplied a thousandfold, and I watched myself helplessly raise a hand towards the door behind which the scurrying sounds of little feet could be heard.

CHAPTER 9
ASHERON

An enraged roar tore out of me that the fiend should have dared attack my woman. With a flick of my hand, I covered the door in a thick barrier of ice to keep Ronika from opening it. With a wave of the other hand, I snapped the bones and claws at the tips of Chaerim's tentacles. She screamed in pain. Shock and disbelief settled on her face that I should have used such an ability against her.

As one, her damaged limbs flopped to the ground like so many beheaded snakes. She tried to reel in her tentacles and resorb them into her body, but I invoked my frost and trapped them in ice spikes all around us.

"Bone magic?" she whispered, dread filling her voice. "How? Luciana severed your tail! She damned you!"

As a sole response, I grabbed one of her writhing tentacles trapped in ice and drained it of its life force. I watched it wither with malicious glee while the demon screeched. She tugged with all her might, merely succeeding in tearing her limb in half. She reeled in her stump, hugging it to her chest.

"No! Mercy!" she cried out when I reached for a second tentacle and gave it the same treatment.

"I warned you to leave what's mine alone," I ground through my teeth in a menacing voice. "It has been too long since I last feasted on the soul of a demon. Now you die."

"A trade, Lord Voror! Mercy for a trade," she exclaimed while trying to slither away from me. "My life for your tail!"

I froze upon hearing those words. As powerful as she was, Chaerim held no sway over me. She likely believed that killing Ronika would have cast me down the spiral of madness all over again. With her crawlers outside swarming the room, I would have been too busy dealing with them to make her pay. She thrived on chaos, pain, and despair. My newfound sanity undoubtedly infuriated her. The sad part was that this gratuitous malice was merely her nature, nothing she had any control over.

Pressing her advantage when she saw me pause, Chaerim resumed talking at an accelerated pace.

"Grant me safe passage, spare my life, and harm me no further, and I will tell you who holds your tailbone. You can be made whole again if you recover it. I am no longer compelling the woman. Grant me this mercy, Asheron, and I pledge to leave this room, not to harm your female, and not to interfere with your business in Hemdell, or your departure thereof. This I pledge."

However devious the demon could be, she would not lie in a pledge. She had valuable information about the location of my tailbone. But why should I grant her a safe passage? I could torture Chaerim and get the information out of her. After all, she had attacked Ronika and thus deserved to die. I would take great pleasure in making it last.

And risk falling back to madness or revolting my woman.

Neither outcome I was willing to gamble on. Furthermore, I needed to get Ronika out of here as soon as possible. As amusing as pissing off the house with our happiness had been, it was retaliating by stirring all the abominations that dwelled within to punish us. The faster I got the information from Chaerim and the sooner I could take my mate to safety. A glance over my shoulder at Ronika confirmed the demon was no longer using her eldritch powers over her. It shamed me that I had not perceived it right away or even anticipated it. I knew better.

"Speak, and make it quick," I ground through my teeth. "Play games, and you will forfeit your safe passage."

Her relief was palpable. She wiggled her tentacles, wanting to free them from the ice spikes still trapping them. But a single look at my face sufficed for her to understand she would remain at my mercy until she satisfied her end of the deal. Although the coldness of the ice pained her, it wasn't inflicting harm.

"The necromancer Cornelius has your tail," she said.

"WHAT?!" I exclaimed.

Ronika's gasp behind me echoed the shock I felt.

"Are you saying the necromancer was involved in my damnation?" I hissed, anger boiling through my veins.

Chaerim vehemently shook her head. "No. He came many days after your fall. Luciana wanted you back. You have been her most loyal protector. You were a powerful guardian before, but as a wraith, you became a wonder to behold. If she could control you with your tailbone, you would be her most powerful weapon."

Seething fury welled through me. The need to go on a murderous rampage clawed at me from within. It took every ounce of my willpower to crush it down. I extended my senses to feel Ronika's soothing presence. She needed me to remain sane so that I could keep her safe.

"And then what happened?" I demanded.

"Cornelius came here many times. Each of their attempts failed," Chaerim said with a shrug. "Luciana allowed him to take it to his home with the strict instructions to devise a method to make it work within the next fortnight or face her wrath. The stench of his fear still tickles my nose. He didn't think he could succeed, and he was right. Lucky for him, a week after Luciana gave him the tailbone, hellfire swept through the house. And just like that, he was free."

"That was centuries ago," I ground through my teeth, a new source of anger blossoming in my heart at her potential treachery. "You said you knew where my tailbone was. I warned you against playing games. How do you know he still has it after all these years?"

She raised her palms in a pleading fashion when I glided closer to her, my claws itching to tear her to shreds.

"Peace, Lord Voror. I am not playing any games. Every year, on the anniversary of your damnation, he comes to Hemdell. He is still trying to summon you with your tailbone. Each time, he tries a different ritual. His ambition knows no measure. Controlling you would be the ultimate achievement. Cornelius wants you for himself. He simply has no idea you are no longer mindless."

My head spun, too many conflicting emotions warring within me. Hope and rage dominated. I could be made whole again. But what if I could indeed be enslaved? I finally got a better understanding of Ronika's despair at the thought of her sire and ancestors becoming puppets to the necromancer.

"I have told you all I know, Asheron. Now please, honor your pledge and grant me safe passage," Chaerim said, her voice tense.

"Leave and give me no reason to end you as I terribly itch to do," I said in a menacing tone.

I extended my hand towards Ronika for her to come closer to me. She complied without hesitation. I unraveled the ice spikes trapping the demon's tentacles. Her whimper of relief awakened a burning desire for me to inflict more pain on her and drain her soul dry. By her frightened expression, she could feel my growing hunger. She retracted her tentacles and swiftly shuffled to the other side of the room, circling as far away from us as possible until she reached the door.

I pushed Ronika closer to the windows before releasing the ice barrier keeping the door shut. When magical energy swirled around the demon, I prepared to lunge at her and tear her limb from limb. However, the pitter-patter of her minions moving away made me realize she was commanding the crawlers to leave. Wise decision. Their attack against us could be deemed as her interfering with our efforts to leave, which would be a breach of her pledge.

As she slithered out of the room, the tips of her broken tentacles trailing behind her, Chaerim glanced at me over her shoulder.

"Good luck recovering your tail, Lord Voror," she said with a malicious grin.

I knew a taunt when I heard one. I couldn't tell if she knew something I didn't, or if she was merrily planting a doubt in my mind to torture me as to what foul play might lie ahead. But there would be time to deal with this later. For now, my sole focus was getting my woman out of this damnable place.

As soon as the door closed behind the demon, I once more sealed it with ice and hastily opened one of the windows. Ronika immediately came into my embrace when I opened my arms to her. Without a word, I flew out, the weight of the world suddenly falling off my shoulders. One look at my delicate human revealed she too had felt the oppressive malice that permeated the air inside washing off her.

Below, the twisted trees in the forest raised their limbs in a vain effort to grab us. But it was the humongous creature stretching over a hundred meters that claimed my attention. The bulging rings of her body glowed a bright green as it writhed with millions of eggs. The bile demon frantically laid more spawn to replace the multitude I had slain on my way in. From this vantage, she resembled a giant caterpillar, with the same obsidian round head and tubular mouth as her offspring.

My nose buried in Ronika's hair, I inhaled her soothing

scent and cast the bile demon out of my mind, as well as the twisted silhouettes of the other abominations haunting the grounds. I quickly crossed the distance back over the gate, the wondrous feel of my woman's body against mine further silencing the madness constantly lurking at the edge of my sanity.

I still couldn't believe that she had fully embraced my wraith… that she had fully embraced me. She even kissed me in my wraith form, without fear or disgust at my terrifying appearance. From her, I perceived nothing but tenderness, affection, and a deep possessiveness. That totally wrecked me. Even my wraith, who abhorred sweet emotions, was melting for her. She was mine. Every facet of me had claimed her, and she had accepted both.

An impossible happiness swelled in my heart. When Luciana damned me, I believed any chance at even a semblance of a normal life had been taken away from me. But now, with this woman, everything seemed possible.

And once I get my tail back…

I landed outside the gate, near the location Ronika had camouflaged her mount. With much reluctance, I set her on her feet and shifted back to my physical form. She dispersed the illusion, making Damar visible again. The horse neighed, pleased to see his mistress. She fed him a couple of apples before turning back to me.

I fought the urge to draw her into my arms.

"*Now*, our agreement is concluded," I said in a neutral tone. "You have what you came for, and I have kept you safe from harm on the way in and back out."

Ronika nodded, although slight creases marred her forehead with a discreet frown. "I am satisfied that you have fulfilled your pledge and are now free of any obligation towards me. But…"

"But?" I echoed when her voice trailed off.

"Will I see you again?" she asked nervously.

My heart soared, but I forced myself to remain stoic. "Do you wish to?"

"Of course, I do. Isn't it obvious?" she asked, as if she was suddenly questioning my intelligence.

A silly grin settled on my face. "Good. Because I intend to keep you."

Her shoulders relaxed, and she returned my smile. Closing the short distance between us, I drew her against me. Ronika lifted her head to receive my kiss, her hands gently caressing my back in the way I loved so much.

Just as I was beginning to deepen the kiss, my spine stiffened with the prescient sense of an imminent attack... from her. Shocked, I pulled away, dreading Chaerim had planted a compulsion in Ronika's mind timed to trigger only once we had left Hemdell. I felt a slight stinging at the back of my head, then the threat warning faded.

Confused, I stared at Ronika, who seemed a bit guilty. Seconds later, a crestfallen expression descended over her features as a red glow emanated around her right hand—a strand of my hair disintegrating. Shock, anger, and betrayal swept through me in quick succession as understanding dawned on me.

I took a couple of steps back, battling to quell the murderous rage that wanted to overwhelm me even as my heart broke. Right this instant, Luciana's face was overlapping Ronika's. I had loved my former ward—not as a lover but like a daughter. She had betrayed me in the worst way, damned me, and abused my trust to take from me to achieve her own ambitions. And now, the woman I was falling for, dreaming of a future with, had just done the same.

I would *not* be used again.

"What do you think you're doing?" I hissed, my wraith claws extruding.

A million thoughts as to all the ways she could use my hair

flashed through my mind. As a non-spellcaster, I wasn't well-versed with occult rituals. I had specific powers, and could enhance existing magic with my spectral energy, like I had done with her wards in Duskwallow. But I couldn't weave a ward of my own or summon a protective shield like she did. Therefore, I had only learned about how to navigate around the magic or creatures summoned by mages and conjurors. Which meant I couldn't imagine what nefarious plans she entertained with my hair.

For the first time since our initial encounter in the burial grounds, Ronika expressed true fear of me. While she made a remarkable effort to silence it, it still radiated in droves from her, further fueling my rage.

"I… I'm sorry," she said, clasping her hands in front of her in a contrite fashion. "I should have asked instead of just trying to take. Please forgive me."

"Why? Why in the seven hells did you try to take a part of me? What did you plan on doing to me?" I snarled, my teeth bared as I advanced menacingly towards her.

Her eyes widened in shock then horror as she was struck by sudden understanding. The genuine disbelief and offended air that took over her face acted like a potent balm on my shattered heart.

"Do to you? Nothing! Nothing at all! I swore to never do you harm, nor do I want to! Surely you can see that I sincerely care for you?" she exclaimed in outrage before her tone shifted back to a more apologetic edge. "I do not want the strand of your hair for myself, but to repay my debt to the Hag. The strand of a wraith's hair was her price in exchange for helping me find a protector to enter Hemdell."

I recoiled, torn between relief that no horrible betrayal had motivated her action, and dread that the Weaver should have requested such a price. What was she up to?

"You cannot take a part of a wraith without it disintegrating,"

I ground through my teeth while trying to sort through the chaos reining in my mind. "We are half-living, half-dead."

Ronika's shoulders slouched, and she unclasped her hands to hug her waist, despair and anger swelling within her.

"She tricked me," she said angrily. "Her and her damn games. I knew there was something shady in her request. I asked her if wraiths even had hair. She said yes, that she wouldn't ask for something that couldn't be given. And yet here we are. How am I to fulfill my end of the deal if a wraith's hair vanishes the minute it is removed from their head?"

"Technically, she didn't lie. Like I said, you cannot *take* a part of a wraith without it disintegrating. For it to remain whole, it must be freely *given*," I said in a clipped tone.

Ronika's eyes widened, hope sparkling in her eyes. The poor female truly had no idea who she was playing with. The Weaver had indeed tricked her. She just didn't realize it yet.

"I…" she paused, searching for her words.

Obviously, she wanted to ask if I would give her one of my strands. But considering how she had initially handled it, she now felt ashamed.

I plucked a strand of my long black hair and held it in front of my face, staring at it while it gently swayed in the light night breeze before shifting my gaze back to Ronika. The timid sense of hope my comment about it being given had sparked in her cranked up another notch as she glanced at the coveted prize between my fingers.

"Do you have any idea what type of spell or magic could be performed using this token filled with my essence and my power?" I asked. "How it could affect me?"

She paled, her lips parting in shock as she realized the dismissive way in which she had thought of settling her ledger with the Weaver. I didn't question that she held no ill intention when she agreed to the terms. Her lack of malice made it harder for her to think of the foul ways people could use what she had likely only considered a rare ingredient.

"Oh Asheron, I'm so sorry!" she said, horrified. "It never crossed my mind that it could be used against you. I… I don't know what to do."

"You could have simply asked," I grumbled before extending the strand of hair towards her.

Eyes wide, Ronika instinctively took it before looking at me with a mix of worry and confusion. "But… You just said it can be used to harm you."

"I asked if you had considered how it *could* be used and whether it would negatively affect me," I corrected. "You are too naïve when it comes to making deals involving the occult. The Weaver is no threat to me."

But she's a threat to you.

This changed things. I had to reprioritize my plans for the evening.

"Go home, Ronika. And settle your affairs," I said in a neutral tone.

Her face fell, and the worried sorrow that emanated from her clawed at my heart.

"You're not coming?" she asked in a small voice.

"I have important things to take care of. They cannot wait," I replied in a noncommittal fashion.

She nodded and licked her lips nervously while carefully fiddling with my hair still held in her hand. "Of course. But… I will see you again, right?"

The timid, almost pleading way in which she asked that last question made me melt from the inside out. As much as I hated that she had sneakily tried to take from me, I couldn't stay mad at her. I smiled and drew her against me. Her almost palpable relief filled my heart to bursting.

"Yes, Ronika, you will. You are mine," I said before claiming her lips in a possessive kiss.

I both hated and loved the way she clung to me with something akin to desperation. She and I would have a lot to discuss after my meeting with the Weaver.

With much reluctance, I ended the kiss and pulled away from my woman. She smiled timidly and carefully placed my strand of hair inside her shoulder bag. I accompanied her to Damar and helped her up.

"I will see you soon," I said before slapping the rump of her mount.

The horse surged forward, and I shifted into my wraith form. For a short while, I flew alongside Ronika, until she was at a safe enough distance from Hemdell before veering South towards the Weaver's domain.

CHAPTER 10
ASHERON

As I approached the gates to the Weaver's estate, a long-forgotten sense of awe washed over me as my skin pricked from the potent energy emanating from her wards. Such power defied logic. But then, very little made sense to us lesser people when trying to understand what drove Cliona Nox. For a second, I wondered if she would force me to seek the blessing of the guardians of her gates to be allowed through. The moment that thought entered my mind, the repulsion magic—which could have burnt me to cinders—relented, granting me safe passage.

I had no doubt it had been yet another one of her little games to remind me of her power.

As if I need it.

I flew over the fence and along the path to her domain. An amused snort escaped me at the sight of the humble shack illusion she had given her dwelling. Although I lacked the magical power to see through the camouflage, I sensed the continued presence of the manor whose halls I had once traipsed through. In comparison, Hemdell paled both in size and magnificence.

I landed in front of the house, shedding my wraith form as I approached the door. It quietly parted in front of me, and I slowly entered. Despite my curiosity at the unusual setting she had chosen for herself, I only had eyes for the woman sitting behind her spinning wheel. A barely visible network of strings sprawled in every direction on the wall by the wheel. Most mortals—including many spellcasters and mage-born—would be oblivious to the existence of this tapestry of their intertwined fates. And ever she spun them in ways only she understood.

"Asheron," the Weaver said in greeting, her eyes remaining on the glowing thread she was spinning.

"Mother," I replied in a similar tone.

"I wondered how long it would take you to visit me now that you have regained control over your mind," she said while pulling at the magical yarn in her hands. "I was starting to feel neglected."

"Forgive me if I doubt you wasted much energy longing for my visit. After all, it didn't seem to bother you for the last three hundred and twenty-five years," I said with sarcasm.

Her foot stopped pumping the pedal that spun the wheel, and she turned to face me. She was as beautiful as in my souvenir. Some subtle changes hinted at the many years that had lapsed since we last talked. Even I couldn't specifically point them out. Then again, I didn't know whether this was her true appearance maintained by magic.

"Your absence is the result of your own choices. I had no control over it, just like I had no control over ending it," she said in a cryptic fashion.

"And yet, you just did," I countered.

She huffed. "*I* did nothing. Your human did, and you responded."

I narrowed my eyes at her. When it came to word and mind games, you couldn't beat her. All you could do was try not to let her crush you.

"Why did you send her? And especially, why did you give

her that charm bracelet? It had no power. I could have slaughtered her," I asked in a stern voice.

She raised an eyebrow in that taunting fashion I so hated, her purple eyes sparkling with mischief. "But you didn't."

"I could have," I argued forcefully. "She trusted you, but you gave her a useless bauble."

She waved a dismissive hand and took on a disdainful expression. "I gave her what she needed to complete her task. The charm didn't need magic because she wielded the most potent one within herself. Faith is what allowed her to pierce through your madness. She only needed to believe it held magic to bolster her confidence. And once again, it worked. So what are you complaining about?"

"She could have died!"

This time, my mother rolled her eyes. "Of course, she could have. You do not deal with the netherworld without putting your life on the line. She knew the risk. I made no mystery of it."

I ground my teeth. Yes, Ronika had known the risk to her life but not the full extent of what she was exposing herself to.

Feeling annoyed, I plucked a strand of hair from my head and extended it to my mother. Her face closed off, and a wave of anxiety immediately knotted my insides. For a moment, I feared she would leave me hanging. Then, to my utter relief, her stool glided forward, stopping right behind her worktable, and she reached for my offering.

She took it, sliding two fingers along its length. It glowed with a white light while she admired it with a mysterious smile. She glanced back at me. The return of the taunting glimmer unnerved me.

"Thank you. You have not wasted the past three centuries, Asheron. Your power has phenomenally grown."

Under different circumstances, I would have been touched by this genuine maternal approval. Although we had never been close, the Weaver had been as good a mother as someone like her could be. But I had different priorities in mind.

"I am glad you find it satisfactory," I said, relieved. "This is the payment you were owed. Ronika's debt is repaid."

She snorted, a cruel glint flashing through her eyes. "It most certainly is not."

"You got the wraith hair you requested," I snarled, taking a menacing step forward, although knowing I would never attack my mother—not that I would ever survive such a foolish endeavor.

"I got *a* wraith hair, which is a very nice gift from a son to his mother. But *Ronika* owes *me*. I never agreed to *your gift* acting as the repayment of *her* debt," she said nonchalantly.

I bared my teeth in anger, which only made her chuckle. "Fine," I hissed, annoyed to have allowed myself to be played by her wretched mind games. "I'll give you another one on Ronika's behalf to settle her debt."

"No," she said in a tone that brooked no argument when I reached for another strand of my hair. "No one but Ronika Ortega will pay me for the debt she incurred."

I stared at her in shock. "You know that's not possible! Don't you realize what it would cost for her to pay you herself?"

"Do you presume to teach *me* how this works?" she hissed back. "Ronika will personally pay me, and that is final."

I shook my head, anger and confusion warring within me. "Why are you doing this?" I whispered, almost more to myself than to her.

"Isn't it obvious?" she asked, tilting her head to the side. She observed me as if I was some strange oddity that defied logic. "The true question is why are *you* not doing it?"

To her, I undoubtedly was.

"If you knew anything about me, then that question wouldn't need to be asked," I replied angrily. "You know I won't do that. So why even set us up like this?"

"You foolish boy," she snapped, her purple eyes glowing, and electric energy filling the room as her temper flared. "Do you enjoy madness so much?"

"Of course not!" I exclaimed.

"Then bind her!"

I shook my head and ran nervous fingers through my hair. "It's not that simple."

"Yes, it is." The harshness with which she spat those words revealed her exasperation with me. "You need an anchor. That's what she is. You like each other. She will give you the peace you require."

"I agree, but she should choose me freely," I countered.

My mother rolled her eyes, then shook her head at me like I was a hopeless case.

"The human already chose you, you fool. While your initial meeting required for her to lie with you once, she didn't accidentally land on your cock the second, third, and however many other times you fucked her."

I flinched at her crudeness. "Mother!" I exclaimed.

She waved a hand in annoyance. "Spare me the prudish act. I have walked this world since the beginning of time. There is nothing I haven't seen when it comes to two souls coming together. You want her, and she wants you. So claim her."

I turned away from her and peered out the window at the impossible garden—which qualified more as a forest—that surrounded her camouflaged estate. Ronika would love to be able to grow some of these powerful plants and herbs for her healing and apothecary business.

If I bind her, she'll be able to.

But at what cost?

My mother's discouraged sigh reclaimed my attention. The disappointed look on her face cut me deep.

"You were always too sweet, too considerate," she mused out loud, as if reminiscing about a mystery she had repeatedly failed to solve. "It hurt you so many times, and still you persist. You never listen to your mother. And where does that get you?" She waved at me as she asked that last question.

That stung and instantly set me in defensive mode.

"She was a child!" I exclaimed, my argument sounding weak to my own ears.

"She was an abomination," my mother snarled. "I warned you not to go back. As always, you didn't listen. Then I told you to kill her, but you convinced yourself you could save her. Instead, Luciana damned you for eternity."

Each of her words felt like a serrated blade stabbing me in the chest. She had warned me. I'd been so stubborn. But how could I have believed Luciana capable of such horror, especially against me? I had been her protector since her birth.

I narrowed my eyes at her, struck by a sudden suspicion. "The hellfire that swept through Hemdell, that was you?"

She lifted her chin defiantly, a cruel smile stretching her lips. "I did what you would not. Luciana could not be allowed to continue unchecked. She would have unleashed the infernal horde onto this world. Plus, she damned my child. Such an affront couldn't go unanswered."

I nodded slowly. Although she had left the comment about avenging me for last, at a visceral level, I knew it had been her main motive. A begrudging wave of love swelled in my heart for the female I would never truly understand.

As a goddess, my mother observed from the sidelines the horrors mortals unleashed on each other over the centuries. While she could nudge fate in certain directions, ultimately, she was merely the hand that spun the threads of people's choices. More than once, mortals brought themselves to the brink of extinction only to rise again. Whatever path they chose made no difference to her.

Or does it?

"Luciana craved to play with demons, so I granted her wish,"

Mother continued with deep malice. "Your father derives great delight feasting on her bones. She should have known better than to try to enslave the son of one of the princes of hell."

This shouldn't have surprised me, yet it struck me like a bolt of lightning straight to the chest. My mother had birthed many children with different powerful beings. My father, Alderan, son of Astaroth, was the most powerful Bone Demon Lord of the seventh circle. There would be no end to the torment he would inflict upon Luciana. As much as I had loved her, even considered her as a daughter, I felt no pity for her fate. In truth, it shamed me to relish the eternal agony she now endured.

My mother speaking again snapped me out of my musings.

"This mortal is your salvation, Asheron. Bind her or fall to madness again," she said, indicating she was ready to end the conversation.

This time, it was my turn to lift my chin defiantly. "I will not bind Ronika by force. She will choose me and our future freely."

Mother took on a bored expression. "As you wish. But remember that she has one month to settle her debt, or I'll come collect."

My stomach dropped, anger and confusion once more surging through me. Mother collecting on an unpaid debt would be far worse than whatever fate I was trying to spare Ronika from by not binding her.

"Why are you doing this?" I asked again, truly baffled.

"I'm saving you from yourself, Asheron."

"I don't need saving! Whether you like it or not, I have to make my own decisions."

"And we both know where it systematically lands you."

I huffed. "What is done is done. Things have changed. I do not need to bind her anymore. Soon, I'll be whole again."

This time, her stunned expression revealed she truly had no idea what I was hinting about. It was nearly impossible to surprise my mother. She often appeared to know your thoughts before they even finished forming in your mind.

"Is that so?"

I nodded. "Chaerim says Cornelius has my tailbone. I intend to recover it."

The way my mother's face closed sent a wave of worry fluttering down my spine.

"What is it?" I asked.

She studied my features for a few moments, the silence—though brief—making my anxiety grow even more.

"You cannot undo the past, my son," she said in an oddly soft tone. "Like you said so well yourself, what is done is done. You are a wraith forevermore, now. Accept it."

"I disagree. The past can partially be undone," I countered. "Tonight, I was able to use bone magic again."

Mother narrowed her eyes, her timeless face taking on a speculative expression. "That's great, Asheron. Then be content."

"Why be content? Do you not wish me to be whole? Is there something you are not telling me?" I asked.

Once again, her face closed off. "I've said all I had to say, my son. Bind your woman or don't. In the end, the decision is yours. I merely weave people's choices, however irrational they may be. Goodbye, Asheron. And remember that Ronika has one month."

She turned away from me, and her stool glided back to her spinning wheel. The door behind me opened with a soft swishing sound, indicating I had overstayed my welcome. I stared at my mother's noble profile for a second longer before turning on my heel and stepping out into the night.

CHAPTER 11
RONIKA

I woke up from a restless night, disappointed—not to say heartbroken—that Asheron never came last night. My overactive imagination bubbled with a variety of speculations laced with paranoia. The main concern revolved around the probability that he had gone after his tailbone. It still boggled my mind that, of all people, Cornelius should have it. But more importantly, the thought that the necromancer might harm him terrified me.

Asheron is powerful. He can hold his own.

He proved as much over and over again last night in that forsaken place. More than once during that nightmarish journey into Hemdell, it had struck me how impossible the task of safely taking me in and out of the manor would have been for most of the other protectors I had in mind. The breadth of Asheron's powers still left me reeling.

They also raised a plethora of questions about my lover.

I couldn't get over the fact that he had personally known Luciana. Worse still, if that Chaerim demon was right—and Asheron's responses to her statements appeared to confirm it—then Luciana was responsible for his damnation. But how? Why would he have agreed to return to that place? According to

Chaerim, he'd been to Hemdell twice in as many days. Why had he gone there on the eve of our mission? Did he go scouting? Had he tried to thin the herd before taking me there?

At least, that explains why he had so clearly known his way around the Manor.

But what of his ability to shatter bones with a wave of his hand? I had never seen or heard of such a power from a wraith. It troubled me how little I knew about Asheron. In fact, I knew nothing. And yet, I couldn't recall forming such a strong bond with anyone before. I genuinely trusted him with my life, beyond our agreement entered into out of desperation.

His anger and hurt once he caught me trying to steal a strand of his hair still cut deep. Why in the seven hells had I not just asked? In more ways than one, he had shown a sincere desire to help me. He could have left me hanging once I found the secret cache empty of the Microlith. Instead, he made sure I had exactly what I needed to be permanently free of the menace that Cornelius represented.

The worst part was that I never even thought of the possible consequences for him. You'd think I was some clueless child who had never heard of the occult. My only excuse was that I'd been so distraught by the nightmare Cornelius had turned my life into that I couldn't properly process anything that didn't involve thwarting his efforts. That didn't make my actions any less selfish and thoughtless. I could only pray that Asheron had truly forgiven me.

As much as I wanted to continue berating myself and speculating over the wraith's whereabouts, I had some serious business to settle. Last night, a quick test confirmed the Endless Purse worked as intended. I could have wept with relief. Nevertheless, as I pulled out the Purse from the safe in my room, my pulse picked up with nerves.

I placed it on the desk near the door and wished for the amount needed to settle the debt. My heart leapt in my chest when the pouch instantly bulged as it filled with my request. Fingers trembling, I parted the flaps open to reveal the pile of money inside. My eyes prickled with happy tears as I started counting the stack of banknotes. To my surprise, the pouch had given me a thousand dollars more than the twelve thousand of my outstanding debt. I shrugged and stuffed the money in my shoulder bag. My bank account wouldn't complain about that little extra.

Initially, I had wondered whether to wish for gems instead that I could sell to the jeweler and use that money to repay the debt. However, not only would that have been an extra step I didn't really want to have to deal with today, but I didn't know that he had that much money on hand for instant purchase of this many gems. Thankfully, unlike many European countries overseas, we didn't have serial numbers yet on our currency. Such talks were making their way through our financial and governmental establishments but had not been adopted yet.

Anyway, I didn't intend to use that purse often. I had no need to be wealthy or extravagant. I just wanted to be able to live comfortably, which had been the case until Cornelius's constant attacks depleted my nest egg. If and when serialized bank notes became a thing, I will have no qualms wishing for gems or gold nuggets instead.

After quickly getting dressed, I hurried to the courthouse to settle my debt on all the administrative and procedural fees the necromancer's filings against me had generated. By the sympathetic looks the security guards and other employees cast my way as I headed towards the clerk, they all thought I was here to sign over my rights due to my inability to meet the payment deadline. The petty side of me reared its head, and I played the part of the defeated woman as I approached the desk with a somber expression.

Brody Soulton, a short, older man with bright green eyes, a bushy brown beard streaked with gray, and a generous round belly, greeted me. The sadness dampening his usually jovial demeanor immediately made me feel guilty for misleading people into thinking I was indeed coming here to grant Cornelius his wishes.

I had known Brody since childhood. He'd been a good friend of my father's and almost an honorary uncle to me. He had helplessly watched this entire saga unfold, his heart genuinely breaking for me. As no one ever won a battle against the necromancer, he and the entire town figured I was merely delaying the inevitable. That had not stopped the gossip mongers from enjoying the drama, some even taking bets as to how many rounds I would last before conceding. A part of me almost regretted not edging a bet in my favor at incredible odds just to further spite those who sought to make a game and profit from my woes.

"Good morning, Miss Ronika," Brody said in a slightly paternal tone. "I did not expect you until tomorrow."

My chest warmed for the old man. Even though he believed this to be a lost cause, this was a subtle way of reminding me that I could technically enjoy my home for one more day before eviction. By signing today, I would be expected to leave by nightfall.

"Good morning, Mr. Brody," I said in a friendly tone. "I considered it, then decided not to delay a good thing."

Right on cue, his eyes widened, and his brow shot up. When my smile broadened, a glimmer of confusion and of timid hope sparked in his green eyes. That further made my heart swell with affection for the older man.

"Delay a good thing?" he echoed cautiously.

"Yes, Mr. Brody," I said smugly, while retrieving the envelope filled with banknotes from my bag. "I'm here to settle my account."

His jaw dropped when I placed the thick envelope on top of

the counter in front of him. He stared at it for a moment, as if trying to make sure it wasn't an illusion before gaping at me.

"*Settle* your account?" he asked, incredulous.

"Yes. Settle *in full*."

The hushed gasps behind me had me glancing around the room. A couple of employees and other patrons had conveniently slowed down going from wherever was calling them or found a way to inch a little closer to the counter where I stood. They didn't flat out invade my privacy but shamelessly attempted to eavesdrop. They didn't need to do that as I made no effort to keep my voice low.

I fought the urge to chuckle at their shocked expressions. By the crestfallen look on the face of one of the guards, he had undoubtedly been one of those to have taken a bet against me.

Serves you right.

Brody Soulton reached for the envelope with an air of pure awe. He started counting the banknotes, his shock and disbelief growing accordingly until he reached the full amount.

"Well, this is... this is wonderful, Miss Ronika!" he exclaimed, the genuine happiness in his voice touching me deeply. "Let me go get your file so that we can finalize the settlement of your account."

"Of course, take your time," I said with a glowing smile.

He hurried to the back of the room and handed over the pile of money to the accountant. He then headed towards one of the many filing cabinets and sifted through the contents of a drawer before returning with a thick folder.

I waited patiently while he flipped through the pages, making a few annotations. He apologized a couple of times for the wait, but I didn't care. What were a few more minutes before the official end of all my woes?

Movement behind the clerk had me glancing up. My stomach dropped at the uneasy expression on the face of the accountant as he approached. He cast a sorry look at me as he came to a stop next to Mr. Soulton and cleared his throat to attract his attention. The older man had been so focused on his task, he hadn't heard his colleague.

He slightly jumped in surprise, then cast a questioning look at the lanky younger male. "What is it, Stafford?"

Stafford gave him the sheet of paper in his hand while casting another sorry look my way. My chest constricted while a million thoughts fired off in my mind. What new catastrophe was about to come crashing down on me? What other loophole had Cornelius exploited to make my life a living hell?

By the air of consternation on Brody's face, he believed my chances of settling my account today had just been crushed.

"What's going on?" I asked, my voice thick with tension.

"My dear Miss Ronika, I am so very sorry. But it appears some late fees and penalties have been added to your balance," he said in a sad voice, while placing the sheet on the counter in front of me. "Stafford just went through the accounting to issue your final receipt when he saw the fees and interest clause. I'm afraid there is an additional amount of one thousand dollars to be paid to settle your account."

My jaw dropped. By the way the clerk's shoulders slouched, he undoubtedly believed shock and despair had prompted my reaction. While shock undeniably featured in it, it wasn't for the reasons he thought. I snorted, finally understanding why the Endless Purse had given me more than I had expected. I had wished for it to give me the amount needed to repay my debt, assuming it would be the twelve thousand stated on the invoice. But it had known the amount was in fact thirteen thousand.

Before I could answer the clerk, a detestable voice rose behind me.

"Problems, Ronika?"

I spun on my heel, stunned to find Cornelius standing behind me with that obnoxious smirk on his pale face. The wretched man rarely strolled about during the day, least of all this early in the morning. Although I knew him not to be a vampire, he certainly acted like one.

"What are you doing here?" I asked in a clipped tone.

"A little bird told me you had just entered the courthouse," he said with false commiseration. "I figured I would come console you myself."

"Console me?" I asked with exaggerated stupor. "For what? I do not need consoling. But I believe *you* might."

He blinked, a frown creasing his brow, and he narrowed his eyes with suspicion. "Why would I need consoling? You have an impossible debt to repay."

"And yet, I am doing it today," I said matter-of-factly, the cruel side of me enjoying dragging this on.

His face hardened. "I believe I just heard Soulton mention the additional penalties and administrative fees you seemed unaware of."

"You mean the extra one thousand dollars?" I asked with fake innocence.

My gaze remaining locked with his, I rummaged through my bag to retrieve the extra money I had previously intended to deposit at the bank once done here. I placed it on the counter in front of Brody.

"I believe this should cover the penalties and fees."

Cornelius grew even paler while the clerk and accountant both gasped.

"That's impossible!" the necromancer exclaimed as he observed Brody count the banknotes.

"It's all here!" Brody said, a broad grin splitting his face while he peered at me with wonder. "This will fully settle your account, Miss Ronika. Stafford will prepare your receipt."

"Let me see this!" Cornelius hissed.

To my shock, he reached over the counter, yanking the pile of money out of Brody's hand even as he was extending it to Stafford.

"Mr. Cromwell!" Brody exclaimed.

Two guards took a step forward, clearly unsure as to what to do. Their duty required them to intervene over what was clearly a criminal act. But Cornelius wasn't someone you messed with without risking serious consequences. In many ways, he was above the law. At least, where common folk were concerned.

I raised a palm, signaling for them not to interfere. "By all means, Cornelius, verify that it's all there. We wouldn't want people to think Ronika Ortega cheated when she once again defeated your plotting and scheming efforts to steal her ancestral property. Count away."

He flipped through the banknotes, magic swirling around him in a vain attempt at dispelling any illusion or glamour spell that might have given regular paper the appearance of money. Teeth clenched, he tossed the money back onto the counter, his eyes shooting daggers at me.

"Where did you get that? I know you don't have these kinds of means," he ground through his teeth.

"There is much you don't know about me," I retorted, my voice dripping with contempt. "I said you would *never* get my property. Try as you may, you will continue to fail."

"You're only delaying the inevitable," he snapped.

I waved a disdainful hand and took on a bored expression. "Blah, blah, blah. I've heard that tune a million times from you before. And we're right back where we started. Come at me all you want, you will continue to fail. I promise you, keep this up, and *you* will go bankrupt long before you bankrupt me."

"Your release papers, Miss Ronika," Brody said in a timid fashion, interrupting us.

"Thank you, Mr. Brody," I replied in a much warmer tone. "A pleasure doing business with you, as always."

Without waiting for his response, I turned towards Cornelius, winked at him in a taunting fashion, then strutted my way out of the courthouse under the flabbergasted stares of the staff and patrons. The string of swear words tumbling out of the necro-mancer behind me only put a silly grin on my face. He had made such a public spectacle of his impending victory over me that this defeat would be even more humiliating than the previous ones.

I was walking on a cloud, a pep in my steps as I returned to my horse. Throughout the journey home, I felt like the weight of the world had been lifted off my shoulders. My mind swirled with plans of all the things I would do, could do, and even ways to expand my shop. The one question plaguing me was how Asheron would fit in that new life, assuming he even wanted to.

All such musings went up in smoke when I found Leander Barlow pacing frantically in front of my shop. My heart sank with worry, and I pushed Damar to go faster. The relieved and vulnerable expression on such a big, hulking man, further increased my concern. Leander was a construction worker whose wife Glinda had fallen ill two years ago. Despite my best efforts, I had failed to find a permanent cure. They came to me after Doctor Osborne gave up on her and recommended she put her house in order.

Her sudden illness made no sense. Before that, Glinda had been a vibrant young woman. At twenty-six, she became one of the most sought-after nurses and caregivers in Willow Grove. Then one day, overnight, she started weakening for no apparent reason. She slept and ate more without ever seeming to get enough. Instead of gaining weight, the petite woman steadily withered, leaving a skinny—if not emaciated—shadow of the beautiful woman she had once been.

Judging by their carriage parked in front of the house, I could only presume he left her inside while waiting for my return. The look on his face when he finally noticed my approach turned me upside down. The love he bore his wife was a thing of legend. With his good looks, comfortable means, and delightful person-ality, Leander could have any woman he wanted. Not for the first time, people had hinted that he should stop living in limbo with this lost cause. After all, he was wasting his best years while prolonging her suffering with magical healing.

Such asinine comments always angered me. Glinda wanted to live. His love and support kept her going beyond what even I had thought possible.

I jumped off my horse before he came to a full stop.

"There you are!" Leander exclaimed, having run to meet me. "Glinda needs you. It's bad. Really bad."

"Bring her inside," I ordered, before rushing to unlock the door.

I made a beeline for the shelves containing my healing and energy tonics. They gave her the jolt of energy necessary to go through regular days. But first, I would do a cleansing followed by an energy spell. The chime on the door resonated as Leander entered. I turned around with a few vials in both hands with the intention of pointing for him to bring her to the examination table in my backroom. However, a single glance at them stopped me dead in my tracks.

Glinda's skin had always been as fair as Leander's was dark. With her light blonde hair and brown eyes, she reminded me of an angel, whereas he was the dark knight protector. Now, her skin looked translucent, her veins bulging beneath. After two years of this slow death, you'd think she was in her fifties instead of her late twenties.

It wasn't her withered appearance that robbed me of words, but the writhing shadowy form latched onto her spine and nape. It vaguely resembled a leech with spindly legs digging into her skin to keep it in place.

By the gods, what is that?

I perceived no particular evil from it, not like with a malicious demon. The magic emanating from it was also rather weak. In the seconds it took me to assimilate all of this, I realized this thing with some sort of parasite feeding off her.

"Ronika?" Leander asked when I just stood there, gaping, my hands full of vials. "Where do you want her? In the back?"

That snapped me out of my shocked daze. I shook my head and pointed at the door leading to my den.

"No. Let's try something else. This way."

"What? Why?" he asked, although he followed me without hesitation.

My wheels spinning, understanding slowly dawned on me as to what we'd been so blind to for the past two years. Leander's steps faltered when he entered the room no client had ever visited before. His unease was palpable as his gaze roamed over the large pentagram on the floor, the altar propped against the wall with magical paraphernalia, and my shelves filled with spices, herbs, scrolls, and various oils and essences.

"Do you remember Ms. Lumley?" I asked, ignoring his discomfort.

He recoiled, confused as to what his wife's former patient had to do with anything.

"I believe your wife is suffering from the same thing that took her," I said calmly while picking up a mortar, and a handful of spices and herbs.

"What?! That's absurd! Ms. Lumley suffered from dementia. She was delusional, seeing things that didn't exist!" he exclaimed, looking unsure whether I still had all my senses.

"Ms. Lumley displayed all the same symptoms your wife is now," I argued, gesturing for him to lay Glinda down in the center of the pentagram. "She was withering and weakening. But more importantly, she was mage-born, which meant she had the power to see things others can't. I don't think she was hallucinating. Ms. Lumley just faded much faster because she was older. Glinda was young and healthy when her sudden illness struck her."

"I... I don't understand. What makes you think that now? What's with the pentagram? I just brought my Glinda here for one of your energy spells," he said, looking like he would have made a swift exit had his wife not been in such a bad state.

Glinda moaned, her frail body trembling in her husband's big, strong arms.

"Leander," I said in a calm and soothing voice, as if addressing a frightened animal, "Glinda needs help right now. We've been friends for years. Have I not always done the impossible to help her?"

He nodded. His eyes misting, he tightened his embrace around her and rested his temple on top of her head. To see such a big and intimidating man so broken by the pain of the one he loved more than life clawed at my heart.

"Then trust me one more time," I continued in the same tone. "This is going to be hard for you to believe, but I can now see that Glinda isn't suffering from an illness. I believe what killed Ms. Lumley moved on to your wife. I can see some sort of evil spirit on her back."

Leander recoiled, and slightly shifted his wife—who he was holding like a bride—to glimpse at her back.

"A spirit? You think my wife is possessed!?" he exclaimed.

"No. This is not demonic possession. I believe it's a parasite riding her, feeding from her. And I believe I can banish it," I added quickly when he seemed about to argue.

A million different emotions fleeted over his handsome features. If not for our long-standing friendship, I didn't doubt for a minute he would have stormed out of here thinking me insane. But on top of the trust borne out of that relationship, the prospect of a potential cure—however unlikely—was too good for him to pass up.

"I need you to trust me, Leander. We can help her once and for all," I insisted.

I could see all the questions warring within him. We probably shared many of them, mainly how come I could see it now and not before. But I suspected either my enhanced magic since meeting Asheron or the parasite weakening from having less and less to feed on from his host was the cause. Or it could be a combination of both.

"Fine," Leander suddenly said with determination, having made his decision. "What must I do? Just place her in the center of the pentagram?"

I nodded. "I will prepare a potion she must drink before I can perform the banishment ritual. The only thing I need from you are three drops of blood and for you to will for her to be freed. The blood of a dearly loved one will strengthen the repulsion power of the banishment. Do not fret, the pentagram will keep the parasite trapped. Nevertheless, just for extra safety, I will cast a protection spell on you to make sure it doesn't go after you as a replacement host."

Leander nodded stiffly and placed Glinda with infinite care in the center of the pentagram. I mixed the herbs and spices in my mortar, grinding them while reciting an incantation. Once done I added oil, blessed water, and Leander's three drops of blood. After carefully mixing it all, I brought it to Glinda's lips. My heart broke further at how weak and emaciated she looked. My last treatment for her dated back a week. But she looked as if she'd been starving for a month since. She struggled even only to swallow it down.

By the time she emptied the bowl, I was silently seething at the wretched creature that had been destroying such an innocent life. I carefully laid her head back down before stepping out of the pentagram. I formed a circle around it with salt, making sure there were no gaps, then placed scented candles at each point of the pentagram. Once done, I cast a protection spell over both Leander and myself, more as an excess of caution than out of any real belief we required it. That creature truly felt low level to me.

"Whatever you see or hear, you must not interfere," I sternly warned him. "And above all, do not enter the pentagram. Your wife may endure some pain during the process. It is normal. Promise you will stay strong and not interfere."

Despite obviously struggling with that prospect, Leander gave me a stiff nod. "I will not interfere. But please, save her."

I smiled then took a deep breath. As soon as I began the banishment incantation, the shadow leech on Glinda's back seized and started writhing even more intensely. In seconds, it shook and spasmed as if lightning bolts were repeatedly striking it. At first, the leech appeared to be swelling on her back. Then it looked more like an invisible hand was trying to pull it away from her. Glinda's previous pained moans gradually turned into whimpers, and then into screams.

I forced myself to block out Leander's tortured voice whispering his wife's name. The poor man was dying with the need to go to her. Thankfully, he kept his word and stood still. After a few moments that felt like an eternity, the first couple of legs at the base of the leech's tail were ripped out of the poor woman's back.

"By the gods! What is that?!" Leander exclaimed with a horrified expression.

I continued ignoring him, focusing on my banishment spell. However, I realized that the leech partially losing its grip on its host had made it visible to Leander, who possessed no magic. One by one, the other claws tore out of her back, each one accelerating the process. When the last one lost its grip, the leech was thrown up in the air. Glinda exhaled a deep sigh, the tension that had stiffened her body bleeding out of her and her shaking fading.

The leech emitted a high-pitch screech, its spindly legs waving in every direction in a desperate effort to try and go back down to its host. But gravity had no power here. I expended even more magic while accelerating the speed at which I recited the incantation. The air around the leech blurred, then a purple spark quickly blossomed into a larger vortex. In a desperate screech, the parasite flailed trying to hang on to the edges of the vortex sucking it in. But it eventually engulfed the creature before closing with a woosh.

"Glinda!" Leander exclaimed once the creature vanished.

"No!" I shouted, when he made as if to go to her. "Not yet."

For a split second, I feared he would ignore my command, but he thankfully caved. I performed a quick cleansing and then cast a protection spell on her before allowing him to pick her up.

Although it would take a few weeks for her to fully recover, a single look at her face confirmed she was indeed free. The milky film that had dulled the beautiful shine of her brown eyes had lifted. The scent of death had also faded.

My throat tightened when she locked eyes with her husband and whispered his name as if she was seeing him for the first time after years of separation. In many ways, it was the case. I blinked rapidly to stem the happy tears welling in my eyes when he kissed her and hugged her tightly while chanting her name with adoration.

"It's gone, right?" Leander asked at last. "She's going to get better now, right?"

"Yes. I believe this nightmare is completely over," I replied with a gentle smile, before turning to Glinda. "Obviously, I will want to see you again a few more times in the upcoming days and weeks just to make sure everything is how it should be. But I'm pretty confident this is it. I will give you some healing tonics to help boost your recovery."

"Thank you," Glinda said in a shaky voice. "You saved me. I didn't know it before, but now I can feel it's gone. It was eating me alive, sucking away my energy and will to live. I can never repay you enough."

"You can by getting better swiftly and making that man of yours happy. He took such good care of you all this time," I said with a smile.

She glanced up at her husband who was still looking at her with adoration. The smile she gave him wrecked me.

"I intend to. I thank the gods every day for placing him on my path," she said, eyes locked with him.

"I love you, my Glinda," he said.

"And I love you, too, my giant."

He kissed her then carefully carried her back to their carriage. I followed with a few tonics and gave them final instructions before sending them on their way.

Once their carriage faded from view, I turned back to look at the house, my heart filling with gratitude for Asheron. He had given me my home back and the power to become the healer I had always aspired to be.

CHAPTER 12
ASHERON

Annoyed to no end, I continued roaming around Cornelius's residence. I'd been in and out throughout the night and most of the morning, searching for the elusive necromancer. Within minutes of first entering the house, I'd found my tailbone. It called to me, and I answered. But I couldn't retrieve it.

Cornelius had stashed it away in a large room that could qualify both as a trophy room and menagerie. Located in the cellar, it contained a mix of artifacts and living creatures, and dormant animated constructs. The menagerie was held in metal cages reinforced by magic. The constructs were the exception, all of them standing side by side, frozen in time, inside a single glass cell.

Although predominantly human in appearance, some possessed animal parts and others mechanical ones. Those abominations resulted from using alchemy and necromancy on the combined body parts from executed prisoners or the unclaimed dead strangers that Cornelius bought for a pittance. He would animate them to serve him, with a glamour spell to hide their hideous appearance from the rest of the population.

On the opposite wall, dozens of relics and powerful artifacts sat on shelves, seeming deceptively unprotected. But formidable magic bound them to the ornate wooden socle upon which they rested. Any fool who simply tried to appropriate these items would learn the error of their ways in the most horrendous fashion.

However, it was one of the glass cases atop pedestals in front of the relics wall that held my attention. Inside, my tailbone, carefully folded into a spiral, sat on a black velvet cushion. Like the other artifacts, impressive magic kept it sealed within. For all my considerable power, I was helpless to bypass them. That meant waiting for the thrice damned necromancer to return from wherever he'd run off to since the previous evening.

I glided back to the main floor to see if I could gather some insight as to when he would come back. The house was surprisingly 'normal' and even inviting. For some reason, I had expected it to be dark and twisted, reeking of foul energy, pain, decay, and despair. While I undoubtedly felt a sliver of negative energy, it was nothing like the omnipresent malice that permeated Hemdell.

Granted, the walls were painted in dark gray shades, framed by varnished wooden beams with elegant, dark brown leather furniture. But the light-colored high ceilings and the immense arched windows kept it from feeling somber or oppressive. Lamps without candles further illuminated the drawing room— which I understood they now called living room or family room. Apparently, they used gas—the same technology as the street-lamps now found everywhere in town. This was but another wonder achieved during the countless years I lost to madness.

I floated past one of Cornelius's animated constructs. You couldn't tell if it had been a man or woman before being reassembled—probably a mix of both. But the servant outfit it wore matched that of a man. It cleverly covered the swollen scars where the limbs had been sewn together, but that had been visible on the naked inanimate constructs in the basement. The ashen texture of the servant's skin and the complete absence of emotion—or of a soul—made it obvious it had been raised from the dead. It busied itself dusting the room, oblivious to my presence. Then again, no one, but another wraith or extremely powerful conjurer, could detect me in my vaporous form.

I started heading towards the back of the house where Cornelius had built a sort of laboratory. Two beautiful young witches and a just as attractive warlock were diligently working there, furthering his research and experiments. During my brief previous visit of that room, a single whiff had sufficed for me to know that he regularly bedded all three, and that they hated each other, probably out of a bitter rivalry for his affection.

Before I could even exit the drawing room, the sound of angry shouts from the entrance stopped me dead in my tracks.

Cornelius!

I raced down the hallway towards the main entrance only to see a couple of human servants scatter, their faces tense with fear. Shock swept through me as I entered the greeting hall and witnessed the necromancer giving into a fit of rage. He latched onto one of his reanimated constructs and began beating it into a pulp. The soulless creature just stood there impassive, while getting torn to shreds. Cornelius's impossible display of strength as he ripped his servant's arm right off, was quickly explained seconds later.

His face and arms became deformed as demonic features pressed forward under the skin and bones. It unleashed its fury on the unresponsive construct, tearing it limb from limb. Terrifying claws extruded from the tips of the necromancer's fingers as he tore at the gelatinous flesh of its victim until total chaos and carnage littered the hall. At least, there wouldn't be any blood to clean.

Cornelius's fury abated at last—or at least, the uncontrollable rage part of it. The demonic presence retreated, returning his face and arms to their normal appearance. He straightened his clothes and ran a hand over his hair to fix it, before marching towards the living area. Heading straight for the liquor cabinet, he poured himself a bourbon and downed it in one go.

"Bested by that weak, pathetic green witch," he hissed while pouring himself a second glass. "How dare she stand up to me?"

If not for my current vaporous form, I'd be grinning from ear to ear to know his plans getting thwarted by my woman had put him in such a foul mood.

"I will break you, Ronika Ortega," he ground through his teeth, his voice dripping with venom. "I would have made you my concubine, now I will make you my whore. I'll have your ancestors and Warden Tree watch as my servants and I take turns defiling you. Then we'll see who has the last laugh."

Instant anger surged through me upon hearing those words. I shifted to my wraith form and advanced menacingly towards him.

"I think not, Necromancer," I snarled.

He yelped and choked on the sip he had just begun taking from his newly refilled glass. Leaning on the bar, coughing, he stared at me in shock.

"Asheron!" he exclaimed, between two coughs. "How... How are you here?!"

I stopped a couple of meters in front of him, my teeth bared. The taste of his fear was whipping my hunger into a frenzy. Despite whatever demon lurked inside him, Cornelius would be no challenge for me should I decide to put an end to his miserable existence.

And he knew it.

"You granted me access the day you housed a part of me inside your home," I said, anger still clearly audible in my voice.

Although I never thought it possible, Cornelius's chalky skin grew even paler. Obviously, he had not expected me to pay him a visit to recover what was mine. After all, he'd gotten away with it for more than three centuries.

"You will leave her alone or face my wrath," I threatened. He blinked in confusion. "She has beaten you fair and square, yet again. Stay away from her and her land."

His jaw dropped, and his eyes nearly popped out of his head in sudden understanding. "The witch?! How in the seven hells is she controlling you?"

He flinched the moment he blurted out those last words.

"Do I look like I'm under anyone's thrall, you fool? Ronika does not control me. She doesn't even know I'm here. Consider this your one and only warning. She is mine and under my protection."

The necromancer swallowed hard, a flurry of emotions crossing his features as he clearly battled to come to terms with the inevitable.

"Understood?" I snarled when he failed to answer quickly enough.

He clenched his teeth then gave me a stiff nod. "Understood," he replied, grimacing as if the words scorched his lips.

I couldn't help a malicious smirk to see him so dejected. It was all the more entertaining that the demon inside him was rattling the cage, aching to surge forward again with another fit of rage. Lucky for him, Cornelius kept him in check. That didn't stop me from needling him about it.

"That was quite the spectacle just now," I said, waving in the direction of the greeting hall. "What have you done to yourself, Cornelius? Are you still even Cornelius Cromwell or just a vessel?"

His face immediately closed off, but not before I glimpsed the spark of shame and hatred that crossed his features.

"I am very much still Cornelius," he said in an icy tone. "Like you, no one controls me. Now, if that will be all, other matters call me."

"I'm sure they do," I said with disdain. "But before I leave, you will return what belongs to me."

"Naturally," he replied with a shrug. "This way."

To my shock, he promptly headed towards the basement, not bothering to check if I was following. That instantly set all of my senses on high alert. I had expected him to try and deny that he possessed it or to at least try to argue that it would be fair for him to keep it or that it would be of no use to me at this point. That he gave in without a fight felt highly suspicious.

When I pointed it out to him, he gave me a mysterious smile that further increased my unease.

"I have no use for it," he said with a shrug as we started down the staircase to the basement. "Believe me, it's not for lack of trying. Having one such as you by my side would have been phenomenal."

"You mean as your puppet," I countered with disdain.

He chuckled and waved a dismissive hand. "Semantics. Luciana made it impossible. The foolish girl was always too impatient, too greedy in her lust for power and discovery. A pity, really. Had she been less controlled by her passions, she could have achieved things that would have made even the gods tremble."

"How did she make it impossible?" I asked as we reached the landing.

"She cut off your tail before damning you," he said matter-of-factly. "Despite being the son of a bone demon, your sire's angelic genetics dominated in you. Your tail remained divine even after the rest of you was damned. You cannot corrupt the divine without a soul to be broken. Had Luciana chopped off your tail after she had turned you, we would be having a very different conversation right now."

"We wouldn't be having a conversation at all," I said, reeling from this revelation as we entered the menagerie. "She would never have been able to chop it off me unless she managed to end the madness her actions plunged me into. And I can assure you that seeing her would have done anything but soothe me."

He stopped in front of the casing containing my tail before giving me an assessing look. "Fair point, Asheron. Which makes me all the more curious as to how you finally managed to emerge from it after all these years. I can only speculate the little witch pulled it off. But how?"

"You can speculate all you want, necromancer. But keep Ronika out of your mind, if you know what's good for you," I said in a grumbling tone.

He chuckled and spoke a few words of power to lift the magic from the casing. "So she did free you. It seems I underestimated her in more ways than one. Thank you, Lord Voror. It mends my bruised ego that I should have lost to someone powerful enough to bring back a demigod from the deepest pits of insanity."

I didn't comment, to focus on assessing my tail for any signs of foul magic on it. While I didn't doubt his story about why he failed to enslave me with it, I wouldn't put it past him to curse it out of spite. Over the years, he'd proven himself to be the type to destroy something that he couldn't have rather than allowing others to enjoy it.

He spoke a few more words of power, this time to release the tail from the pedestal and cushion it sat on. Cornelius then waved at it while staring at me with a taunting glimmer in his deep blue eyes.

"There you go, Asheron. Yours for the taking." A malicious smile stretched his lips when I continued to stare at him without reaching for the tail. "Do not fret, Lord Voror. There is no curse or other negative magic on it. I swear it is still exactly the way it was on the day Luciana took it from you. Death magic has no power over the divine."

While my gut continued to scream danger at me, I didn't doubt the honesty of his words. But I also felt at a visceral level that he was preemptively enjoying what he believed to be my imminent demise or him exacting on me some form of retribution.

Against my better judgment, I picked up my tail. To my relief, I indeed felt no evil magic and triggered no defense mechanism. Instead, a delightful warmth spread through my hand holding it. Even without it reattached to my spine, I almost felt whole again.

"See?" Cornelius said mockingly. "No harm, no foul. But you and I should really reach an agreement. I do not only have servants and puppets. There are others who work for me of their free will."

I snorted with disdain. "Not out of free will, but out of thirst for power. They whore themselves out to you for any scraps you can give them."

He shrugged. "Don't we all do it in one form or another? We give to others what they deem of value, often with much reluctance, in exchange for what we need. Whether you give your body, your blood in battle, or the sweat of your brow through physical labor, you're still selling yourself to someone to make a living and to achieve your goals. In the end, we are all whores. It's just that some of us don't do it on our backs."

"That's one way to put it. But I do not need or want anything from you that I haven't gotten back already."

"If you say so. Do you wish me to reattach it for you?" he offered, gesturing at the tail in my hand.

I stared at him in disbelief that he should make such an outrageous offer. "I'd rather whore myself out to a pack of trolls than to let you put a hand on me."

He stiffened and his teeth clenched when he heard me echo the words Ronika had spoken to him on the day he had come to pressure her at her house to sign over the deeds to the house and offered for her to become his concubine.

"As you wish," he said in a clipped tone. "I believe our business is concluded."

"It is," I replied. "See that it remains as such by staying away from my woman."

"I will not do anything to cross you, Lord Voror," he replied in a mysterious tone. "Enjoy your tail… until we meet again."

That he had not flat out said he wouldn't mess with her didn't go unnoticed. As did that last little taunt. He knew something I didn't. But I firmly intended to figure it out sooner than later.

"Farewell, Necromancer," I said before gliding out of the room and back up the stairs.

By the time I reached the greeting hall, two human servants—one man and one woman—were already almost done cleaning the carnage their master had left behind. The female noticed me first. She yelped, slapping a palm to her chest before taking a few steps back. The man cast a startled look at her before peering around the room with a frightened expression, probably expecting to see a still enraged Cornelius returning. But when he saw me advancing in my wraith form, he looked like he couldn't decide whether to faint or empty his stomach on top of the remaining pieces of hacked flesh.

To my pleasant surprise, the instinctive bloodlust their reaction should have triggered barely tickled my wraith. The image of Ronika's beautiful face immediately flashed before my mind's eye. My mother's words resonated in my head. My woman was indeed my anchor… my peace. I ignored them as they frantically backed away from me, plastering themselves against the side walls as if they wished they could melt into it.

I opened the door then shifted into my sheerest form without fully becoming vaporous. I couldn't transport physical objects otherwise. Thankfully, with Cornelius's estate being a bit out of the way, there wouldn't be any witnesses—other than his servants—to see me traipsing through the sky with a long tail made of bones in my hands.

As I began my descent near Ronika's house, I noticed her accompanying a couple out of her shop. A fragile-looking woman snuggled in the arms of a big and muscular man. Considering her weakened state, I would have expected the woman to look sad and worn. But her expression mirrored the glowing smile etched on the man's face.

I glided inside the shop through the door left open and continued to the backroom where Ronika normally performed healings and examinations. I placed my tail on the counter and debated if I should use the side door into the private part of her residence instead. Before I could make a decision, her quick footsteps resonated outside.

"Asheron?!" she called out.

I froze. How in the world did she know I was here? Even though I hadn't been fully invisible, Ronika had not been looking in my direction when I arrived. She'd also been so focused giving instructions to her clients that she shouldn't have been aware of my presence.

"Asheron?" she called out again, her voice much closer.

On instinct, I shifted to my vaporous form a split second before she entered the backroom. Her eyes zeroed in on my position, and a happy smile illuminated her beautiful face.

"You're back!" she exclaimed.

Stunned, I shifted back to my physical form. She ran to me and threw herself into my arms. I embraced her, and we exchanged a tender kiss. I lifted my head and gently brushed her hair from her face, still confused.

"How did you know I was here?" I asked.

"I felt you arrive," she said as if it was self-evident.

"*Felt* me?" I echoed.

She nodded. "It was like a tingling. A little bit like the first time I felt your aura, but much more agreeable. It was super brief. I figured you had just flown inside."

"But you saw me when you entered the room, even though I was in my vaporous form," I insisted.

"Right. About that, something just happened that I believe to be related," she said sheepishly.

She described what she witnessed when Leander, the burly man, brought in his wife, the fragile woman called Glinda. My jaw dropped as she continued with the banishment she performed.

"I'm hoping this will be the end of the illness that had slowly been killing her," Ronika said in a hopeful voice.

"I can confirm that it is," I said with awe. I smiled when her brow shot up in surprise. "It appears you now have the power to see wraiths," I explained.

"Wraiths?! That thing was not a wraith, was it?" she asked, taken aback.

I nodded. "Yes, it was. We come in various forms. Our power level varies greatly based on what magical predispositions we possessed before the curse and how badly the ritual went when we were damned. Wraiths such as the one you banished are the weakest form. They are fairly mindless parasites. Leech is an appropriate name to describe them. Unlike with a demonic possession, those leeches do not try to control or influence the host in any way. They simply latch on to them and feed off their life force until they wither and die, at which point they move on to a new host."

"Blast! I was right then that it migrated from Ms. Lumley to Glinda," she whispered with angry disbelief. "If only I had known then, I could have saved her, too, and spared Glinda all this pain."

"You cannot blame yourself for this," I gently chastised her. "In truth, I am speechless that you are able to see us. It appears you and I have formed a greater bond than I thought."

"That's a good thing, isn't it?" she asked with a sliver of

worry in her voice. "I mean you're not unhappy about us growing closer, right?"

"I couldn't be happier. You are mine," I said in all sincerity.

As much as I worried about my effects on her, seeing how I was enhancing Ronika without causing harm further gave me hope for a future that didn't involve binding her.

"I kind of remember both you and your wraith saying something to that effect," she said in a playfully seductive tone.

I tightened my arms around her in a possessive fashion. "We certainly have. And I made sure Cornelius was aware of it as well."

She stiffened, and her eyes widened in shock. "What?!"

It was my turn to give her a summary of what transpired at his estate, from his hissy fit to me recovering my tail.

"By the gods! I wish I could have seen him losing his mind," Ronika said with an evil chuckle. "Seeing him seething at the courthouse had been a blast. I can only imagine how much better it must have been watching him go into full rage. Thanks for telling me, this made my day even better. You even have your tail back," she added, glancing at it with an air of wonder.

"Thanks to you," I said, my heart swelling with deep affection for my woman as I gently caressed her face. "You have given me my life back. You have made me whole again."

"As you have done for me," she replied, the tenderness settling on her face moving me to the core. "You've not just made my life better, you've made it perfect. Meeting you was the greatest thing to have ever happened in my life. You say I'm yours, but you are mine, too, Asheron. I don't ever want to let you go."

"My Ronika," I whispered, my heart filling to bursting.

I claimed her lips in a passionate kiss, pouring into it the depth of the emotions she had awakened in me, and that I had never felt before for anyone.

Her hands caressing my back sent a delicious shiver through

me. By the gods, I would never tire of the possessive and eager way she touched me. I'd never wanted to belong to a woman the way I did her. I became hers the moment she broke the madness. Ronika didn't realize it just yet, but she truly owned me.

A bolt of desire exploded in the pit of my stomach when she raked her claws alongside my exoskeleton in that way she knew I loved. I growled in approval and deepened the kiss. What first started as an expression of tenderness and gratitude soon evolved into something much different. The moment I broke the kiss, Ronika's lips wandered down my neck to my chest, and her hands roamed with increasing boldness all over my body.

While I was fully naked when shifting back to my physical form, she was much too dressed.

I eagerly lifted her dress, annoyed that it forced her to stop kissing and caressing me so that I could take it off her. Finding her bodice and drawers underneath further aggravated me. I almost extruded my claws to rip them right off her.

In my impatience, I merely yanked her bodice down. Thankfully, it wasn't one of those boned and tightly laced ones that seemed to be trending among women in this era. I lifted Ronika up and sat her on the counter, my mouth latching onto one of her pinkish-brown nipples. I hungrily sucked on it while my hand fiddled with her drawers. To my delight, that loose undergarment parted open between the thighs, giving me direct access to my woman's burning core.

My fingers wormed their way to the slick petals of her slit. The scent of her arousal had blood rushing to my groin and made my mouth water. I slipped two fingers between her folds and inside her sheath. The wet heat of her inner walls greedily squeezed my fingers, drawing them deeper within. Each contraction resonated directly in my cock, which strained against the confines of my protective loin plate made of bone scales.

Unable to resist, I grabbed Ronika's hips and drew her behind to the edge of the counter. She yelped and slapped her palms on top of the wooden surface for support. I spread her wide while crouching and buried my face between her thighs. Her strangled cry sent even more blood rushing to my already engorged cock. I emitted a painful groan as I extruded, grateful for the instant relief.

With one hand, I moved aside the wretched fabric of the drawers that kept getting in my face while I sucked on her little nub. The fingers of the other hand continued moving in and out of her as she began gyrating in response to my touch. By the gods, she tasted exquisite! I could gorge on her divine essence for all eternity. Hanging on to both my horns, she lifted her pelvis for greater contact with my face, needing more. I accelerated the movement of my fingers making love to her, thinking with much chagrin about what else I would be doing to her right now if my tail were reattached to me.

Soon, I will.

When her legs began to shake around my face, I picked up the pace of my ministrations even more. My blood boiled with the need to ride her, but I would have her fall apart for me once first. As much as I wished she was clawing at my spine right now, I reveled in the intensity with which she tugged at my horns, like she was drowning in a sea of pleasure and hanging on to them for dear life. But it was the sound of her moans filling my ears and the desperation with which she whispered my name as she neared the edge that was driving me insane with lust.

And then her climax slammed into her.

She pulled at my horns so hard as she cried out, I almost expected them to tear right off. The pain shot straight into my cock in a blissful, fiery blaze that almost had me spilling. With a beastly growl, I jumped to my feet and impaled her on my throbbing shaft. It burned going in. But that pain, too, was delectable, fanning the flames surging through me.

Ronika's startled gasp stretched into a raspy moan as I immediately set a frantic pace. Even as she continued to fly high, she released my horns to wrap her arms around me. Her nails digging into my back made me spill some of my seed. That broke something inside me. With a feral growl, I buried my fangs in her neck as I began pounding into her.

She cried out, her nails digging deeper into me. I had not planned on finding my release so soon, but my seed shot out of me in powerful spurts while the divine nectar of her life's blood flowed into my mouth.

By the gods! I would die with pleasure. This was too much. Her tight sheath squeezing and stroking my cock with each thrust was sending fiery tendrils scattering in my loins, through my veins, and to every cell of my body, setting me on the verge of combustion. And that pure ambrosia I greedily swallowed was just more fuel for the inferno consuming me from within.

Another savage shout escaped me as I forced my fangs out of my woman. I could drink her dry in my endless hunger. I reclaimed her mouth, moaning against her lips as she feverishly caressed me with a possessiveness that tugged at my heart and soul. She was mine, and I was hers. Even now, my seed coursed through her, like a magical aura infusing her being with my essence.

I broke the kiss to peer at her. Seven hells, she was breathtaking. Disheveled, her lips swollen by my kisses, her face flushed with pleasure, and her undergarments half falling off her, my woman glowed with a powerful aura of sin, lust, and unbridled passion. She looked like Aphrodite herself.

A sex goddess I wanted to see fall apart for me at least one more time.

Relentless, I slipped a hand between us to massage her clitoris. Despite spilling my seed, I didn't soften. Just as I was beginning the next round of my sensual assault on my woman, the chime of the shop's door resonated, announcing the arrival of some visitor. Ronika stiffened and started pushing back, panic settling on her flushed face.

"Hello?" a male voice called out from the front.

"Give me a minute! I'm coming!" Ronika shouted, her voice labored as she frantically tapped on my shoulder for me to stop thrusting into her.

How in damnation had we forgotten that the front door wasn't locked? But it didn't really matter to me. All I cared about was the feel of my woman around my cock, and my determination to hear her scream my name again while I filled her to the brim.

"She is coming, but not for you. Go away!" I shouted back in a voice so growly, it was barely intelligible to my own ears.

Under different circumstances, the patron's muffled gasp, and Ronika's both outraged and mortified expression would have been hilarious. But the searing desire for my woman consuming me left no room for this type of obnoxious interruption.

"Ashe—!"

I swallowed her attempt at chastising me with a voracious kiss while I pounded into her. There was no question he could hear the thumping of my thrusting into Ronika, and the slapping sound of flesh meeting flesh. Annoyed with the mortal still lingering in the shop—and who seemed unsure what to do—I summoned my frost, spreading it all over the floor. Although I couldn't see him from this angle, I clearly heard his gasp of alarm. The stomping of feet was soon followed by the chiming of the door as he wisely made a quick exit. I spread my frost to the door, sealing it shut. I'd be damned if we were interrupted again.

Yes, Ronika would be coming some more... for me.

CHAPTER 13
ASHERON

After she extracted some hardly sincere apologies from me for how I handled the intrusion, Ronika spent a non-negligible amount of time discussing with me the matter of my tail. No words could express how deeply her genuine concern for my well-being touched me.

She no longer needed me. Her troubles with Cornelius had been solved. Even without my threat to him should he bother her again, Ronika could have handled anything else he threw her way with the Endless Purse. As she had no thirst for power, and no ambition other than to put her magic to use for the welfare of others, her wish for my presence could only mean real affection, and not a ploy to exploit me.

Like me, she had perceived no evil magic or curse on my tail. Nevertheless, she insisted we bring it to Vigil, her Warden Tree. I followed in her wake as she headed towards the majestic tree. He could have passed for the Watcher's little brother. The knots of Vigil's trunk also formed what clearly resembled a face, slimmer, longer, and more youthful than the one from his kin in Duskwallow. Very few families were blessed with such a protector. No wonder Cornelius so desperately coveted her lands.

As we closed the distance with him, Vigil shifted a couple of his roots, making a clear path to his wide trunk. A few of his lower branches slowly swooped down, closing around Ronika in a paternal embrace when she reached him.

In that instant, I finally understood the protectiveness the Watcher had displayed towards my woman that first night in Duskwallow. She was a daughter of the land, bonded to one of the ancient guardians. He would have felt it the minute she approached him.

"Vigil, this is Asheron," she said almost timidly, the way a maiden would introduce a suitor to her sire. "He's very dear to my heart."

Under different circumstances, I would have simply found this adorable. But to my shock, a wave of nervousness surged through me. What if Vigil disapproved of me? As a Warden Tree, he was an important—even revered—member of the family. Although his rejection wouldn't automatically mean that Ronika would cast me out of her life, it would undoubtedly create some tension.

"Asheron, this is Vigil. Technically, he's been our bloodline's protector since the dawn of time. But to me, he's just family," she added with great depth of affection in her voice and on her face.

Vigil emitted a rumbling sound, and one of his limbs gently brushed against Ronika's arm.

"Greetings, Vigil," I said respectfully. "Ronika loves you deeply. She has gone to great lengths to protect you from those who sought to use you for their nefarious designs."

"With your help," she added, her beautiful brown eyes sparkling with gratitude.

Vigil rumbled again. Although he didn't give me a paternal caress like he had with my woman, the way he waved one of his branches struck me as a thanking gesture.

"Vigil, we have a special request for you," Ronika said in a more serious tone.

She quickly explained to him our dilemma. To my pleasant surprise, the Warden Tree didn't hesitate to accede to her request. One of his thickest roots further emerged from the ground, almost forming a small table in front of him. Ronika gestured for me to place the tail on it. I complied. No sooner did I release it than a series of tiny vines wrapped around it. They began to glow at the same time as the runes adorning what could pass for Vigil's forehead.

I held my breath, dreading what the verdict would be. Ronika's hand slipping into mine startled me. I gave her a sideways glance, only to find her eyes locked on my tail. Another wave of emotion swelled through me in light of the tension stiffening her back. That she should care so much further filled the gaping hole that had expanded in my heart and soul over the centuries of my damnation.

When his runes took on a pure white glow, my throat tightened, and a sensation I hadn't felt in centuries pricked my eyes. I couldn't remember the last time I had welled up. In truth, I never thought a wraith would be able to shed tears. Although I didn't, this was the closest I came to doing it upon seeing this confirmation that no curse desecrated my tail.

Ronika's joyous squeal had me bursting out laughing while she hopped on her feet and clapped her hands. Even Vigil seemed amused by her reaction as he waved his leaves in a musical rustle. He released my tail from the luminous vines, and my woman picked it up with something akin to reverence before extending it to me.

I didn't take it.

"Would you do me the honor of putting it back on me?" I asked, my voice slightly shaking with overwhelming emotions.

She nodded without a word. I suspected her own throat was

just as constricted. After a last thank you to Vigil, we headed back inside and made our way up to her bedroom.

No special ritual was required. I lay belly down on her bed and held my breath while she gently rubbed two fingers over the small recess at the base of my exoskeletal spine where my tail had been severed.

"Here goes," she said in a soothing voice.

Seconds later, an intense cold stabbed the small of my back. I gasped at the connection, the freezing sensation rapidly evolving into countless prickling impressions, as if a thousand needles were poking at me along the length of my spine. It shifted into electric sparks that spread throughout my body all the way to my extremities.

It was only when Ronika started calling my name in a worried voice that I realized I was breathing loudly, in short bursts, like someone on the verge of hyperventilating. The gods only knew why I was doing that. As strange and unsettling as this entire experience felt, I wasn't in any actual pain or distress. I was merely stressed and a little overwhelmed.

Forcing myself to control my breathing, I took her hand and gave it a gentle squeeze.

"All is well, my Ronika," I said in a reassuring tone. "It just feels strange. I will need a moment to adjust."

"Oh, good!" she breathed out, her relief palpable.

The odd lightning sensation lasted a short while longer before fading. Although a part of me wanted to scream with joy at finally being whole again, another felt crushed and depressed. I wouldn't say that something was off, but it also wasn't how it used to be. Something was missing. And then an intense sense of peace washed over me followed by a surge of power. I could feel my bone magic returning instead of the timid sliver I had reclaimed since meeting Ronika.

However, at a deeper level, my wraith chafed. Of course, the angelic essence in my tailbone would clash with the cursed nature of my wraith. But it didn't trouble me. Like he had with Ronika, my wraith would adapt to this other facet of me. After all, joy and hope were anathema to a wraith who thrived on pain, terror, and despair. And yet, he couldn't get enough of Ronika's happiness.

I shifted to the side to look at her with a smile.

"How are you feeling," she asked, her face intensely studying my features for any signs of pain or discomfort.

"I'm feeling fine," I said in all sincerity before carefully wiggling my tail. My heart soared at its instant responsiveness. "It works!" I exclaimed with a silly grin.

She giggled and caressed my hand still holding hers. "No pain at all?" she insisted.

I shook my head. "My tail doesn't pain me. Something feels odd at the base of my spine, but not in a worrying fashion. I think I just need a bit of time to assimilate having it a part of me again after so many centuries."

She nodded with that same serious look on her face. "You should rest for the next day or two," she mused out loud. "I would also suggest you avoid shifting into your wraith form for a little while until you've fully bonded again with your tail."

"I was thinking the same," I conceded.

"You're not going to give me a hard time? You're not going to tell me that lame nonsense men love throwing around about how rest is for the weak?" she asked with overly dramatic shock.

I laughed. "There was a time, I likely would have given you such an answer. But when you are as ancient as I am, you start acquiring some wisdom."

"I'm glad to hear it," Ronika said, only half joking. "Speaking of how ancient you are, you are overdue to tell me about yourself. As you are bedridden for the foreseeable future, now would be a good time."

I smiled and nodded. Tugging on her hand, I made her lie in bed with me. As soon as she snuggled against me, I felt annoyed at the clothes between us. I almost asked her to remove them before revising that opinion. Her naked body against mine was too great a temptation for me to resist. Seeing how unbridled I became once I unleashed my passion on her, giving in to my desires with my freshly attached tail would likely be a recipe for disaster. Deciding to play it safe, I wrapped a possessive arm around her while gathering my thoughts.

"Where do I even start," I said pensively. "I am one of more siblings than I can count or will ever meet. My father, Alderan, is a prince of hell, and one the most powerful bone demons in the seventh circle. He leads a few of the legions of his father, Astaroth."

"You're the grandson of the Duke of Hell?!" Ronika exclaimed, her eyes all but popping out of her head.

I snorted. "One of far too many. I'm but a grain of sand in the endless and harsh desert of his progeny. We have no rapport, and I doubt he is even aware of my existence—or that he cares."

"Still, talk about having connections in high places. Or rather, really deep ones," she said, looking unsure if she was impressed or worried. "How did he meet your mother?"

I chuckled. "I doubt *he* went after her and suspect she just decided she wanted him and didn't give him much of a say in the matter."

Her jaw dropped. "Your mother whipped a prince of hell into submission? Who is she? Lilith?!"

This time, I hesitated. "Truth be told, I do not know who my mother truly is. She has gone by many names over the centuries. She's undoubtedly one of the most powerful beings I've ever met. I believe she's a goddess, one of the Ancients. But she loves surrounding herself in a shroud of mystery and secrecy. Then again, in our world, knowledge is power, and you don't want to give others power over you."

She nodded slowly in understanding.

"Mother raised me through my early years. It was an unusual

experience. She wasn't the affectionate and nurturing type. I was left to my own devices most of the time with various tutors of otherworldly origins. But that didn't make her a bad mother. She was always keenly aware of what was going on with me and woe unto anyone who threatened me."

"I can't begin to imagine what it must have been like, especially the *otherworldly* tutor part. My own mother had no use for my father or me. She left us shortly after my birth and never looked back. But go on. I'm fascinated!"

I smiled and gently caressed her cheek. "We moved quite a bit back then, but it was always in the Scandinavian countries, in villages with many other non-human children like me. Well, some were human, but mage-born. That allowed me to have a somewhat normal childhood."

"I wondered about that," she said pensively. "What was it like?"

"Dangerous," I said with amusement. "Some of them, especially the Cambions, tended to have fairly volatile personalities. That was to be expected with demon-born children. The problem was that many of them had been sired on human women with little to no power of their own, and who often didn't know how to raise those children and rein in their darker nature."

"I can only imagine," Ronika said with a frown. "But what of your tutors, your mother, and other supernatural beings in the region? Couldn't they help?"

I pursed my lips while reflecting on a way to answer without breaking some of my pledges of silence.

"Let's just say that people helped when and where they could. But you can only go so far with some of them. For many, the best solution was merely to cast them into the abyss to be raised by their sires or their kin. Others, like a few friends I made, could be helped but required steady and nearly constant guidance. I soon realized I enjoyed trying to push them in the right direction. Ultimately, they had to make the choice of their own free will as to which course of action they would take. I just offered alternatives and explained why a certain path would be better for them and the community as a whole."

"Lord Voror!" she exclaimed with sudden understanding. "I was wondering why that demon kept calling you that way. You became a Voror—a form of guardian angel in Scandinavian lore!"

I smiled and slowly nodded. "Guardian *angel* isn't the term I would use, even though I do have angelic blood. But the fallen don't exactly refer to themselves as such anymore. A guardian spirit would be more appropriate."

"You weren't a wraith back then, though," she argued.

"Correct," I conceded. "However, I always had the power to make myself invisible to others. Some of the parents, especially the mothers in the surrounding countryside, either had no idea a demon had sired their child or were desperately trying to hide it from their spouse. As you know, many demons enjoy seducing women, impregnating them, before vanishing. They consider it a sport."

"When it comes to that, demons aren't the only ones to behave in such a disgusting fashion," she said with contempt, before her face softened. "So you secretly guided them into less destructive behaviors?"

"I did, and it worked." The pride in my voice resonated loud and clear. "There are no words to describe what it feels like when you help save someone from themselves. Most of them are not evil. They didn't choose their nature. Instinct usually drives their actions. But with the proper tools, they can control those instincts instead of being controlled by them. And once I got them on a solid enough path, I would move on to the next Cambion. Sometimes, I would watch over two or three of them simultaneously."

"Your mother must have been proud," Ronika said with admiration.

I snorted. "My mother always felt I was too sweet, whereas my father was unimpressed. I had spent some time with him in hell. He wanted me to be a guardian in the seventh circle. But punishing villains never appealed to me as much as preventing them from falling to begin with. Thankfully, they didn't get in my way or interfere with the path I had chosen for myself."

"That's good," she said with approval before taking on a serious expression. "And that's when you met Luciana?"

"I didn't so much meet her as feel her. She was so powerful that her very birth felt like a tear in the veil. I instantly knew that she would either become extremely good or terribly evil. There was no question that I had to protect her."

"And I'm guessing she was evil?" Ronika asked in a gentle voice.

I shook my head. "Luciana wasn't evil, at least not in the traditional sense. While some of the things she wanted to do or try would be deemed evil by societal and moral standards, to her it was simply a matter of sating her curiosity and answering the million questions going through her mind. The way she looked at it, everything was worth testing, exploring, and learning from. I merely guided her choices without attempting to crush her inquisitive nature. It just required some creativity to allow her to accomplish as many things as she wanted but in a way that would cause no harm to others or herself."

Ronika shifted, and her index finger absent-mindedly traced the bone scales on my shoulders while she reflected on my words with a slight frown.

"The way you describe it, things seem to have been going well with her. Where did it go wrong?"

"Things were going extremely well. She was thriving. Between her beauty, charisma, and great intelligence, Luciana was adored by just about everyone. Her father worshiped her. By the time she turned fourteen, she had sufficiently mastered all the principles I taught her so that my presence really had nothing more to offer her. So I left and moved on to a different ward."

"Did she balk when you abandoned her?"

It was my turn to frown. "I did not abandon her. I left but still kept an eye on her. At first, I would visit once every three months. Then, it was every six months. And finally, once a year. She had always been a beautiful girl and was quickly growing into a stunning young woman. But on her nineteenth birthday, I found out she'd been married off many months ago. It made no sense."

"Why?" Ronika asked. "In that era, wouldn't that have been deemed a little old for a woman? I believe fourteen was a fairly common age for a girl, especially with arranged marriages between wealthy houses."

"You are correct," I conceded. "But Luciana's father adored her. It made no sense to me that he would marry her to a man old enough to be her grandfather, and who she clearly felt nothing but contempt for."

"Did her family need money?"

I shook my head. "No. The Delacroix family had great wealth of their own. That's when I learned that her father had discovered his wife's indiscretion which resulted in the birth of Luciana. As she was the only child they conceived, her father realized he was in fact left without an heir. I don't think this hurt him more than realizing the girl he had adored since her birth was in fact not his child."

"That was not Luciana's fault, though," Ronika argued.

"I agree. But his pain and anger were too great. Therefore, he punished both his wife and her child. That had been the greatest mistake he could have ever made. Hemdell was obsessed with Luciana. He knew she didn't love him but would have given his soul to win her affection. So he gave her anything and everything she wanted."

"Making it possible for her to indulge in all the things she shouldn't, and that you had spent years teaching her to resist," she said with sudden understanding.

I nodded grimly. "Naturally, I went to visit her. The things she had access to were truly troubling to me. I tried to reason with her, but she had grown extremely stubborn. To be fair, I think bitterness fueled her actions. She felt betrayed by both her parents, and especially her father, who she had also adored and loved more than her mother."

"So she delved deep into the dark arts, unrestrained, and unfettered," Ronika said, matter-of-factly.

"That's quite the understatement. After Hemdell died, with full access to his wealth and resources, she totally surrendered to her obsessions. When she begged me to come guide her again because she was losing herself, I came without hesitation. Not only was it my duty, but in many ways, Luciana was like a daughter to me."

"So she did try to fight it!" Ronika exclaimed, her eyes flicking between mine, searching.

I heaved a sigh of both anger and disgust then shook my head. "No. She was way past meaningless things such as morals and righteousness. It was a trap from the beginning. As I had no reason not to trust her, I just followed her when she guided me into her den. I didn't see the conjuring circle. She had cleverly camouflaged it. By the time I felt its magic close around me, it was too late. I was caged and paralyzed."

"Oh no! I'm so sorry," she said, her voice filled with sadness and empathy as she gently caressed my chest in a soothing gesture. "I can't imagine how painful it must have been for you to be betrayed by someone you cared so deeply for."

"It broke my heart," I said, anger—not pain—surging deep within as I reminisced about those dark times. "But all such sentiments vanished the moment she cut off my tail. It felt like my soul had been ripped right out of my body. From that moment forward I just sank deeper and deeper into an abyss of agony."

"She tortured you?" Ronika asked, anger seeping into her voice. "But why? Why did she turn on you?"

"Although it was torture, which lasted for hours, Luciana had not deliberately set out to torture me. Or rather, that had not been her goal. My suffering was merely a side effect of the ritual she was attempting to accomplish," I begrudgingly admitted.

"What did she want?" Ronika asked, in no way mollified by my words.

I shrugged and lazily let my hand roam over the soft curve of her shoulder and down her arm before settling on her waist.

"She wanted what most of the conjurers and spellcasters who ended up turning into wraiths coveted. Luciana was attempting to harness my powers for herself. She desired eternal youth and endless power. Wraiths are created when life or death magic goes horribly wrong and either the conjurer or the sacrifice is subjected to unbearable pain and despair."

"So that means her ritual failed," Ronika said with a frown. "She sacrificed you but gained nothing, not even control over you with your tail."

"To be honest, I do not know to what extent her ritual succeeded or failed. I just wanted to die so the pain would end. My thoughts alternated between that and wanting revenge, to inflict as much pain as I was enduring. There would be no mercy, no limit to the debauchery with which I would unleash my wrath."

"That's how you descended into madness," she said in a sympathetic voice, her arm wrapping around me to give me a gentle hug.

I returned her embrace and placed a soft kiss on her forehead. "Giving in to the madness numbed the endless agony that was destroying me to the very core of my being. I don't know how I left Hemdell. More than once, I felt myself dying during that nightmare. I don't remember anything of what occurred after that or over the past three centuries. Besides the occasional flash of rampages I've been on, everything else is a blur. And then I heard your voice calling my name."

"That entire time?" she asked, stunned. "This was your first time regaining control over your senses since that night?"

I nodded. "On a few occasions, I believe I came close to emerging from the madness. It was never quite enough to fully pull me out. But there was something different about you, something powerful. Your emotions were crashing over me like a tidal wave of peace, determination, and strength. It cut through the thick curtain that had been fogging my mind. I couldn't remember ever feeling something like that since my damnation. The minute humans detect my presence, nothing but dread pours out of them, which further fuels my need to kill and destroy. I wanted more of what emanated from you. I hungered for that peace. You were the anchor I had needed to latch back on to sanity."

Ronika's eyes misted, and a warm emotion settled over her beautiful features. "I'm so glad I found you, and that I could free you. A part of me almost wants to go thank Cornelius for being the catalyst that brought us together."

An evil chuckle tumbled out of me. "That's the main reason I didn't kill him already."

She laughed and snuggled closer to me, her hand gliding down my side then to my lower back. I suspected she was going for my tail but couldn't quite reach it.

"So how does having your tail back change you?" she asked with undisguised curiosity.

"My tail fully restores my bone magic powers. I do not believe I used them at all during the madness. After you first awakened me, I couldn't invoke it at all. But over the following days, it sparked a little. And a bit more by the time we reached Hemdell. And moments after you reattached my tail for me, my bone magic surged through me with the same strength as before. My tail also gives me greater self-control and helps dampen the madness."

"That's amazing. Now that you're restored and have your mind back, what are your plans? What do you want to do?"

Although she spoke the words nonchalantly, the slight tension in her voice didn't go unnoticed.

"I could be a Voror again. I'd love that," I said sheepishly. "Since my awakening, I've been roaming the land. It is mind boggling to me how humans and supernatural beings now interact so openly. Conjurers and those who dabbled in the occult used to hide for fear of being burned at the stake. Now, you have storefronts on main streets and openly advertise your services. Beings who could use a mentor abound in these parts."

"There certainly are," she said approvingly. "You could do a lot of good. But where do you live right now?"

Once again, I didn't miss the underlying tension in her question.

"Wraiths do not need to sleep," I said with a shrug. "It is only my physical form that requires rest and normal sustenance. But so long as I remained in my wraith form, I had no need for a home. Now, that will change."

"You could stay here," she offered, a most adorable redness creeping onto her cheeks.

The swiftness with which she had offered confirmed she had been looking for a way all along to get to this point. Although I had hoped for such a proposition, I needed her to fully under-stand the hurdles we would face should we proceed.

"I am a bone demon hybrid," I reminded her cautiously. "From what I've seen so far, demons do not live openly among humans here. I've seen them and other beings—like shifters and fae—living freely with mortals in some of the surrounding villages, but not here. I don't know that the local population is ready for one such as I."

She shrugged and waved a dismissive hand. "Vampires, demons, and fae already live among us. They simply cast glamour spells like Cornelius does with his undead servants. With my enhanced magic—thanks to you—I could cast a similar spell on you so that you could come and go unhindered."

"That would be an acceptable option," I said with a smile.

She beamed at me, the tension stiffening her shoulders fading away as she pressed herself against me. "I think it's a great option. Anyway, times are changing. In a matter of a few years, I expect supernatural beings will also live openly among us. Willow Grove loves to boast about being the most avant-garde city on this continent. Having neighboring small towns be bolder than we are won't be acceptable in the long-term. Soon, you'll be able to strut with those sexy horns of yours and wag that bone tail on Main Street in broad daylight."

"Sounds like a plan," I said, drawing her tightly into my embrace.

"Then we have an agreement, Lord Voror," Ronika said, lifting her face towards mine.

"We have an agreement, my Ronika," I whispered back before claiming her mouth in a possessive kiss.

CHAPTER 14
RONIKA

The following week went by so quickly it left me reeling. Between Glinda's *miraculous* healing and my defeating Cornelius, I became the talk of the town. People flocked in masses to my humble shop. Whether they wanted a wart removed, some performance enhancing tonic, glamour spells to give them a more youthful appearance, or proper healing for more complex conditions that traditional medicine couldn't resolve, they all came to me.

At this rate, I would seriously need to consider hiring help to handle anything that didn't require my personal touch. It both thrilled and overwhelmed me. Like every business owner, I wanted to achieve a certain level of success. But I had no dreams of global domination and no wild ambitions of great wealth. To me, true success was making a positive difference in the lives of my patrons, establishing a rapport with people who eventually became as much friends as they were customers, and being able to pay the bills doing something I loved.

Therefore, this heavy influx of people scared me. I didn't want this to become impersonal like I was operating some kind of factory. That said, novelty always attracted the curious and gossip mongers. I figured things would slow down and return to more normal levels in a few weeks.

Still, the steadily increasing strength of my magic left me speechless. I had come to the conclusion that having sex with Asheron was the cause. His seed wasn't like normal human semen. Although I felt his release inside me, it quickly shifted in nature into something different that left no stickiness or mess behind. The closest thing I could compare it to was raw energy that spread through every cell and organ in my body, enhancing me.

I regularly wondered to what extent my power would keep growing as Asheron and I pursued our intimate relationship. The gods knew he had stamina for a legion. That also raised many other questions. With things still being early between us, I didn't want to speculate too much about our future. But it would be foolish of me not to think of the long term.

The Hag stated I couldn't get pregnant from a wraith. Was that a permanent fact or did a potential workaround exist, should we get to a point where we would like to start a family? Did getting reunited with his tail change anything in this calculus? Assuming we could conceive, what would our offspring be like? Would they be classified as Cambions as well?

A Cambion was the offspring of a human and a demon. Technically, Asheron was half demon. But I had no clue what his other half was. And now that he had been turned into a wraith, what did that even make him? From all the lore I had read, wraiths had always been humans cursed into this half-dead state.

I had far too many questions and nowhere near enough answers. Sadly, Asheron knew even less. It wasn't like he'd had some wraith mentor to teach him the ropes. Considering his otherworldly nature, it made every assumption about him no more than conjectures and speculations.

For all that, for the first time since the death of my father, I was truly happy. Helping Asheron connect with this new era and showing him all the societal and technological evolutions that had taken place over the past three-hundred and twenty-five years was amazing. He was like a child, curious and eager to absorb all the wonders that surrounded him.

To my delight, not only did my glamour spell work perfectly on him, his control over his physical form—which I suspected was enhanced by his tail—allowed him to fully neutralize his aura. No one who brushed past us as we traipsed around town and attended plays at the theater even flinched or expressed the slightest unease.

We were truly pulling this off.

Asheron had even narrowed his choice down to three young Cambion candidates that could use his guidance. When he mentioned trying to figure out which one he would start with, I bit my tongue wondering if he ever got compensated for his work. Not being materialistic—and now thanks to the Endless purse—whether he brought any money at home truly didn't matter to me. I was more than happy to be the provider. But he was the one who shocked me by revealing he held considerable wealth and properties in a few of the Scandinavian countries where he had lived.

It turned out that he had indeed gotten paid by some of the parents who knew of their child's true nature and sought out his aid. Furthermore, his mother had set him up with substantial sums of money over the years growing up. Having no real needs for spending, he just saved it all. Centuries of interest had increased his wealth to what he called obscene amounts.

As he still had no true use for any of it, he did not intend to charge for his services, but would have some of his assets transferred to a local bank so that he could spoil me.

Who was I to argue with such a plan?

Yes, life was good. The only two small clouds remaining on the horizon were settling my debt with the Hag, and the lingering discomfort in Asheron's spine.

The boom of activity at the shop kept me too busy and too tired at night to make the trip to the Weaver's estate. And to be honest, what little time I had left in the evening, I'd selfishly devoted to spending with my man. I didn't overly stress about it as I had the payment in hand and still three weeks left to bring it over to her.

My concern was with Asheron. On a few occasions, I caught him wincing and stretching his back as if it pained him. When I questioned him about it, he merely mentioned some soreness which sometimes flared where his tail had been reattached. Obviously, I examined him. A simple healing spell took care of the mild redness and immediately brought him relief. But it made me nervous that at the end of that first week, the redness kept returning.

And then things went downhill.

On the eighth day, after one particularly restless night, Asheron left to go see the ward he had settled on. That evening, he did not return. As it was his first time switching back to his wraith form since getting his tail back, I feared something had gone terribly wrong. The next day, I did not hear from him or see him. Worried, and not knowing where to look for him, I cast a recall spell that would compel him to come back home. When that failed, I attempted a seeker spell to pinpoint his present location. To no avail.

The worst part was that I couldn't even feel a connection. It was as if my attempts to reach out to him were getting lost in the ether. It was like reaching out for something that Turned out to be an illusion or sending a letter to a nonexistent address.

It was like Asheron had ceased to exist.

When two more days went by without any news from Asheron, I gave in to panic. He never would have just vanished for four full days without finding a way to let me know something was keeping him away. My imagination ran wild with speculations. Had something gone wrong with his ward? Had he turned out to be as evil a Cambion as Luciana had been? Was it the tail? Had something caused his madness to return?

When further attempts at both recall and seeker spells continued to fail, I decided to pay a desperate visit to the Hag. She had known where to find him that first time. Surely she would have some insights as to his whereabouts. Long before the sun started lowering on the horizon, I grabbed my shoulder bag, making sure Asheron's hair was safely tucked inside, and headed to the stables.

The Hag normally didn't receive anyone during the day. I could only pray she would make an exception this time. It was already mid-afternoon. If not, I would camp outside her gates until she let me in.

To my dismay, as I was walking Damar to the front of the house, I found Cornelius outside with an expectant look on his face. My blood turned to ice, and a sense of foreboding crashed over me. His beaming smile when his eyes met with mine heightened my unease.

"Cornelius, what are you doing here? What do you want?" I asked in an icy tone as I closed the distance between us.

"Hello to you, too, my dear Ronika. I'm doing great, thank you for asking. How are you faring?" he replied with obnoxious enthusiasm.

"I don't have time for your little games. I asked you a question. What do you want?" I snapped.

A smug smile settled on his lips while a malicious glimmer sparked in his green eyes. "I just wanted to see how you were faring. I haven't felt your friend's energy around here in a while. I hope he's feeling well. That he's feeling... whole."

My blood drained from my face as shock and horror descended over me. Was he here fishing? Was he gloating? He knew something and was either here to get confirmation or to taunt me about a certainty he already had.

"What did you do?" I hissed, taking a menacing step towards him.

"Me?!" he exclaimed, with exaggerated stupor while pressing a dramatic palm to his chest. "I have done nothing, my dear. But your response leads me to believe that something unfortunate has indeed happened to the Voror," he added with fake commiseration. "I did warn him to be careful what he wished for. How sad to have broken out of the madness only to fall victim to something far worse."

"You foul creature," I spat as both anger and fear twisted my insides. "If you mess with him in any way—"

"*I* have nothing to do with what befell him," Cornelius said, interrupting me with evil glee. "His own poor choices have once again cursed him. But fear not, little green witch. Once this has all played out, I'll pick up the pieces… all the pieces," he added, giving me a lascivious slow once over that made my skin crawl.

"Go burn in hell, you scum!" I snarled before jumping onto the back of my horse.

I took off with the sound of his victorious laughter chasing after me. His words confirmed something terrible had indeed happened to Asheron or was currently happening to him. I pushed Damar hard, guilt gnawing at me for forcing him to maintain a punishing pace. A sixth sense was shouting at me that time was of the essence. If I didn't find him tonight it would likely be too late.

When the imp statues watching over the gates of the Hag's estate immediately opened them upon my approach, I could have wept with relief. Although I had cast some healing spells on Damar on our way here, my poor mount looked exhausted. I would make amends later. For now, my priority was to find and save Asheron.

I didn't even bother tying Damar to the post and just ran to the front door of the hut. Like on my previous visit, the door parted on its own before me. I rushed inside to find the Hag once more sitting behind her spinning wheel.

"I need your help," I exclaimed, foregoing any proper greeting. "Asheron—"

"Miss Ortega," she interrupted in a casual tone, "you've come at last to settle your debt."

"Asheron needs help. He's missing. I've been looking for him everywhere, but I can't—"

"Ronika!" she once more interrupted, this time with a cold and sharp tone. "You have a debt to settle. I have no interest in whatever matter you wish to discuss. Honor our contract, and then I will *maybe* consider entering into another one with you."

I cursed under my breath in annoyance, then a second time out loud when I realized I had left my bag on my horse in my hurry to come talk to her. Turning on my heel angrily, I ran back out and fumbled in my efforts to detach the bag from the saddle, half tearing it off in my impatience. I ran back inside to find the Hag had moved from the spinning wheel and was now sitting behind the worktable like during our first audience.

I sifted through my bag with restless fingers until I retrieved the small box in which I had placed the strand of Asheron's hair. With much care, I plucked it out and extended it to the Weaver. She stared at me with the oddest expression before reaching a hand to accept my offering. The moment I released it, the strand of hair glowed red between the Hag's fingers before dissolving in a shower of tiny specks that then vanished into thin air.

My blood drained from my face at this horrible déjà vu.

"What?! That's not possible! That hair was given. Asheron *voluntarily* gave it to me. It can't vanish like this!" I exclaimed.

"And yet, you clearly saw that it did," the Hag said nonchalantly. "As you said yourself, Asheron gave it to *you*. Not to *me*. You cannot take and keep a part of a wraith that has not been freely given to you personally."

"Then all the more reason for you to help me find Asheron!" I exclaimed. "He'll be able to—"

"My contract is with *you*, not with Asheron. *You* must pay the debt, and only then can you request more assistance that may or may not be granted," she said, cutting me off yet again.

I gaped at her in disbelief. "How in the seven hells do you want me to pay you if I can't transfer a strand given to me by a wraith?"

"Figure it out," she said, looking bored.

In that instant, I wanted to claw her face and beat her into a pulp. The gods knew I'd never been the violent type, but I was worried sick for Asheron, and she was just stringing me along with nonsense.

"Enough of the stupid mind games! Why don't you just tell me what you want?" I snapped.

She raised an obnoxious eyebrow, looking at me like one would a bratty child throwing a tantrum. "I told you what I wanted, a wraith's hair."

"And you know damn well I can't give one to you," I shouted back.

She shrugged and stared at me with an unbothered expression. "Then you're out of luck. I suggest you find a way to do it before you lose Asheron or before your deadline runs out."

I closed the distance between us and pressed my palms on top of the table, leaning forward with an urgent look. Although she didn't move, the Hag narrowed her eyes at me. I realized that this sudden approach could be deemed threatening, as if I was lunging at her. That she might retaliate in preemptive self-defense should have frightened me, but I was too worried for my man.

"Before I lose Asheron?!" I echoed. "Is he hurt?"

"Maybe, maybe not. But that is neither here nor there. About your debt, what are you going to do?"

I straightened and stared at her in shock. "Why are you doing this?" I whispered in disbelief, angry tears pricking my eyes.

"You, too?" she asked, looking both amused and a little blasé. "I'm getting asked that a lot lately."

"What?" I asked, baffled by that nonsensical comment.

She chuckled and waved a hand. "Never mind that, it's not important."

And it truly wasn't. Asheron was somewhere likely seriously hurt, and the only person who could help me was playing stupid games. I ran my fingers through my hair, fisting them at the nape while I paced around the room, my mind racing in search of a solution. There was one, I was just too blind to see it. Beings like her thrived on riddles. It was their way of assessing your worthiness. But I had no patience for this. Time was running out for Asheron. I could feel it in my bones.

I dropped my hands in defeat and came back to stand before her. A tear of both anger and frustration slid down my right cheek.

"Look, I don't know what you want from me, but I really need you to help me find him. I can't give you what we agreed upon. But ask me anything else, and if it's in my power to give it to you, I will without hesitation. Please help me," I pleaded.

She studied my features with the strange fascination one would while examining a creature that shouldn't exist in the real world.

"You really care for him," she said with a bemused tone.

"I do," I said fervently. "With all my heart, I do. I'm begging you, please."

Her gaze slowly roamed over me before stopping on my left shoulder. She gestured at it with her chin.

"You're shedding," she said, matter-of-factly.

"What?" I whispered, the unexpected response giving me whiplash.

She gestured once more at my shoulder with her chin. I

looked down to notice a clump of three strands of my blue hair I had shed, probably from running my fingers through it moments prior.

Annoyed, I grabbed them and made to toss them on the floor.

"DON'T!" the Hag shouted, startling me.

I froze, my arm still raised from initiating the throwing gesture, and my hand fisted around the strands.

"You stupid girl," she hissed angrily. "Are you truly so naïve and ignorant in the ways of the dark arts that you would throw one of the most potent magical ingredients that could be used against you onto the floor of one such as I?"

I felt myself blanch. She shouldn't have had to mention it. Obviously, I knew better. Hair, nails, blood, and saliva were but some of the parts easily removed that contained the essence of the person you wanted to affect with magic, be it light or dark.

"I'm… I'm sorry," I said, distraught. "Yes, I know better. I just can't think straight right now. Asheron needs help."

Her face softened, and she gave me a stiff nod. To my shock, she opened her palm towards me.

"Give it here," she said calmly, leaning forward.

On instinct, I started to extend my hand towards her to comply, then froze. I gaped at her, my mind refusing to accept the thought suddenly trying to make its way in. Eyes locked with mine, she held my gaze unwaveringly, her face taking on an intense expression. My blood turned to ice, and a cold shiver ran down my spine.

That's not possible. It cannot be.

"Go on, Ronika. Give it to me," the Weaver said in a calm voice.

For a moment, I considered running out, getting on my horse, and riding as far away as possible from this forsaken place. But Asheron needed me. My hand shaking, while a sense of despair and inevitability weighed me down, I acceded to her request and placed the small clump of hair in her palm.

The tension on her ageless face bled out, and she straightened. I stared numbly while she untangled the three strands. A yellowish glow—similar to that of a flame—ran their entire length before fading.

"Thank you, Ronika Ortega. Your debt is settled. Our deal is concluded."

"That's impossible," I breathed out, shaking my head in denial. "Our deal was a wraith's hair. I am human."

"Why do people always lie to themselves as if it will somehow change reality?" she mused out loud. "You stopped being human the first time you laid with a wraith."

"I *am* human," I insisted stubbornly. "I'm still me, just with more magic. Look at me!" I exclaimed, waving at my body. "I am made of flesh and bones. I sleep, eat, bleed, and do all the things that humans do. Becoming a wraith requires life or death magic going terribly wrong. I didn't do any of those things and didn't suffer the endless agony and death needed to return as a wraith," I argued, more to convince myself than her.

"You're not human anymore. You started becoming a wraith on that first night, and then a bit more every time you took his seed within you," she explained nonchalantly, sounding even a bit mocking.

"If that's true, then you both violated our agreement," I retorted in desperation. "You both pledged I would come to no harm!"

The Hag snorted in amusement. "You aren't harmed. You were merely changed and enhanced. Nowhere in our agreement was it stated that you would not be changed. Like you said yourself, you're still you, just with more magic."

"And when madness takes me over, you'll still claim you didn't cause me harm?" I snarled.

She gave me an obnoxiously indulgent smile. "The only madness that could possibly take you is the mental illness humans are prone to. A wraith's madness comes from the torture and agony before they become half dead. You transitioned through love."

That struck me like a bullet through the chest. Was that even possible?

"You embraced Asheron… all of him," she continued in a serious tone. "No living being can survive a wraith's touch."

"I survived it. Asheron controlled the deadly touch of his wraith," I argued.

"There is no such thing," she countered with a dismissive gesture of her hand. "The wraith form systematically leeches life on contact. That's why Asheron was always careful to only ever touch you in his physical form or partially phased. Never in his wraith form. But the more you took his seed, and the more your mortal form died, giving way to your wraith. So much that you not only physically embraced his wraith but also started intertwining your heart with his. This bond can only be formed between wraiths."

My head was spinning. I felt wobbly on my legs as I struggled to come to terms with the insane words she was speaking. A friction sound behind me had me glancing over my shoulder. Despite my frazzled state, I welcomed the sight of the guest chair sliding from its position by the entrance all the way to me. I let myself drop into it while still trying to make sense of the chaos in my mind.

"So you're saying I am damned for eternity?" I asked at last.

"You are not damned, child. You are merely transformed. But if you truly hate the prospect of remaining what you have become, there is still time to revert it," she said with an unreadable expression.

I straightened, hope swelling within me. "Really?! How?"

"Sever all ties with Asheron," she said in a factual tone, although I didn't miss the underlying coldness. "You must never see him again, and especially never lie with him again. In time, his essence within you will fade. Considering how saturated you are with it right now, it will take at least a year before you return to your former self."

That struck me even harder. The prospect of never seeing him again felt like a thousand daggers were stabbing me in the heart. And yet, I stunned myself by asking more questions.

"And what will be the side effects?" I asked, licking my lips nervously.

Although subtle, her face closed a bit more. "You will sustain no side effects. By the time his essence has faded from you, you will simply be back to the way you were before you came here the first time."

I nodded slowly, my mind still reeling, before I narrowed my eyes at her. "What if I had not come here tonight? You said it is early enough now to revert it. How much longer before it would have been too late?"

"It takes forty-five days of regular couplings before it becomes irreversible."

My jaw dropped in understanding. Forty-five days… only a couple of days shy of the total amount of time that would have passed between my first night with Asheron in Duskwallow and the deadline the Weaver gave me to repay my debt. Technically, she ensured I could make an enlightened decision, even if it was at the last minute before it would be too late. While I was starting to get a sense of what kind of game she was playing, countless questions remained.

"Does Asheron know what this is doing to me?"

She snorted again, this time with the air of discouragement one expresses when faced with a hopeless case. "Asheron is clueless when it comes to his own nature. How could he not be? It's not like he can walk up to another wraith and ask for guidance when all of them are lost to madness. That's why there's so little literature about them. He is now the third wraith in existence to have found his anchor."

"His anchor?" I echoed, confused.

"The one person who can root him in reality and bring back his sanity. *You* are his anchor."

I blinked, having not expected that answer, and least of all that it would send such a warm feeling spreading through my chest.

"So he had no idea that us having sex was turning me into a wraith?" I insisted.

My stomach dropped when she hesitated.

"Asheron knew that giving you his seed would enhance your magic," she said carefully. "He doesn't know that continued sex with you beyond those forty-five days will permanently turn you. He thinks that pursuing your relationship without binding you to him will spare you from potentially falling to madness."

"But you said I can't fall to madness since I transitioned with love," I challenged.

"That's correct. But Asheron doesn't know that," she said in a self-evident tone.

"Then why didn't you tell him?!" I exclaimed, baffled.

"Because he would have left to protect you from himself. He hates what he has become and refuses to condemn you to the same fate. But that's just because he doesn't understand his true nature and the beauty of what he could be once properly anchored," she said in an almost wistful tone.

I gaped at her, shock and outrage swelling through me at yet another revelation. "You set this up from the start! You used me to free him!"

Her face twisted in anger, and her eyes took on a reddish hue that turned my blood to ice. For the first time, I truly feared she would turn her wrath on me.

"Set you up? Stupid human! I have gifted you my son, a demigod! He's bestowed upon you the type of power people kill for. And you're here sniveling over the loss of some useless humanity? Ungrateful wench! If you like your pathetic life so much, then get back on your horse and return to that home

Asheron helped you keep out of Cornelius's clutches. Have no fear. You got what you wanted, and your debt is repaid. Go, and make sure I never see your face again."

"Your son?!" I breathed out, flabbergasted. Why in the seven hells would he have kept something like that from me?

"You truly are an open book, Ronika Ortega," she said, shaking her head with disapproval. "My children are sworn never to speak of our bond… for their sake."

"If he is your son, why wouldn't you help me find him? He is hurt, isn't he?"

"That is none of your concern," she replied dismissively.

Anger once again flared inside me. To my shock, I angrily slammed my fist on top of her table. "Like hell it isn't! I don't give a shit whether he's your son or not. I care about him. While you're sitting here playing mind games, I know he's hurt. I can feel it in my bones."

"Hurt isn't the appropriate term," she said in a mysterious tone. "He's dying."

"WHAT?!" I shouted, jumping to my feet.

"His tail is killing him," she said in a conversational tone before gesturing at my chair. "Sit."

I wanted to argue, but I dropped back into my chair, my head spinning and my heart aching. "That's not possible! We tested it. Vigil confirmed there was no curse on it. There was nothing that could harm him. Did Cornelius—?"

"The necromancer has nothing to do with it," she said in a curt and dismissive tone. "I warned Asheron to leave that tail alone and bond with you. But that boy has always been stubborn. Your Warden Tree is correct. His tail is pure, it is as divine as he was before his fall. His wraith is cursed. It cannot coexist with the divine."

My eyes widened in understanding. "So then we need to remove the tail again!"

"No!" the Hag said forcefully. "Remove it again, and it will permanently kill him."

"There must be a solution! Surely you know what to do?" I exclaimed.

"There is. You must bond with him," she said in a calm voice.

"How?"

"Permanently become a wraith," she replied. "You must anchor him to the mortal realm and especially to Vigil."

My head spun as I struggled to make sense of her words. "Vigil? What does my Warden Tree have to do with anything?"

"As your bonded mate, Asheron will become a member of your bloodline. This will grant him Vigil's protection. Warden Trees possess powerful magic."

"Vigil tested his tail and saw nothing wrong with it," I countered. "But now you're telling me that the tail is in fact killing Asheron."

"Vigil tested the tail. He did not test Asheron," the Hag said in a tone that implied she was starting to question my intelligence. "As my son isn't part of your bloodline, Vigil could not test or aid him. But once your blood courses through Asheron when the bond is complete, Vigil will be able to establish a balance between his cursed and divine halves."

I nodded slowly, my eyes flicking from side to side as I replayed her words through my mind to properly assimilate them.

"So if I bind with Asheron and bring him to Vigil, he will be healed, correct?"

"Yes."

"Where do I find Asheron?" I asked.

She tilted her head to the side, her gaze assessing. "You will bond with him and permanently become a wraith?"

"Of course," I replied, annoyed by this additional delay.

"Why? Just moments ago, you were complaining about—"

"With all due respect," I said, interrupting her, "we don't have time for your games! Asheron is out there dying and needlessly suffering. He saved my life in Duskwallow when he owed me nothing. He spared my father and my ancestors from being turned into Cornelius's mindless puppets. He helped me save my home and Vigil. And thanks to the way he's enhanced my magic, he allowed me to save customers I deeply care about and who would have died otherwise. So if becoming a wraith is what I must do to save him in return, I will do it. I owe him that much. He has suffered enough and deserves peace, even if that turns me into…"

"Even if that turns you into a Planewalker," she continued in my stead when my voice trailed off. Her oddly maternal tone took me aback. "Wraiths come in many forms. You banished a parasitic version, and you mated with an angelic one, while most others are human conjurers of varying powers. All of them were turned through agony, torture, and complete despair."

"A Planewalker?" I asked.

"It's a very rare type of wraith, one who was turned by love. There are only two others in existence. It will grant you biological immortality, the power of flight, lightning, frost, and enhanced green witch magic. You will not have the power of dread or bone magic like Asheron, but you have no use for those. And, as I stated earlier, there will be no madness. You will still need to eat and sleep. In all the ways that matter, you will continue to live like a normal human. You can even have babies."

"Why didn't you tell Asheron all that? Why let him go through all this anguish and uncertainty?" I asked, once more baffled.

"Because he would have told you."

"That's exactly the point!" I exclaimed, my tone making it clear this was obvious.

"Then I wouldn't know if love or greed made you choose my

son. I wouldn't have known whether you deserved for me to kill you or let you live."

My jaw dropped. "What?!"

She smiled. Despite its taunting edge, I didn't miss the hard glimmer in her eyes. In that instant, I realized that had she believed I was using her son, the Weaver would have indeed killed me.

"You chose well, Ronika Ortega. Take your carriage to Devonshire forest. He is in the field close to it. You will not see him, but you will feel him from the road. Bring him back to your home and perform this ritual."

She quickly went over the steps for the bonding ritual and then the healing.

"Thank you," I said, my heart soaring. "What do I owe you for this?"

She chuckled. "Were I a better person, I would have given this information for free, since it involves one of my sons. But everything has a cost."

The Hag burst out laughing when my face dropped.

"Fear not, little girl. You have already paid with the two extra strands of wraith hair you gave me. Goodbye, Ronika Ortega. Take good care of my son."

CHAPTER 15
RONIKA

The journey back home felt like an eternity and a day. I hated that I couldn't go straight to Asheron, and that I had to stop to get my carriage first. At least, Devonshire forest wasn't too far from my house, and it was in the right direction. I would have been livid had I been forced to go to the other side of town and then backtrack to Asheron's location.

For a brief moment, I considered ignoring the Weaver's instructions and going straight to the forest's edge. But I knew better than to challenge her. First, if Asheron was in as bad a state as she implied, he would likely be unconscious or unable to hold himself up. He would end up falling off Damar or significantly slowing our ability to ride back together on his back. Second, in spite of her twisted mind games, the Hag had never led me astray. And if he truly was her son, she would want even more for me to succeed in rescuing him.

That thought still blew my mind. It explained so many things and simultaneously raised a million more questions. Now I understood what he meant by saying he didn't quite know what his mother was but believed her to be a goddess. In her own way, the Weaver confirmed as much by claiming she had given me a demigod when she set me up with Asheron.

A part of me felt manipulated, and another felt flattered beyond words that she would deem me worthy of her son. I still reeled about the fact that I was a wraith. Or rather a Planewalker... I much prefer that title. It sounded a lot less ominous and had less negative stigma attached to it. If everything she said was true—and I had no reason to doubt her—then this transformation was truly a blessing and not a curse. It would mean that Asheron and I could be together forever instead of him risking falling back into madness once my mortal life expired.

At long last, I reached my house, relieved not to find that wretched necromancer still lurking in the vicinity. After harnessing Damar to the carriage, I threw in a blanket on the seat next to me, then hastily made my way towards Devonshire. It took an endless thirty-minute ride before I felt the unmistakable tingle of a wraith's presence about half a mile from the start of the forest.

I advanced a short distance more before stopping the carriage as the tugging sensation grew to its maximal intensity. The pull undeniably came from the left side of the road. I blindly ran into the open field, using the tingling as sole guidance. About fifty meters in, I finally glimpsed a silhouette sprawled in the tall grass ahead.

"Asheron!" I shouted with a mix of relief and fear.

I rushed to his side, my heart breaking at the terrible state he was in. Lying face down, his skin had taken on an ashy-gray tinge. The flesh around the exoskeleton of his spine was swollen. By the reddish and yellowish hue, severe infection—and maybe sepsis—had set in. A sickly smell emanated from him. His body was shaking, and his skin was alarmingly cold to the touch.

Pained moans rose from him in between shallow, labored breaths. When I turned his head and called out his name, he weakly battled to open his eyes. They were glassy.

Judging by the disturbed trail behind him, Asheron had tried to crawl to the road after crashing in the field. My heart further constricted as I berated myself for waiting this long to ask the Weaver for help. He'd been agonizing here for days while I sat home speculating instead of taking decisive action.

I cast both healing and numbing spells on him, knowing they wouldn't do much. But it would slightly dampen the pain and give him the energy needed to hang on until we could bond and get Vigil to help him. Although he remained confused and mostly out of it, that light healing seemed to provide the small boost I had hoped for. Asheron appeared a bit more aware, a glimmer of recognition even sparkling in his eyes. He opened his mouth to say something but only an unintelligible rumbling came out.

"You're going to be all right, sweetie," I said in a comforting tone. "We just need to get you to the carriage so that I can take you home, and we can heal you. Your mother told me what to do. Can you get up?"

As he was far too heavy for me to carry, I cast a lightweight spell on him. It wouldn't be enough for me to pick him up, but it allowed me to help him stand. To my surprise, I turned out to be far stronger than I expected. It still was nowhere near enough for me to carry him like a bride, but it made it easy for me to support most of his weight as I took him back to my carriage. He was stumbling on unsteady feet, forcing me to half drag him through the field.

The tortured moans and grunts emanating from him cut me deep. My eyes pricked with repressed tears for the unbearable pain I knew him to be enduring. Each step had to be sheer agony. My throat tightened when he cried out as one of the swollen blisters on his back burst open. I felt a warm liquid trickling down my arm supporting him. I couldn't tell if it was blood or pus, but the sickly smell went up another notch.

When we finally made it to the road, as gut-wrenching a

challenge awaited us, merely trying to get him inside the carriage. By the time we succeeded, tears were freely rolling down my cheeks from the debilitating pain he was feeling. I wrapped the blanket tightly around Asheron and gave him a sip from the waterskin I thankfully always had on my horse or in my carriage. After so many days in the field, he was dehydrated, as proven by his cracked and parched lips.

The journey back home brought a fresh new round of agony for my poor man. The rocking motion of the carriage caused friction on his raw back. He hissed or groaned each time we hit a bump. I struggled between speeding up to the maximum so that we could arrive faster or slowing down to reduce the impact of the rough road on his wounded back. In the end, I elected to make haste.

At long last, we got back to the house, and I cast another healing spell on Asheron just to give him the sliver of extra energy so we could make it to the garden. By the time we reached Vigil, Asheron was half delirious. I tried to lower him carefully at Vigil's feet, but he collapsed. If not for my Warden Tree's prompt reaction, it would have been a bad fall. But a series of vines shot out from the base of his roots, catching Asheron, and gently lowering him to the ground.

I rushed back inside to get a knife and promptly returned. Kneeling next to my man, I made an incision in my wrist then pressed the wound to his lips to make him drink. At first, I feared he would resist or be unable to swallow. But the moment the first drop of blood touched his lips, Asheron's hand flew to my forearm, latching onto it with bruising strength as he greedily started drinking from me.

I lay down on my side in front of him, and whispered words of encouragement, while ignoring the pain in my wrist. He started partially shifting. Instead of it being his lower body, it was his upper half that shifted to his wraith form. To my shock, he suddenly let go of my wrist, grabbed me by the nape, and brought my face closer to his. I cried out when he buried his vicious wraith teeth in my neck. For a split second, I thought he would rip my throat out. Thankfully, he merely drank with a voracity that soon had me feeling lightheaded. A part of me wanted to tell him to stop, but I kept quiet. Despite his current delirious state, at a visceral level, I knew his wraith would stop before he caused me grievous harm.

I wrapped my arms around his partially shifted body, surrendering myself to him.

The relief I felt at him slowing down the amount of blood he was draining from me was short-lived. Beneath my hand, the swollen skin surrounding his spine was growing burning hot. His exoskeleton started moving, ebbing and flowing like a wave. It took me too long to realize it was actually trying to tear right off his back. His body was rejecting his exoskeleton and tail.

He tore his fangs out of me and cried out in agony.

"Vigil!" I shouted, not really knowing what I wanted him to do, only that he needed to do something.

Instantly, large vines started wrapping around us, binding us together. Vigil's thick roots rose from the ground forming a wall around us, the one behind Asheron pressing inward to prevent his spine from moving.

Asheron's previously freezing skin was like burning all over to alarming levels. Against me, through the fabric of my dress, it felt like holding a steaming pot fresh off the fire. Ignoring the increasingly uncomfortable searing heat and the terrible screams from Asheron, I began reciting the incantation the Weaver had given me then made a slight incision in his neck. Like he had done with me, I began to drink his blood.

My lips instantly tingled, and a terrible burning sensation spread inside my mouth and down my throat. You'd think I was drinking acid. Blocking out the pain, I continued drinking until my entire body felt ablaze. I recited another incantation, my voice scratchy and raw. With each word, the unbearable heat emanating from Asheron steadily decreased, as did his trembling. The dullness in his eyes faded, and awareness returned.

"Ronika," he whispered once I finished the incantation, his voice just as raw, but laced with surprise and a bit of confusion.

"Bond with me," I said.

He blinked, shock followed by fear settling over his features.

"No," he slurred. "I won't curse you."

"We are destined," I countered, each word painful as if I'd swallowed shards of glass. "I'm already a wraith. I repaid your mother with my own hair. Bond with me and let me be your anchor."

I could feel him struggling with himself, trying to resist. But his wraith took over, and he fully shifted into his ethereal form. For a second, I feared it would drain the life force from Vigil. Thankfully, my Warden Tree remained unscathed. Like in Hemdell's secret study, his wraith pulled me closer into his embrace and leaned forward to kiss me. His cool breath instantly soothed the burning in my throat and through every cell of my body. Simultaneously, magic threads emerged from his luminous chest and seeped into me, wrapping around my heart.

Our pulses synchronized, and our breaths, our bodies, our very souls became one. He was in me, around me, fully intertwined with me. A soft glow surrounded us, and a magical tingling enshrouded us. It took me a moment to realize it was Vigil's magic penetrating us through his glowing vines.

But my ability to form thoughts faded as did our joined heartbeats. They slowed down more and more, and then stopped. Surrounded by the soul of my beloved and of my Warden Tree, I died.

CHAPTER 16
ASHERON

For three days, I diligently looked after my woman. The morning after she and Vigil saved me, I brought her back to her room, bathed her, and watched for any sign of things having gone awry. I still couldn't believe she had done this for me, and worse that I complied with it.

The selfish part of me rejoiced that we were one, that she was mine, and I was hers for eternity. Ronika had made me whole in every way. Even my tail was once more in harmony with me, despite the cursed part of my being. I just wanted her to wake up so that I could make sure she was all right, that my foul blood had not corrupted her.

A familiar surge of energy had me jerking my head towards the window. Letting go of Ronika's hand, I rose to my feet from the edge of the bed where I'd been sitting to glance at the back-yard through the window. To my shock, I observed my mother with her palm pressed against Vigil's trunk. One of his vines gently rubbed her forearm in a friendly caress.

Just as I was wondering what in the seven hells my mother was doing here, I noticed a series of magical trees, herbs, and exotic plants that only existed in my mother's garden in all of Willow Grove. It was an incredible gift to my mate.

Mother suddenly looked up at the window over her shoulder. Our gazes connected, and a taunting smirk stretched her lips. Moving away from the window, I headed straight for the door to go have a conversation with her. Finding her already standing behind the door when I opened it seconds later startled the living daylights out of me.

"Damn it, Mother! You know how much I hate when you do that," I growled.

She laughed. "I know," she said with an unrepentant grin.

I growled again in annoyance, which only made her smile further. I backed away as she stepped into the room. To my dismay, she slowly circled around me, examining every inch of my body. Her hand settled on my exoskeleton and slid down to my tailbone. I could feel her tremendous magic testing and assessing. It always felt odd being touched by my mother. She had never been the hugging or affectionate type. Although her examination was clinical, I felt as nervous as if I was being evaluated for my personal performance or worth.

For some reason, I always felt like I was a disappointment to both my parents, even though they never gave me actual cause to think so.

"You are in harmony again," she said approvingly.

"I am," I replied softly as she finished circling around me to lock eyes with mine. "You all saved me."

She shook her head before walking up to the bed. Sitting at the edge, she reached a hand to Ronika's face and gently caressed her cheek. That seriously took me aback. I couldn't recall the last time I had witnessed my mother acting in such a maternal fashion.

"*We* didn't save you. *She* did. This girl loves you," mother said, her fingers absent-mindedly playing with Ronika's blue hair while she continued to study her features.

It was my turn to snort. "She barely knows me."

Mother glanced at me over her shoulder with a 'seriously' expression. "Are you truly going to once more challenge something I say?"

I flinched and lowered my eyes, properly chastised. Apparently mollified by my silent submission, my mother turned back to my woman.

"The bond is strong," she continued with the same approving tone. "It was done well. She did *very* well. For such a fragile and naïve little thing, your mate is formidably strong. She's the perfect match for you."

"She may be strong, but I've damned her," I said in a dejected tone. "How do I protect her?"

"From what?" Mother asked as if I made little sense.

"From madness, of course!" I exclaimed in an obvious tone.

My mother rolling her eyes with extreme annoyance left me speechless.

"You know, the only thing that will cause this poor girl to go mad is your nonsense," she said with aggravation. "She's not damned. She's merely enhanced. Ronika wasn't tortured or cursed. She chose to transition out of love. Your mate can explain it all to you. I'm not having that conversation twice."

"You already did?" I asked, feeling stupid the minute the words left my mouth.

Obviously, they'd had that conversation. As delirious as I had been during the healing and bonding process, I clearly recalled Ronika stating that she was already a wraith since she had repaid her debt to my mother with a strand of her own hair. Thankfully, my mother simply ignored my last question, having likely guessed I'd realized my own stupidity for asking it.

"You must guide her through her powers," she continued. "It will be confusing and maybe even a little scary for her at first. But she is gifted. Her magic was stunted and trapped within.

Your bond has unleashed it. She will be a magnificent healer in the near future."

"But will she be happy? Will she grow to resent what I did to her?" I blurted out, voicing the fears that had steadily festered inside me since I awakened in the garden.

Instead of the tongue lashing I expected, mother smiled at me with that rare maternal expression that always warmed me to the bone.

"Stop fretting, my son. No one in the universe can make either of you happier than each other. She is your other half."

I heaved a sigh of relief, embarrassed to be so emotional in front of her.

"Thank you for saving me and for finding her for me," I said affectionately.

She snorted. "You certainly didn't make it easy."

I chuckled. "Where would be the fun in that? I thought you loved a good challenge?"

She smiled. "You have a point. But next time your stubbornness gets you into trouble, please see that it doesn't involve me looking for a solution for three hundred and twenty-five years. I do have other brats to keep out of trouble."

I gave her a sheepish grin. "Right, let's avoid a repeat of that. However, Cornelius might be a problem. There is something very disturbing inside him. I was never fond of how ambitious and power hungry the necromancer used to be. But I don't think the ruthless monster he has become is him. I think that thing inside him—"

"Leave Cornelius alone," my mother interrupted in a stern voice. "He is not your concern."

"But—"

"ASHERON! I said leave. Him. Alone. For once in your life, listen to your mother. He has his purpose."

The harshness in her voice and in her expression sent a cool shiver down my spine. Anyone else likely would have run for the hills by now.

I gave her a stiff nod. "As you wish, Mother."

"Good boy," she said in a much softer tone. "Speaking of which, when will you tell her that the Endless Purse didn't just conveniently happen to be so easily accessible right next to the observatory by accident?"

I stiffened and gave her a stern look. "She doesn't need to know."

Mother shook her head and examined me like I was an anomaly that defied all logic. "You spent an entire week traveling to the ends of the world to recover the one artifact that could save her home. You fought your way through Hemdell a first time to place it in the study for her. And then you battled your way in a second time the next day so she could miraculously find it. All that, and you take no credit for it?"

"I wanted her to like me for me, not just for what I could do for her," I begrudgingly admitted. "Anyway, it needed to be in Hemdell for her to be able to bind it on time. Her magic would have been too low and taken too long elsewhere."

The glimmer of approval in my mother's eyes did strange things to me.

"So you do understand more than you let on," she mused out loud.

I didn't quite know what she meant by that but decided to leave it alone. She rose to her feet and glanced out the window. I followed her gaze.

"Those are impressive new plants in the garden," I said as a thank you.

She gave me a taunting smile. "Every last one of them is unique. You gave her the power to maintain them. Like I said, she will be one of the greatest healers of these times. For a human, she has an unusually beautiful soul. It is what allowed your angelic essence to realign with what you became."

She glanced at Ronika and caressed the back of her hand one last time. My throat tightened that the woman who had not only captured my heart but literally owned it would earn my mother's approval.

To my shock, she walked over to me and pulled me into her arms. I froze at first, before returning her embrace and burying my face in her hair. A wave of emotions choked me while she gently caressed my hair and back with a maternal affection I couldn't recall her ever giving me past my toddler years.

"Be happy, Asheron," she said, before releasing me. "You have suffered enough. Just learn to listen, and you'll suffer less in the future."

I let go with much reluctance and chuckled to hide my embarrassment.

"Yes, Mother, I will try," I said, proud that the firmness of my voice hid how this far too rare display of affection had deeply touched me.

"Pfft!" she said, with obvious disbelief. "You will always be a hopeless case. Goodbye, Asheron. Come see me again with your firstborn," she said while heading towards the door.

"I love you, Mother," I blurted out.

She stopped, one hand on the door frame, and looked over her shoulder at me with a mocking expression.

"Of course, you do," she deadpanned, as if I'd stated the obvious.

I snorted and opened my mouth to reply, but a soft moan from Ronika had me jerking my head towards the bed.

"I think she's waking up at last," I said with excitement while rushing to her bedside.

When my mother failed to respond, I glanced back at the door to find it wide open and my mother nowhere to be seen. I shook my head with an affectionate smile before refocusing on my woman.

Another full hour would go by before Ronika awakened at last.

"There she is," I said tenderly.

She blinked, temporarily disoriented before regaining her bearings. Her eyes widened with sudden awareness, memories of recent events having likely come flooding back to her. Her hand darted towards my chest, touching me as if to make sure I was real.

"Asheron! Are you okay? Is your tail—?"

"I'm fine, my Ronika," I interrupted gently. "You saved me and healed me."

"So it worked?" she asked, her eyes misting while a happy smile settled on her face.

"It did," I confirmed before guilt swept through me again.

"I'm sorry for making you a wraith. I didn't mean to bind you to this life."

She gave me a 'Are you stupid?' look eerily similar to the one my mother had given me just a moment prior.

"You're sorry for turning me into something amazing?" she said in a chastising tone. "Me becoming a wraith was inevitable."

She then launched into a detailed recounting of her meeting and conversation with my mother. This took me through a whirl-wind of emotions, from shock to anger, to joy, then right back to anger.

"I can't believe her," I ground through my teeth. "Why didn't she just tell me rather than let me agonize for weeks over the fear of harming you?"

"Don't be mad at your mother," Ronika said while rubbing her palm over my chest in a soothing fashion. "She was right. By not knowing, she made sure I chose you freely, because my heart belonged to you, and not because I saw you as someone who could benefit my ambitions."

I looked at her with awe, my heart swelling with love. "I

can't believe you did this for me," I whispered, my hand reverently caressing her hair.

"I did it for us," she replied matter-of-factly. "From that first night in Duskwallow, you were mine, and I was yours. A part of me would have died without you. Every day, since then, you have occupied every last one of my thoughts. The prospect of never seeing you again was unbearable."

"But you know so little of me," I argued weakly.

"I know what matters," she said with a shrug. "For the rest, we have an eternity to find out. The important thing is that you are now once more whole and that nothing and no one can ever harm you again. In truth, I thought Cornelius had gotten to you. That wretched monster knew something would go wrong. As did your mother."

She added that last line by giving me a pointed look. My face heated, and I gave her a sheepish expression.

"She says you never listen to her," she gently chastised.

"I don't," I admitted with an embarrassed chuckle.

"Then maybe you should start to," Ronika replied in the same stern tone.

"I just might. By the way, your customers are getting worried," I continued, eager to switch the topic. "Apparently, the entire neighborhood heard demonic screams emanating from your backyard. When you failed to show up for three days in a row, the wildest rumors started spreading like wildfire. They think Cornelius did something to you out of spite."

My poor Ronika couldn't seem to decide if she wanted to laugh or be horrified.

"Does it make me a horrible person that a part of me wants to let the rumors continue to run wild if only to get Cornelius in trouble?" she asked with a mischievous glimmer in her beautiful brown eyes. "But I will be good and go reassure them."

I chuckled in approval. "Good. Many of them genuinely care about you on a personal level. More than once, I considered letting them know all was well. However, I doubted they would have appreciated a bone demon greeting them, then trying to convince them that you were temporarily out of commission after bonding with him. But that you were fine, nevertheless."

She laughed, the faraway look in her eyes hinting she was visualizing the scene. My chest swelled with love for her.

"My Ronika," I whispered with a world of affection, "you are my heart. You are my everything."

"As you are mine," she whispered back.

I leaned forward and captured her lips in a tender kiss, pouring all the depth of my feelings for her in it. She returned it with the same fervor. Whatever misgivings still lingered in the back of my mind faded in that instant. I could feel the wraith within her, but it was just another facet of her, devoid of the darkness mine had. She was my light, my anchor, my love.

With much reluctance, I broke the kiss and rose from my sitting position at the edge of the bed.

"Come, my Ronika. Let's go feed you. You must be starving by now," I said gently, extending a hand towards her.

She looked a little surprised, her eyes flicking from side to side as if to assess her actual hunger level, while instinctively reaching for my hand.

"I'm not actually hungry, but I could use a bite," she said, shifting to the side into a sitting position at the edge of the bed.

But before her feet could even touch the floor, her legs blurred as light brown smoke, the same shade as her golden skin, formed around her as her lower-body turned into her wraith form. She gasped in panic as her shadow skirt started rising up, up, and still farther up until she was dangling upside down. I burst out laughing.

"Someone is itching to fly," I said with both amusement and excitement at the thought of zipping through the skies with my soulmate by my side. I shifted into my wraith form and straightened her. "Well then, my mate, let's teach you how."

EPILOGUE
RONIKA

The following weeks turned out to be the most confusing and the most thrilling of my life. Although I remained human in all the ways that mattered, I had this entire new side of me to learn and master. I felt like a toddler taking her first steps. Then again a hatchling dreading its first flight would likely be a more appropriate comparison.

Saying I had a few false starts and accidents would be the understatement of the century. If not for Asheron babysitting me every step of the way, I would have crashed and broken every bone of my body more times than I can count when my wraith decided now was a good time to take a break while I was hundreds of meters up in the air.

At first, I feared he would tire of how dependent I had grown on him. But Asheron loved it. I soon realized that beyond his genuine love of helping others, my man ached to feel needed, wanted. I didn't understand it. Even though his mother wasn't the overly affectionate type, there was no question she loved him. And he was well-aware of it. So I couldn't quite figure out where that insecurity stemmed from. As I couldn't get enough of him pampering me and watching over me, it worked out for the best. Especially since I loved returning the favor.

For the first week following my transformation, I closed the shop, only answering the most urgent calls. I didn't want to have to explain to my customers why I was dangling upside down with my legs turned into smoke and my dress bunched under my armpits because my wraith was itching to fly, and I couldn't keep her under control just yet.

The fact that I'd almost set my own house on fire by inadvertently summoning lightning after accidentally cutting myself while chopping vegetables reinforced my decision to keep my patrons at bay for their own safety.

It took me a full month to finally agree to try and pass through a solid wall in my vaporous form. Initially, shifting that far used to bring me to the brink of a panic attack. Despite seeing Asheron do it countless times, I kept fearing that a gust of wind would scatter the invisible smoke I had turned into, and that I would never be able to return to my physical form. Once I had gotten over that particular fear, another one kept me paralyzed.

What if I tried to go through a wall and my stupid wraith decided it no longer was in the mood to play, and I shifted back to my physical form with most of my organs still in the middle of that wall? Asheron tried to reassure me multiple times that we didn't actually go through the wall but through the tiny—sometimes almost invisible—openings around apparently solid surfaces. But that didn't change the fact that even if I was going through a peephole, if I returned to my physical form mid crossing, I would die.

With infinite patience, he first had me use that ability with an opening large enough to let a big dog through. As I gained confidence, we went with smaller and smaller openings, until it was something no bigger than the tiny space under a closed door. More than once during that process, I argued that I really did not need these types of abilities, but he insisted that I fully master all my new powers so that—should the improbable need arise for me to use them—I wouldn't rue the day I had opted out of learning them.

In the end, it proved quite useful when he and I went on romantic escapades together. In our vaporous form, we had no limit as to where we could go and what we could do. This included entering the lairs of the most dangerous creatures in the world—even witnessing the live birth of a hippogriff—without being noticed or distressing them. It had been all the more amazing that I had always believed they hatched from eggs. But it turned out griffins did, not hippogriffs.

I was happy, truly happy. Aside from falling madly in love with my wraith, my shop was booming with customers coming far and wide for my healing and tonics. With my insanely enhanced magic, I got to handle far more serious cases that had confounded traditional physicians and magic healers alike. The fantastic garden the Weaver had gifted me also allowed me to create new potions, tonics, and ointments that sold right off the shelves and addressed a variety of needs that no one else were able to meet before or not at the same level of efficiency as I now did.

Asheron, too, was thriving. He had found himself a couple of wards he was looking after. On the side, he also acted as a vigilante, taking out roaming monsters terrorizing the countryside, or eliminating evil doers threatening the peace and safety of Willow Grove. I was fully aware that this was a way for him to feed his wraith, who still required to drain the lifeforce or soul of his prey. That didn't bother me in the least, considering who he was feeding on. Thankfully, as his physical form also fed on regular food, he didn't need to leech a target too often.

As an added bonus, with his bone magic fully restored, Asheron occasionally assisted me with patrons who had sustained severe injuries, from a simple fracture to a compound one, or something more extreme like a shattered spine or vertebrae. My patrons referred to him as my bonesetter husband. They had no idea how accurate they were.

And husband was indeed Asheron's new title. While common law spouses didn't stir outrage and pearl clutching here as it did in some other states or countries, official marriage was still seen with a more favorable eye, not to mention all the legal benefits that came with it. We debated long and hard about what kind of wedding we wanted, then settled for a simple private ceremony at the courthouse.

Visiting the courthouse always reminded me of Cornelius. The necromancer no longer bothered us. I would lie by saying I hadn't derived extreme pleasure from rubbing it in his face the first time Asheron and I ran into him in town. He had been so certain his tail would have killed Asheron, and that he would have then been able to come back after me and my house.

There was something delightful about being petty to miscreants.

Obviously, he wasn't invited to our wedding. But the courthouse clerk, Brody Soulton, was moved to tears when I asked him to give me away. Glinda—now fully healed and with her youthful and delicate beauty restored—acted as my matron of honor, while her husband Leander stood as Asheron's best man. When we returned home, an insane feast sat on our dinner table, and new exotic plants had been added to the garden. We didn't need to ask who that present was from.

Although we both wanted children, Asheron and I agreed to delay for a few years, maybe even a few decades, if not centuries. As we were essentially biologically immortal, there was no rush for us since we wouldn't age. My family had never been rich. We'd earn enough to meet our daily needs, but not to splurge or spoil ourselves with anything too extravagant.

Now, I could explore the world without limitation. Between mastering my new powers, running the shop, living my wildest dreams, and deepening the bond with Asheron, my life was already as full as it needed to be. But more importantly, the day we had children, I didn't want them to spend their lives hiding in plain sight. Although Asheron didn't mind having to wear a glamour spell to traipse around town, I wouldn't do this to my kids.

It would be a while before non-humans could openly live here in Willow Grove and be themselves without being ostracized or stirring a panic. With Vigil and my ancestors buried in our backyard, moving elsewhere was not an option. Therefore, we intended to wait until the right time to start our family.

But that didn't mean we couldn't enjoy practicing.

My husband was insatiable. And I certainly did not mind! I'd always considered myself more of the traditional type when it came to sex, but being married to a wraith, and being one myself —although I was technically a Planewalker—opened the door to a world of new possibilities. While not an exhibitionist, I'd discovered my favorite place to get naughty was not the privacy of our bedroom.

On the first anniversary of the fateful night Asheron and I met, we celebrated the event with another round on Duskwallow's altar. This time, I did last through the night instead of falling into a coma-like state thirty minutes in. Halfway through, having apparently not learned from what befell their kin, a handful of Shadow Flayers decided to drop by once again.

We paused our frolicking for a little snack. I rarely ever fed through leeching a target's lifeforce. It had taken me a while to feel comfortable with that mere concept. But doing so on monsters—human or otherwise—I had no problem with. The fact that it was merely a transfer of energy, not me actually tasting their flesh, made it easy. And to be honest, my transformation had awakened a slightly predatory side of me that didn't mind coming out to play. To suddenly be the one sending such vicious creatures running for the hills proved both thrilling and invigorating. There was something to be said about being the hunter instead of prey.

I devoured one, and Asheron gorged on the other three. He put that abundance of fresh energy to good use with round two of our first-year anniversary, making me sing arias until sunrise on the stone altar.

Two months later, on the first blood moon after our anniversary, we flew side by side over Hemdell. It was my first time returning here. With my enhanced wraith vision, I finally saw the true faces of the horrors that lurked in the shadows. Had my stunted human eyes allowed me to see what surrounded us at the time, I never would have gone through with it. Once more, I thanked the gods for the calm determination and stoicism Asheron had demonstrated that night. His strength had given me the confidence to see this through.

We pursued our flight farther north to the Denholm River, which separated Willow Grove from Wolfmoon Mountains, the land of the Lycans and shifters. We raced each other and danced over the water under the red glow of the blood moon.

Our wraiths kissed, and our hands roamed over our ethereal forms while our pulsating hearts glowed against each other's— his red, mine a golden-yellow. Intimacy like this transcended sex in our physical form. As wraiths, our shadows intertwined. Even though I knew which parts belonged to him, and which ones belonged to me, we were also one. I felt Asheron and his emotions on both a physical and spiritual level. His pleasure was mine, and mine was his, mutually enhancing our enjoyment of our coupling.

And yes, beneath the billowing shadows of our wraith forms, there were tangible parts, including our hearts and naughty bits. The first time Asheron had slipped his wraith fingers inside me with their terrifyingly long claws, I had shuddered at the thought he would maim me. Where it likely would have been the case in my human body, my wraith form only writhed with pleasure.

Nothing could harm us in our ethereal state, except a divine weapon wielded by a holy knight.

Despite his angelic genetics, Asheron was everything but holy.

As we swirled and soared through the night sky, my beloved first made me cry out in ecstasy with his wicked touch, then by impaling me on his length. And what a magnificent cock it was. Dark as sin, it possessed the same ridges with a scale-like texture as in his physical form, but each crease of the ridges glowed with the same red pulse as his chest. One after the other, his thrusts sent waves of bliss spreading through me.

I burned from within, lightning sparks going off through every fiber of my being. With the intense golden-yellow glow from my chest, and the bright red one from his, our ethereal forms glowed like a shooting ball of fire in the sky. Only the wind whipping past us kept us from combusting.

As our pleasure built towards its apogee, our threads sprung forth, binding our hearts together as we became one, body, heart, and soul. There was no beginning, no end, just overwhelming pleasure and incommensurable love. With one voice, we shouted in ecstasy, liquid bliss flowing between us in an infinite loop.

We glided under the blessing of the blood moon, our hearts beating as one, basking in each other's love. Our eyes locked. Even though words were unnecessary, I couldn't help but to speak them.

"I love you, Asheron."

"I love you, too, my Ronika. My heart. My soul. My eternity."

THE END

CLIONA NOX

SHADOW FLAYER

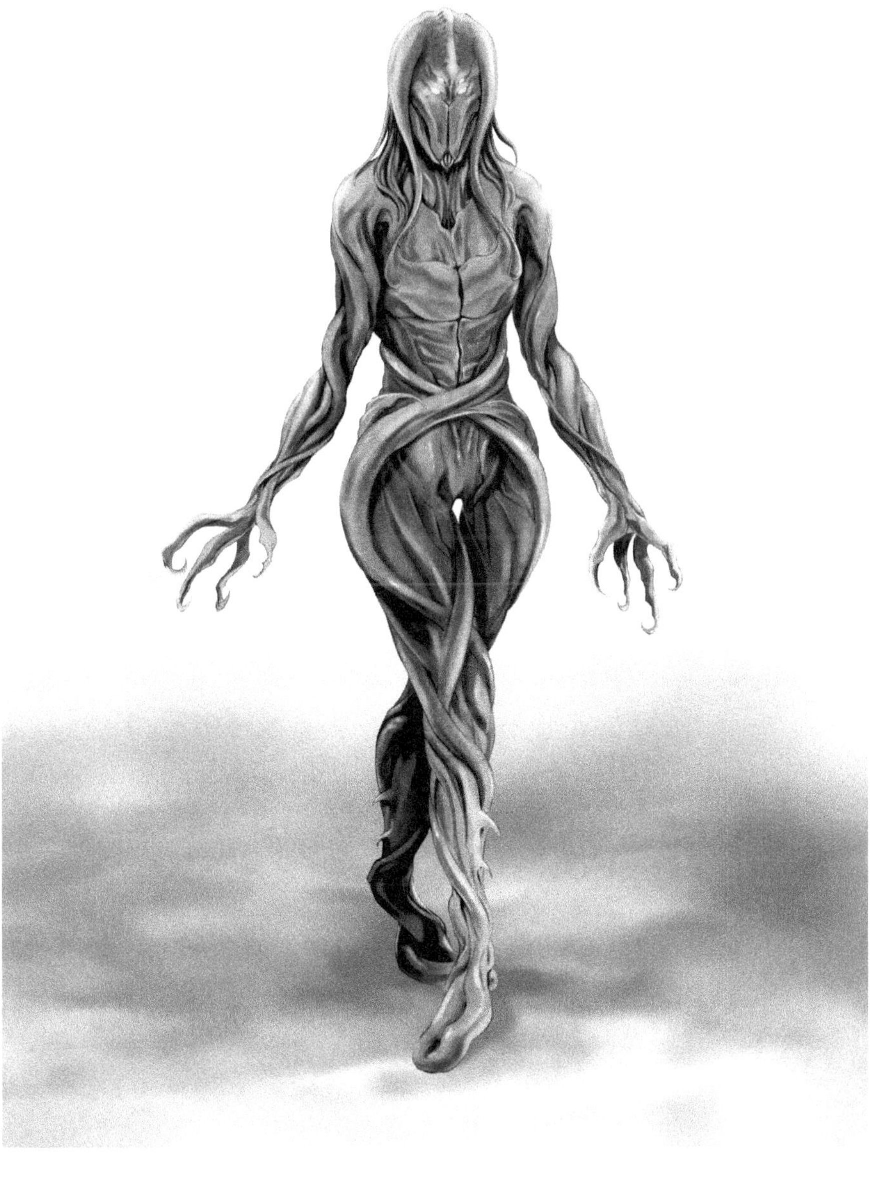

SHADOW FLAYER

BILE SPAWN

CRAWLER

CHAERIM

BILE
DEMON

ALSO BY REGINE ABEL

THE VEREDIAN CHRONICLES

Escaping Fate
Blind Fate
Raising Amalia
Twist of Fate
Hands of Fate
Defying Fate
Imperial Fate

BRAXIANS

Anton's Grace
Ravik's Mercy
Krygor's Hope
Keran's Dawn

XIAN WARRIORS

Doom
Legion
Raven
Bane
Chaos
Varnog
Reaper
Wrath
Xenon
Nevrik
Rogue

PRIME MATING AGENCY

I Married A Lizardman

OTHER
True As Steel
Alien Awakening
Heart of Stone

ABOUT REGINE

USA Today bestselling author Regine Abel is a fantasy, paranormal and sci-fi junkie. Anything with a bit of magic, a touch of the unusual, and a lot of romance will have her jumping for joy. She loves creating hot alien warriors and no-nonsense, kick-ass heroines that evolve in fantastic new worlds while embarking on action-packed adventures filled with mystery and the twists you never saw coming.

Before devoting herself as a full-time writer, Regine had surrendered to her other passions: music and video games! After a decade working as a Sound Engineer in movie dubbing and live concerts, Regine became a professional Game Designer and Creative Director, a career that has led her from her home in Canada to the US and various countries in Europe and Asia.

Facebook

https://www.facebook.com/regine.abel.author/

Website

https://regineabel.com

Regine's Rebels Reader Group

https://www.facebook.com/groups/ReginesRebels/

Newsletter

http://smarturl.it/RA_Newsletter

Goodreads

http://smarturl.it/RA_Goodreads

Bookbub

https://www.bookbub.com/profile/regine-abel

Amazon

http://smarturl.it/AuthorAMS